There Is No Mrs. Gezunterman

by

Kevin Mednick

Savvy Press

SAVVY PRESS

© Kevin Mednick 2012

ISBN 978-1-939113-04-7
LCCN 2012951141

Cover art by Leah Mednick

Published by Savvy Press
http:www.savvypress.com

for Kathleen

Jeff -
chapter 8 is just
for you -
Ken

A long habit of not thinking a thing WRONG, gives it a superficial appearance of being RIGHT, and raises at first a formidable outcry in defense of custom.

–Thomas Paine, *Common Sense*

Part One

Chapter 1

When the answering machine message said, "This is Mrs. Gezunterman. I have Sarah's shoes," Max Rodriguez suspected the messenger was acting on behalf of his mother, who was trying to reach him from the other world. After the message appeared twice more that week, Max was certain. But what was his mother trying to say?

The calls had been made to the telephone in the Rodriguez family room. It was the only phone in the house, as Max's father allowed no others. Until it was time for bed that was the room where the whole family—Max, his little brother and sister, and their dad—lived. They did homework there, watched TV, ate meals, read the newspaper, and surfed the net. It was the busiest part of the house, which meant the messages were heard not only by Max but by everyone, and Max was not the only one who had an opinion as to what they meant.

"She's telling you to get up off your ass and get a job," Chuck Rodriguez said.

Max ignored him.

"You could hook up a gadget to the phone that would record all incoming numbers," said Amanda. "That way, you could just call this Mrs. Gezunterman back."

"I don't think so, little girl," said Max. "I think we're dealing with something bigger than a telephone number here."

Max sensed the conversation was at the point where the next comment from his father might turn things ugly, and that neither of them wanted it to go that way.

Amanda saved them both.

"But who is this Mrs. Gezunterman?" she said.

"That's what I have to find out," said Max. He shut off the TV, jammed his feet into his sneakers, and announced, "I'm off to the library. The quest begins."

"Wow," said Chuck. "I'll call the papers."

Since graduating from college two years earlier, Max had set out on many quests, each beginning with a trip to the library. He never made it, and each time he returned home, his father questioned his use of the word "quest," because it contained, Chuck said, the suggestion of action.

"I walk a fine line," Max would say. "My college instincts tell me the library is the place to refine and redirect my quests. But I learned from Mom that insight can strike you anytime and anywhere and that you have to be open to it. So while the library is a good place to start, it's not the only place."

"He's going out to a bar," said Benjamin, who, at age fifteen was Amanda's other older brother. Benjamin had brooding, dark eyes and scrutinized life from underneath a ledge of thick, black hair. He sought the simplest explanation to things. Ben didn't know it, but there was a bar in Wheaton that had placed seven or eight books on a shelf above the entranceway and called itself The Library.

But Amanda, with her round face and green, trusting eyes, disagreed. She said Max wouldn't be going through all this just for a beer. Max's sister had little to say that was negative about anyone except Benjamin, whom she sometimes called pond scum. She'd picked up that phrase from a Ranger at the Salt Pond Visitors Center at Coast Guard Beach in Cape Cod, where Chuck had taken the family after the funeral to lick their wounds, a trip that had been a disaster. What Max recalled most about it was his father's startling admission, three days into the vacation, that leaving their home at that moment in time had been a mistake.

"Mommy would have known better," Chuck had said.

True to Max's word, it was the public library that he headed toward every time he walked out the door after having said, "The quest begins." He just couldn't get there. The reason was a world view he considered "more evolved" than his father's, though Max was only twenty-six.

Max felt a constant readiness an almost palpable sensation of receptivity that freed him from his father's work ethic even as it shackled him to the man's refrigerator. He was open to anything, so open that the slightest distraction, the faintest movement, the quietest sound, or smallest urge derailed his train of consciousness and placed him on an alternate set of tracks. This day it was the smell of coffee, languid and thick, coming from Dr. Java's Coffee Emporium that cost the library a customer.

It was a smell Max would not have smelled but for his decision to walk to the library. Max often opted for footwork over wheels, convinced as he was that the forces of nature and karma were more readily received in that mode of transportation than while driving.

He had a distance of about three-quarters of a mile to cover, starting from his family's share of the subdivision on Alameda Street, near Reade Road, then one block south to Hilltop Street, past the high school and through the parking lot of the Grand Union mall. The library was waiting just beyond the mall's eastern border.

He set out at a brisk pace, leaving behind the pine-treed, one-third acre lot with the two-story brick structure that had been his family's home ever since Amanda was born. He thought he had enough momentum to get there, but Dr. Java, perched in the ready position near the Grand Union to pick off stragglers, reached out and pulled him in.

Max had dressed for the occasion, which meant a T-shirt that was clean and without holes. Towering a full half-foot above his father, he had long arms and legs as well as the hands and feet of an even taller man. His looks were a combination of his father's complexion and hair and his mother's bone structure, especially her narrow chin. Most dominant were the dreamy green eyes that came from his mom and conveyed the sense of accessibility that so troubled his father. Dark but sparse facial hair came and went along with Max's motivation to shave, giving him a rumpled look. All in all, his appearance said: *Sure you can talk to me. I'm not going anywhere.*

Inside the cafe, Max considered the choices of lattes, coffees, and mochas that appeared on the wall under the menu's motto: "The Place For Intimate Conversation." As anyone who'd ever squeezed into one of the closely spaced tables and chairs could attest, conversations were intimate only as far as everyone outside the building was concerned.

He bought a plain cup of coffee and sat down in one of the Dr.'s cushioned chairs, dangling one bony leg over its armrest. Pouring sugar into his brew sufficient to sweeten his latest capitulation to forces beyond his control, he heard the man at the next table say: "Now how would I know where her shoes are?"

Thought Max, *I wonder if I should even turn around.*

He did. The speaker was in his late forties, gray but still handsome and trim, in a rugged, muscular sort of way, and he was talking into a cell phone. He wore a dark expensive suit and had the tan seen on people who are exposed to the sun all day, like homeless people and wealthy people who have multiple homes in sunny places. Opposite him was a blond woman about half his age. She sat politely eating a double fudge brownie while her companion spoke.

"How does a teenager lose a pair of shoes anyway? She can't drive. Any place she went, you had to take her, isn't that right? So where were you in the last week? Look, tell her to calm down. Yes, I'll spring for another pair if it's that important. Good-bye."

The talker and his friend got up to leave. She was slender with long legs, wore a black, leather skirt and high heels, and stumbled toward the parking lot with the tan man's hand supporting her at the elbow. They got into a black vehicle. As it pulled out, Maxwell Rodriguez, standing at the window of Dr. Java's, scribbled the model, BMW 740I, on his napkin with a pencil he'd grabbed from a passing waitress. He also wrote down the license plate: CHAZ.

Max sat back down and nodded his head in self-approval. Then he finished his coffee and headed back home.

Chapter 2

Scott gave the old woman a one-armed hug and escaped into his red Saab. His brother Keith gave her a full embrace and got into the passenger seat.

"You know, I don't think I've ever seen you hug her with both arms," said Keith.

"I don't want her to get the wrong idea."

"She's your mother."

"Exactly."

They headed down Balltown Road in Niskayuna, New York, toward Route 7 on their way to the Thruway. Although it was only mid-June, the Sunday traffic heading south was already getting heavy.

"I'd say it was a good visit," said Scott. "She was particularly pleased with my new position." Scott had recently been named director of Pinewood Park, a residential treatment facility for substance abuse.

"Oh, yeah."

"I could tell by the way she said, 'For this you want I should be happy?'"

"I thought the clue was when she said, 'You should be Head of Orthopedic Surgery at some hospital, better.'"

"She always says that." Which was true, and she'd been saying it since Scott had dropped out of medical school after one semester a quarter century ago. His mother had told him it was cruel "beyond words" to make her deathly ill and deprive her of the family physician all at once. Since then, she'd reminded him of his misdeed a thousand times and every time she did so, words eluded her. But even his brother had asked him why he'd bothered starting if he was going to stop so soon.

"I went on a lark," Scott had said. "My freshman biology class had a bunch of pre-meds in it and I was the star. They said I had a head for science, so I declared pre-med. When I got to med school, I was a fish out of water. All my quirky people were gone and it was just me and the hard drivers. I was interested, but that wasn't enough. Those kids had more than interest. More, even, than passion. They had a fire going. That's what it was going to take, and I just didn't have it. So I left."

They were about to get on the Thruway. Keith reached into the back seat and pulled something out of his attaché case.

"Listen to this CD," he said. "I've been saving it for your birthday, but I think you need it now."

Keith slipped the disc into the stereo, turned up the volume, and the first notes of Jackie Wilson's "Higher and Higher" filled the car. "Oh, yeah!" he said, the two syllables coming out of his mouth quickly, like jabs from a prizefighter: O Yeah! Scott could feel his brother's words hit his ribcage.

They hit the repeat button a couple of times each until reaching Exit 24, and should have passed by as the road turned toward New York City. Suddenly, Scott veered into the exit lane.

"What if we take this exit?" he said. His brother stared across the width of the car. Exit 24 led to a different highway. Keith's wife and kids were waiting down in Rockland County. Scott had no wife, not anymore.

"I don't know where it takes us," said Scott. "I think Massachusetts. Maybe to the Berkshires."

"And beyond that?" said Keith. He usually looked at the road even if someone else was driving, but just now he did not take his eyes off his brother. Both men were smiling.

"Beyond that, Captain Columbus, is the end of the Earth." And through the tollbooth they went.

After about a dozen repeats of "Higher and Higher" and three or four rounds of Marvin Gaye's "I Heard It Through the Grapevine," they were past Albany on Route 90. The green hills of western Massachusetts were beckoning when the "check engine" dashboard light came on.

"Damn," said Keith. "We may be resorting to wind power after all."

"It's okay," said Scott.

"What do you mean, it's okay? Do you know what the problem is?"

"I've no idea."

"Do you know what we should do? What if the car's about to blow up? Should we stop?"

"I'll pull over, shut the engine off, and leave the stereo on."

"That's good. It'll scare away wild animals."

"No, I'm telling you," said Scott, "It'll be all right."

They pulled over and sat on the side of the road and the Isley Brothers came on, singing "It's Your Thing." They started moving back and forth. Soon, the car was shaking as though the Saab itself was a fan of soul music.

"You don't think we should call for help?" Keith yelled over the music.

"No, just keep listening. It'll be all right."

A gray Pathfinder pulled up in front of them and out stepped a shapely woman in tight jeans and a tank top. The look on her face, as she walked back toward the Saab, gave Scott the impression that she'd been thinking of something very funny and had stopped her car just to let him in on it.

She reached the car and looked in through Scott's open window.

"How can you lose," she laughed, "with the stuff you use?"

Given that the Isleys had just asked the same exact question, the brothers were a bit short on words, but the laughing lady helped them out.

"What's the trouble? I'm pretty good with cars."

"Check engine light," Scott managed to say. "It's on."

"How's the car running otherwise?"

"Okay. Fine. It's just that the light came on and . . ."

"Pop open the gas cap cover."

"But I filled up less than an hour ago."

"Who's running the show here, buddy?" she laughed.

Scott popped and the brothers piled out of the car and followed the lady in jeans to the rear left fender, where she reached in and plucked out the gas cap, which was lying loose underneath the lid.

"I could've sworn I put that thing back on," said Scott.

"Then you didn't tighten it. You have to tighten it so that it clicks three times. Otherwise, a sensor goes off in the computer, and the check engine light comes on. Take it to the dealer when you get home and they'll reset it. The car's all right."

"Thank you. That's a relief. How do you, I mean, who . . ."

"The first repair is free," she laughed, and walked back to the Pathfinder. "After that, you'll have to pay. Drive safe, boys."

The two men remained standing as she drove away.

"Okay," said Keith eventually, tapping his brother on the shoulder. "That was something. Now let's go home."

Scott wouldn't budge.

"Scott. Come on."

"Wonderful, wonderful." Scott was murmuring.

"Yeah, she wasn't bad, but I've . . ."

"I must find her."

"Why? So she can teach you how to fix transmissions?"

"I must see her again."

Ten minutes later they were still standing there, Scott facing tomorrow's sunrise, Keith searching Scott's face for clues. Scott put his hand on his brother's shoulder. It was the first Scott had moved since the laughing lady had departed.

"Must find her," he said.

Scott's unblinking eyes were fixed on the point where the laughing woman's SUV had disappeared from view, and he was murmuring again, but this time it sounded like singing. A vaguely familiar tune, but not the soul music they'd been listening to. More like something from a Broadway show.

"What's that you're singing?"

"Was I singing? Listen, Keith. I must find her. I must find her now."

Keith looked at the ground and shook his head. "Right," he said. "You must find her now."

Chapter 3

Alexander Hammermill had long since dispensed with distinctions between meals, opting instead to consider all time spent between arising and retiring as "eating time." He felt there was only so much discipline one could muster in a given day and all of it was needed for his artistic endeavors. Parsing time along the lines of designated meals when he was always hungry anyway burned energy he could not spare.

Alexander had lost count of how many times he'd sat down for a meal on that Sunday, not that he'd been keeping track, the effort factor being of concern. Yet, as he approached his big table once more, he stopped briefly to straighten a bronzed wall plaque that had nothing to do with eating or art. It was a certificate of incorporation for something called T.U.L.P.

Treat Us Like People or T.U.L.P., a not-for-profit corporation of the State of New York was formed for the purpose of: "The protection, furtherance, and enrichment of the human spirit in all endeavors relating to the interaction between said spirit and the corporate and government entities, duly formed and/or elected, which run, profit from, govern, or purport to govern, this great nation."

Hammermill called the verbiage "legal gobbledygook," but as its author was "damn proud." And it was abstruse enough to convince the clerks at the Department of State in Albany that some legitimate corporate purpose had been stated.

When it began, little more than a year and a half ago, Alexander wanted nothing more than to go on a fishing vacation. That's how he puts it even though it is hard to conceptualize a vacation for one who has never had to work, which is why Alexander's wife, Cindy, was always careful to call it a "trip." He called Tango Airlines and an unknown representative—identifiable only by the eight hundred number that brought Alexander to her telephone—spoke to him.

Thirty minutes later he had a reservation, a confirmation number, and a seat on a plane from Albany, New York, to Fort Myers, Florida, leaving February 14th, and returning February 23rd, with a stop in Atlanta, Georgia, each way. The ticket was to be paid for with member points deposited into his Tango Air Miles account from his American Express account. The transfer to his Tango account would take three to five days, after which he was to call back and have the ticketing transaction completed. The ticket would remain on "courtesy hold" for fifteen days, during which time he could cancel if he chose.

Alexander hung up the phone thinking he was set. Tango Airlines thought otherwise. Three days later he called for his tickets. After twenty minutes of Tango's Muzak and recorded messages, Alexander found himself connected to another representative, name of Sandra.

"Sandra! It's Alexander."

"How can I help you?"

"Don't you remember me? I made a reservation with you just last week."

"Do you have a confirmation number?"

"Absolutely. But do you remember?"

"It wasn't me. What's your confirmation number?"

"I didn't think it was you either, Sandra. Why don't you transfer me to whoever took the original reservation?"

"I can't do that."

"Sure you can. Isn't there some notation in your computer that tells you who it was?"

"We cannot release our representatives' names."

"I'm not asking for her name. Just put me through to her extension."

"I can't do that."

"Why not?"

"It's not our policy to do that."

"Okay. Can you help me then?"

"Confirmation number?"

"QPU5RT."

"Hold on for a moment." Five minutes later: "Thank you for holding. How can I help you?"

"How can . . . I'd like to ticket, uh, buy the tickets, I guess. With Tango Sky Miles."

"I'm sorry. You cannot purchase these tickets with Sky Miles."

"What do you mean *cannot*? When I made this reservation I told the lady whose name you won't tell me that I was using Sky Miles."

"That's impossible."

"Oh, really?"

"Yes, company policy doesn't allow the use of Sky Miles on those dates. But even if it did, that flight is sold out."

"That's impossible."

"No, it's not. That flight was sold out six months ago."

"Come on now, Sandra, I'm getting the feeling you're not joking anymore."

"I'm not joking."

"But I have a confirmation number. I'm confirmed."

"You have confirmation of a fare."

"What do you mean, a fare? That's a fare with a seat attached to it, right?"

"No, it's just a fare."

Alexander gazed through his kitchen window at the distant lights beyond.

"I've a confirmed fare on a flight, but the fare is for a seat that doesn't exist because the flight is sold out, and was sold out before I was confirmed on it, and even if the seat did exist before I bought it, I still couldn't pay for it the way it was agreed I'd pay for it because Tango doesn't allow its customers to pay for seats on that date with Sky Miles, though your representative, whose name you won't give me, did not tell me that when I made this reservation a few days ago. Have I got that straight?"

"I wouldn't put it that way."

"But that's the way it is."

"Not at all, sir."

"Let me talk to a supervisor."

"Fine."

That's when things got bad. No, the other representative had not been mistaken, the supervisor said. No, she would not tell him who had taken his reservation or where she worked. She, the supervisor, would deal with it and that ought to be—that would be—good enough. After all, they were Tango Airlines, a big company, and it was their policy to resolve all customer complaints satisfactorily. And since it was the policy of the big company to do this thing, Alexander was wrong—he thought her tone implied he might be insane—to suggest that the thing was *not* being done satisfactorily. And by the way, his Sky Miles, recently converted from his AMEX account, would not be returned to that account. Company policy forbade it. He was welcome to reserve another flight on Tango any time he wanted. She'd even help him right then and there.

Someone was listening. The recorded advisory that said, "This call may be recorded or monitored," was for real. And that someone was taking notes.

Her name was Irena Poppadapoulos, age 47, wife, mother, Tango senior supervisor, subversive. She'd had it with big company policy, and two years of listening to her subordinates do exactly as they'd been instructed convinced her she had to do something about it. Listening to Alexander Hammermill put her over the edge.

She contacted him and told him what she'd been thinking. He told her it was just what the doctor ordered, and T.U.L.P. began to take shape.

Chapter 4

"We'll get back on the highway, get off at the first exit we come to, and look for her at the first town we hit," said Scott. He'd recovered from his stupor and returned to the Saab.

"You're okay to drive?" said Keith.

"I'm okay to *fly*."

"Oh, please."

"I'm telling you. I feel as though my body could lift off, like it has no mass."

"It's all the drugs you did when you were a kid. You're having flashbacks. Here, I'll put that CD back on. That should help."

"No. I've got this tune roaming around in my head and I don't want to lose it. It's been there ever since she drove away. You can't put anything else on until I place it. I can't tell whether it's a jazz standard or a show tune."

"Hum a few bars."

Scott hummed.

"I don't know what it is either, but I know it's a show tune," Keith said. "So now you're humming show tunes? You feel light and you're humming show tunes? Scott, you've suffered a stroke. We should call for an ambulance."

"Oh, come on. You know what Mom says. You're not a real doctor. You're only a psychologist."

The first town they came to was West Stockbridge. Walking it from end to end twice, slowly, took ten minutes. No gray Pathfinder. They entered a deli where a worker who appeared to be Indian was standing on a ladder, fiddling with a security camera placed above the doorway.

Scott said, "Having problems?"

"Yes," the man on the ladder said. "Just since a few moments ago. The damn thing is on the blink and I don't know why. All the cameras are out. And not only that, but when I first tried calling my security company, my cell phone wouldn't work. The phone came back, though. But the cameras are still out. It's like they were hit by lightning."

Scott bought a Dr. Brown's black cherry soda. Keith, a Diet Coke, and the two of them sat on a bench outside the store.

"Look at the traffic signal," Scott said, gesturing.

The town had one traffic light, a blinking yellow, at its east end.

"What do you notice?" Scott asked his brother.

After a few seconds and several sips of his soda, Keith said, "It's irregular. It's blinking to an irregular beat. So?"

"So the security system was out at the deli, the man's phone didn't work, and the traffic light is on the fritz. She's been here."

"Okay, spaceman, that's it. Give me the keys. I'm driving home."

Had Olivia's Lookout faced the opposite direction, Jane might have been able to pick up Scott's red Saab in her binoculars as it whisked the brothers out of West Stockbridge. But as they scooted home, she was finishing her bagel and iced tea and gazing down upon Stockbridge Bowl. She wouldn't change a thing except, perhaps, for the home at the water's edge she dreamed of owning one day.

The parking area she was in led to hiking trails, but she could not understand why anyone used them, as the Lookout itself "could not be topped," as she liked to laugh, to her daughter's dismay.

A curved stone wall rimmed the lot. Beyond it, acres of open space—a gap in the forest—stretched out along a hillside below, disappearing into the distant waters of the Bowl. Trees on either side of the opening framed the view so that it was stark or colorful or lush, depending on the season, but always beautiful. The smells were summer verdant, like this day, or autumn dry or springtime redolent of wildflowers that staked claim to the open space. Even in the dead of winter the spot was sublime. She knew.

A couple with Jersey plates on their car hopped out and asked her for directions.

"It's the oddest thing," the woman said, "our GPS was working fine all the way from Parsippany. We got up here and went on this hike. And now, all of a sudden, it won't work. Completely on the fritz. Can you tell us which way to Lenox?"

"Right coming out of the parking lot here, bear left at the bottom of the hill. You're only a few minutes away. But I wouldn't sweat the GPS," Jane laughed. "Once you pull away, it'll come back to you. Trust me."

So the woman laughed and Jane laughed and the people from Parsippany pulled away. Jane returned to her view, wondering, just for a moment, why the big, strapping man who'd been behind the wheel of the lost car hadn't been able to ask for directions.

"When it comes to the tough stuff . . . " she laughed.

Chapter 5

At 9 A.M. on Monday, Max awoke, the rewarding burn of the last night's effort still warming his bones. His dad had left for work ninety minutes earlier. It would be at least an hour before the phone calls started. By then, Max would be able to say he'd showered, eaten, cleaned the kitchen, made the beds and checked the *Times Union*. Still, the conversation would proceed as follows: "I take it you've looked at the paper by now."

"Yes, Dad."

"And am I correct there are still no jobs for a young man with a bachelor's degree in philosophy and no work experience to speak of?"

"Yes, Dad, you're still right on the money."

"Y, Estoy correcto que todavia hables español, no?"

"Si."

"Just checking. I have to go. I have work to do. You know, work."

Max knew his bachelor's degree in philosophy did not open the floodgates of opportunity. But due to the union of Chuck, a native Colombian, and Max's foreign language teacher mom, he and his siblings had built-in linguistic advantages, and as Chuck had mentioned more than once over the past years, every school system in America was desperate for Spanish teachers.

"I can't see myself teaching," Max would say.

"I can't see myself with an adult son who doesn't work," Chuck would say, "but here I am."

Max did work from time to time, here and there. It was a here, now, and tomorrow job that eluded his grasp, although "grasping" was not how Max's father might have described his son's job hunting style.

The previous summer Max worked on a road crew, holding the red flag, but the job ended when the road repair was finished. He next found work when a landscaping crew headed by a former high school classmate arrived at his home to do the fall cleanup. It was outdoor work, and Max was promised it produced the deep tans and taut muscles that made women curious about which kind of seed to plant in sunlight and which to plant in shade. It snowed early that year, and Max's new friends, though willing to sow seed whenever and wherever possible, were forced to seek more sheltered employment. Max, though, could not move on.

"This lawn thing is a part of me now," he said. "It's burrowed into my bones for the winter, and I fear I won't be able to cast it out until spring."

"Does that mean you're not gonna work again until it gets warm out? Cause if it does, Dad is not gonna be happy," said Benjamin.

That spring, Max had taken a job pumping gas and doing minor car repairs at a Thruway rest stop close to home. "The highway is like a vortex," he said, "and I'm right next to it. People are going so far, so fast. At any time, I could be sucked in and land who knows where."

"Yes," said Chuck, "but you keep coming back here. Maybe you're not standing close enough."

Benny and Amanda were spending their days in the Town of Wheaton Recreation Program, Benny as a counselor and Amanda as "just a kid." Max had been coming back home each night, but he'd also been going each day to the rest stop and working, something that held off his father's anger only for a time. In just a few days, Chuck's attitude had shifted from "At least you have a job" to "Do you intend to grow old at that place?"

Max went to work as usual at 11 A.M. At about 6:45 P.M., near the end of his shift, he caught a whiff of fragrance and a snippet of conversation coming from a gray Nissan Pathfinder.

He'd been standing out at the gas pumps, a spot from where he could watch the final minutes of his shift expire with little risk that someone pulling into the garage, some eighty feet away, might force him into a last-minute repair.

When the Pathfinder pulled up to the full service island, he waved off the kid who was supposed to do the pumping and ambled over to the SUV himself.

The inside, as far as Max could see when he peeked through the window, was messy in a way that made Max feel good. No one category of objects dominated the space. It was more like a free-for-all—candy wrappers, boots, clothing, a hairbrush, books, a fan, garden tools. He couldn't tell if there *was* a back seat or just more items piled underneath what was visible.

The Pathfinder's occupants, two women Max guessed to be in their mid-thirties, stepped out of the SUV to stretch, and Max heard one of them say: "That was the best vintage store I've ever seen. Usually, the stuff is junk."

"I know," said the other, the one whose jeans were not quite so tight, "and there was so much of it. Where did he find so much stuff?"

"Excuse me," said Max, to the first one. "That's a lovely perfume you're wearing. What is it?"

"I'm glad you noticed," she said.

Max also noticed a complete lack of facetiousness or sarcasm in her tone, although she was laughing. In fact, it was her laughter and not her voice that carried her words to his ears. "It's bath oil, not perfume, and I don't think it would work for you."

"If you don't mind my asking, is this a vintage clothing store you're talking about?"

"Yes," she laughed, handing him two twenties. "It's on Route Nine in one of those strip malls north of Latham. I think it's called Your Father's Child."

"No," he said.

"I'm afraid so. I had a rough time with it, too, but once you're inside, you get over it." Laughing still, she got into her SUV and turned the key. Her friend got in on the other side, and off they went.

"Thanks," he said as the Pathfinder pulled away. Then he raised his eyebrows, tilted his head, and announced to no one, "I'm on my way." It wasn't much of an escape, since the clock by then read 5:30, but Max counted every minute saved from tedium as a victory. He slipped into his ancient Buick, adding, "And who knows if I'm coming back."

It took him only twenty minutes to drive down the Thruway, up Route 87, and find the clothing store on Route 9. It shared space in a strip mall with a health food store, a chiropractor's office, and a travel agency.

He opened a door that led him to an open courtyard with a tile and brick floor. Lining the inside walls of the courtyard were snapdragons and marigolds, and if not for something else, their scents would have stopped Max right where he stood.

It was the kind of moment when his mother would have said, "You have to be thankful for these bursts of clarity." Nancy Rodriguez had lots of expressions like that. Chuck sneered at them, but Max loved them. He'd upgraded this particular expression to "Cloudbursts of Clarity," and he was having one now. It was telling him that the reasons he'd had to pump the gas for the lady in the Pathfinder, left work early to come to a vintage clothing store—even why he'd spent the last two years bouncing from one odd job to another—were staring at him in the form of a display of bronze statues in the middle of the courtyard.

The most prominent one was about three feet high and was of an oak tree in full bloom. The display itself was about five feet by five feet. Surrounding the blooming oak were three others, all of them placed around a flowing stream that meandered around the trees. But those other trees, all smaller, were barren, hidden from the sun by the overshadowing central oak.

Max walked slowly around the statues, stopping at various points to make sure he was seeing what he thought he was seeing. After the first ten minutes, he realized the piece had no title on or anywhere near it. That caused him to stay an additional half-hour.

"What's the statue called?" he finally asked the store's proprietor.

"What would you call it?" the man said. He was standing behind a counter and a cash register, clad in gabardine slacks and a 1950s rayon bowling shirt. He looked out at Max from inside a round face that featured deep-set, mournful eyes in which Max detected a slight twinkle. A Russian face, Max decided—soulful and saddened by all the generations of long, brutal winters that had come before it. It was a face Max liked.

"I'd call it The Banker," said Max as he watched the twinkle ripen to a gleam. "Yes. The Banker. I don't see how you could call it anything else." The owner opened his cash register and took out a card.

"Here's the sculptor's name and address. He lives nearby. You'll have to call before you go because it's impossible to find the place without detailed directions. Give him my name."

"Which is?"

"Mario Lambruzzo."

Max looked at the card while Mario called a phone number. The card read: "Alexander Hammermill **T.U.L.P.** Treat Us Like People."

"It should be called 'The Banker,'" Max said after Mario introduced him over the phone.

"That's exactly right," the voice on the line said, "but for some reason, people don't see it that way. Why don't you come by and tell me about it?"

Max scribbled directions on the business card Mario had given him and took off.

The trip was not as complicated as Max had been told. Only the last two turns were difficult, coming as they did without warning. The first one, a hard right off of Route 146, could have been the entrance to any of the half-dozen subdivisions he passed along the way. But instead he found himself on a dirt road surrounded by undeveloped forest and looking for "one extremely gnarled oak tree."

He found it, and soon thereafter the sculptor's house, on which a hand-painted sign advised, "We were here first." He brought his car to a halt and got out. Approaching the house, he heard what sounded like gunfire ring out from the far side of an open garage, and his right shoulder began to dip. A back door to the garage opened and a huge, bearded man dressed in overalls and carrying a rifle stepped through. Max stopped moving except for his shoulder, which continued to sink as his body leaned toward the sunset.

The big man strode directly at Max, the rifle dangling from his arm like an iron toothpick. By the time he got within arm's length, Max was listing over so far he could have picked up pebbles.

"You feelin' all right, son?" The man raised his rifle the short distance it had to travel to tap the outside of Max's lowered shoulder.

"Sure. Why do you ask?"

"'Cause you look like if I just stand here and count to ten or so, you'll keel over all by yourself."

"No, I'm okay."

"Oh, I get it. It's the rifle. Afraid of guns, aren't you. Never fired one. Wouldn't own one. Et cetera. Et cetera. You stop me now if I say something off the mark."

"No, no, you're doing pretty well so far."

"Hey, are you that fellow I spoke to on the phone a few minutes ago?"

"Yeah, that's me."

"Well, isn't that something. I throw this stuff out there into the void year after year and suddenly they're breaking down my door."

Max looked around. Other than him and the giant, there was no one.

"I'm Alexander Hammermill. I'll tell you what. Let's you and me go out back and exorcise that fear of firearms you've got and then we'll talk about my statue. Here, you take it."

With that, Hammermill jammed the rifle sideways into Max's chest and turned and led the way back through the garage.

The artist dwarfed Max, yet he walked quickly and smoothly. Max had to trot to keep up. The grace of movement, the strength and confidence of stature were unmistakable. Max was certain he was following a ballplayer.

"Football," Max shouted, trying to regain some of his composure while the two made their way through the garage. "I'm guessing you played football, and maybe basketball, with that height. And I bet you were some pitcher too."

"Classical piano," said the man. "I never liked sports. You feeling like Charlton Heston yet? You've been holding on to that rifle for a good thirty seconds now."

"I'm okay," said Max, straightening up.

The garage was filled with paintings. Some were on easels and some were leaning against walls. There were also statues, some on pedestals and some on the ground, along with buckets filled with brushes, hammers, and chisels. It was an enormous studio.

Behind the garage was a narrow opening in the middle of tall pine trees. At its end, about thirty or forty yards away, was a high wooden wall plastered with targets. Hammermill loaded the rifle, gave Max some quick instruction, and told him to "let 'er rip."

Ten rounds later, the targets had suffered no new wounds.

"You're doing this on purpose, right? Nobody shoots that bad."

"No. I'm trying my best."

"But it's fun, right?"

"Well . . ."

"Liberals. Okay. Come on in. Let me show you around."

Back inside the garage, Max was shown two paintings of a moose ("The same one. Can you tell?"), and dozens of works in progress that were of different sizes and shapes that Max could not identify. After a few minutes a woman appeared. She was less than half Hammermill's size, and looked as ordinary as he did not.

"My wife Cindy," said Alexander, extending his arm toward her. "Cindy, this is Max Rodriguez." Cindy was holding a plate of cookies.

"We rarely get company," Cindy said. "It's a treat for us."

"Mario told me I wouldn't be imposing. I guess he doesn't speak for you, but I got the impression it would be okay."

"Yes, yes," said Cindy. "It's fine, really. It's just that few people see what Alexander is trying to do with his statues. But you did, Max, and we're glad you came by. Just what did you think would be a good name for that statue?"

"The Banker," Max said.

"Quite so," said Cindy. "Quite so. That's nice to hear. You'd be surprised how many people want one just like it but have no idea what it's about. Why, some people insist that particular work is about global warming or the drought in Africa."

"That's hard to believe," said Max.

"There are some real kooks out there," said Alexander.

Alexander traced Max's line of sight, which had now shifted to the moose. "You can have it, you know. I've got two," Hammermill said.

"I've no money to pay for something like this," said Max.

"I don't work for money," said Alexander.

Max, Cindy, and Alexander moved to the kitchen for more cookies and hot chocolate. Like the rest of the house, the kitchen was designed in the colonial style. It had white, wooden slat doors held to their doorjambs by black iron hinges, and an open hearth darkened from use. Cindy fetched white plates painted with images of horse-drawn carriages.

Max sat down at the wooden kitchen table and learned that Alexander Hammermill did not work for money because his grandfather had made a fortune selling Spam to the U.S. Army during W.W.II. Those profits, since invested and diversified into blue chip stocks, office buildings, and other holdings provided more money than the Hammermills could ever need.

Cindy and Alexander were on their own little island in the middle of a sea of subdivisions. The entire area, including the subdivisions, had originally been owned by the family.

"Developers were descending on us from all directions," said Alexander. "I wasn't trying to make more money. I just couldn't help it."

"So we came up with this idea," said Cindy.

"Yes. Cindy did, actually. We called it our Island Plan. We sold off the estate except for forty acres right in the middle and a strip of land coming off it about one hundred yards wide for access to the main road."

"No one knows we're here," said Cindy. "Builders drive by on Route 146 and think, 'Too bad, somebody already developed it,' and the people in the houses around us assume some horrible creature lives out here in the woods, or maybe it's forever wild or a toxic dump. Whatever it is, it's enough to kill their curiosity. We're insulated."

"But we do like friends to visit," said Cindy, smiling, "and we do go out. It's not like we're hermits, but coming home for us is something special."

Cindy Hammermill was from Virginia, where her family had been involved in real estate development near Williamsburg. Max grinned wildly every time she spoke. In addition to the cookies, the table had a bowl filled with peanuts sent up by Cindy's "Daddy."

"I believe our new friend has never heard a southern accent before. Is that right, Max?"

"Well, we didn't get many southerners at Madison."

Relaxed as he was by the glow of newfound friendship and a stomach full of hot chocolate, cookies, and peanuts, Max felt the winds of a new direction kicking at his heels.

Chapter 6

"Don't you think we should've told him?" Cindy Hammermill said. She was snuggling against her husband's side. They were in the master bedroom of their island home, between the suburban continents of Fox Run Drive and Appian Way.

During the summer, their house was hidden by vegetation. The sound of Alexander hammering metal statues into form rang out loud and clear, but no one ever bothers to track down a sound.

In winter, people nearby had to be able to see the lights from their home, but the Hammermills assumed those people thought they were seeing lights from some other subdivision, or maybe from some convenience store they'd never actually located from the street. And it's the rare suburbanite who puts on boots and a coat to go exploring where his car won't take him. The Hammermills could've been constructing a landing zone for Martian spaceships. Their secrets were safe in the suburbs.

"Why, a visitor reeled in by your art work, Alexander. We've seen nothing like that in years. Don't you think it's a sign?"

"I do," said Alexander. "But I'm not sure what it's a sign of. He didn't ask anything about the organization. We did agree to certain rules, you know."

"Yes, rules. But as I recall, it was rules that got the organization going in the first place."

When they'd met at the Hammermill place a year earlier, Alexander learned that Irena Poppadapoulos was a woman about whom other people said, "Oh, Irena. The Greek." She'd grown up in a Greek community, learned to speak Greek at home, and married a Greek man with whom she raised two Greek children. She attended a Greek Orthodox Church, taught Greek at a Greek school, volunteered at a Greek community center, and vacationed in Greece every summer. It was her frequent plane rides back to the home country that gave her the idea of starting a travel agency so she could help other Greek families go back and forth to Greece. After the Internet put her agency out of business, she used her contacts in the industry to land the job at Tango Airlines in Atlanta.

"I know the business," she'd told Alexander. "I get along well with people, and I'm happy to have found a cheap way to fly to Greece. But the customers who used to be my friends and relatives are now adversaries, and I don't like that. I never thought there was anything adversarial about going on vacation. The customers want to go and the airlines want to take them.

"But the part about the airlines wanting to take the customers applies only to customers who behave as the airlines want them to. Once customers start asking questions, once they start requiring a level of service above the bare minimum, the airlines just want to get rid of them. So the idea is to construct service systems that are so frustrating that the customers will give up and go away.

"I used to tell that to my husband and he'd say, 'Aren't the airlines afraid of losing the business?' and I'd say, 'No, not really. They figure the exasperated customers from our airline will go to other airlines, but the exasperated ones from those airlines will come to us, so it's a wash. Not only that, but once customers have been defeated by one airline, the fight has been taken out of them. You see, they really want to go to Florida or Mexico or New York very badly. So they'll take whatever we dish out and say thank you. They're actually easier to handle the second time around.

"What we're doing is punishing people for fighting for decent treatment. That's what's going on here. If you dare stand up and say, 'Hey, this isn't fair,' we smack you down. That's my job. I'm a smacker supervisor."

She'd told Alexander Hammermill that listening to his call had not only inspired her but that she considered it a sign of the rightness of her cause that her new partner turned out to have not only the will but the resources to put their new organization on the map.

Alexander had been convinced there was more than enough anger and frustration out there to give the new organization momentum and he'd felt they should remain flexible enough to follow that energy where it took them. That meant few rules, no entry fee, and little structure. The one exception to the rule about no rules was that anyone who said the word "policy" had to go sit in the corner until further notice.

The organization grew by word of mouth and people seemed to like it that way. New members were personally recruited by existing members who found themselves, by chance, in position to witness another person's moment of truth.

Within three months T.U.L.P. had a computer division which had to be split up into software and hardware sections because the two divisions didn't get along. A telephone switchboard manned by a live human being at all times served as a hotline. A psychologist trained in anger management was available twenty-four hours a day. Hammermill paid for it all.

Next came the banking division, which became the most militant arm of the organization. Spurred on by its first recruit, a building contractor named Gus DeMauro, it circulated emails Irena Poppadapoulos feared were coded messages to militant sleeper groups of home buyers. DeMauro had been recruited by the chief of software, who'd been in a bank in Mountain View, California, when he'd overheard Gus trying to pay off a loan. It wasn't until the contractor had raised his voice that the software chief had noticed him. It was just before closing time on a Friday at the end of a month, and the bank was crowded.

DeMauro had been dressed in jeans, a blue work shirt, and brown work boots. He was no more than five and a half feet tall, bald, and covered in dust. Large forearms and a back too broad for the rest of his body gave him an almost comical look.

"What do you mean, I've got to pay three more days of interest?" Gus had said to the young assistant manager.

"That's the time it'll take for your check to clear," the manager had said.

"Baloney. The bank I'm writing this check on is across the street. There. Look. You can see it out your window. It's the brick building between the two Thai restaurants." When DeMauro had gestured, several people standing in line had turned to look.

"Normally, it's five days, sir. We're cutting it to three because you're a valued customer."

"You're goddamned right I'm a valued customer. Do you know how much money flows through my account here? So let me pay the thing off now. I'm here now. It doesn't take you five days or three days or three minutes to verify that my check is good, and you know it. In fact, you can call my other bank on the phone. Better yet, just walk across the street and verify that the money's there. That's what this valued customer wants you to do. I'll wait."

"I can't do that, sir."

"Why not? And don't tell me it's company policy."

"It's company policy."

"I'm writing you a check for what I owe today and I'm not giving you an extra three days of interest. You do what you want, but if you come after me for the three days interest, I'll come back here and break your neck."

"Excuse me?" the banker had said.

"You heard me," said Gus, who handed the banker a check and smiled. "And I mean every word of it." He'd then made a twisting motion with his hands, as if snapping the head off a chicken, and walked out the door.

The software guy had followed him out to the parking lot.

Chapter 7

Scott was still wondering how to find the laughing lady when he walked into his office on Tuesday morning and turned on the stereo. His staff knew to avoid disturbing him when music was on because it meant he was concentrating intensely on his work. What they usually heard coming through the door was classical, with a heavy emphasis on Bach and Mendelssohn, composers they'd learned to identify because Scott gave spot quizzes. But there were also strange chanting sounds and guitar picking and a fast-paced, wild-sounding music that Dr. Berk, one of the visiting psychologists, told them was Klezmer music.

When he became Director, Scott moved into the large corner office, installed a pair of used B & W speakers he'd found on Craigslist, hooked them up to an old receiver that had been gathering dust in his garage, and set about expanding the myth of his tuneful ruminations.

Scott couldn't concentrate on anything when there was music on, other than the music, but his patients could. They could begin to think seriously about the things that had laid them low and brought them to that place, and what work was needed to regain their health. A music collection broad enough to challenge anyone's ability to name a genre not covered in his iPod was Scott's opening gambit of choice to a population not given to opening up.

For those not susceptible to that approach, Scott's fallback was a framed, poster-sized photograph of a sunset scene in the High Desert in New Mexico that hung on his wall. The picture invited comment from everyone who saw it, just as the scene had done when Scott viewed it with the photographer many years before.

After leaving medical school, Scott decided to look for America.

"Like in the song," he'd said to his bewildered mother, whose head was still spinning. "I want to find what those other kids in the class have. I don't want to back into a career. I want to run to it, with my arms open wide."

"Song, schmong," she'd said. "They had tickets to success, and so did you. And you gave it up. Such *narischkeit* I can't believe."

Most of America was west of where he was, so that's the direction he pointed his car. He saw the Finger Lakes and the Great Lakes, Niagara Falls, and Chicago, where a city filled with blues clubs nearly broke his heart.

"It's because you feel the music as much as they do but you can't play it like they can. That's why it hurts so much," his brother told him over the phone.

After three days in Madison, Wisconsin, he was sure he had it figured out, and wrote his brother a postcard that read: "Beautiful town, wonderful people. I'll get a Ph.D. in English Lit. and teach. Come visit."

But by the time the postcard had been delivered, he'd met an English teacher at the university who told him the students complained bitterly about reading authors like Faulkner, whom they called "irrelevant," and Hemingway, whom they called a "pig." Writers being studied now were increasingly selected on the basis of ethnicity and color.

"I love Faulkner," Scott had said. "And Hemingway *was* a pig, but his books are great."

"Forget it," she'd told him. "You've no chance."

Heading west, he spent two full days driving through endless corn fields. At night he stayed in motels carved into them and read Steinbeck's *Travels With Charley*. "Eat hardy," he wrote to his brother. "We'll never starve."

He made his way south to the Grand Canyon, where he floated down the Colorado River for one glorious day that ended with him spending an hour considering, then rejecting, the idea of becoming a park ranger. That night, in a honky-tonk in Flagstaff, he sat in with a rock and roll band that had a female singer who was working her way back to Santa Fe. The next morning, they headed out together. A year later they were still together, with Scott not yet having figured out if it was sunsets over the desert or the six and a half percent commissions he kept earning at her father's real estate firm that had kept him there for so long.

The girl's name was Julia, a skinny, intense young woman with a cocaine problem that was evident from the first night they met. Scott, whose own use had ended in college for no reasons other than it cost too much and his fear it would damage his nose, discovered he had a knack for saying the right words and doing the right things to help her through the worst of her addiction. She loved him for it, and so did her parents. He found a rehab facility for her and guided her through recovery and two relapses.

Eighteen months after coming to New Mexico they were married, but when his new father-in-law offered him a piece of the business, he stunned the man by turning him down. Instead, he returned to school, this time to get certified as a substance abuse counselor. Now it was his turn to return to the facility that had cured his wife, but as a therapist.

"This is the gig I've been searching for," he wrote Keith. "Med school was closer to the mark than I thought."

He loved the work and felt he had a real gift for it. It wasn't long before he was promoted to assistant director of the facility, although he continued to sell the occasional piece of real estate for his father-in-law to pick up some extra cash.

The day after his twelfth anniversary Julia left him for a doctor who'd just been appointed Head of Orthopedic Surgery at a hospital in Santa Fe, and Scott moved back East.

Chapter 8

"I'd like to see it too. Can't we just wait till it comes out on DVD?"

"Alexander, honey, you know how I like seeing movies in the theater."

"I know, but . . ."

"You like seeing movies in theaters just as much as I do. You just don't like the Rialto, for some silly reason. But it's the only theater around that shows foreign movies."

"It's not the theater. It's the people who go to that theater. They're all so . . . so . . ."

"So like us?"

"It's that liberal look. They're all so predictable. They . . . they wear sensible shoes, every one of them."

"Alexander, are we not going to the movies because liberals wear sensible shoes?"

"No, but would it kill them to just once put on a shoe that wasn't orthopedically correct? And their clothes. So sensible. In muted colors and earth tones. If they're really feeling their oats they'll wear something mauve. That's as wild as they get. Mauve.

"And they all read *The New Yorker*. Last time we went the fellow in front of us was reading up until the moment the lights went out. He didn't want to waste a minute. The whole world has to know how intellectual he is. If he'd had a flashlight, he'd have turned it on and read during the coming attractions.

"And the gray hair. All the women are gray. All the men are gray."

"You're gray."

"I know, but every one of them? What's politically incorrect about hair coloring? Can't they be liberal with dark hair? Would it be a crime?"

"Is there anything else?"

"If you must know, yes."

"Tell me, dearest."

"It's their cars. They pull up there, one after the other, in those midget, fuel-efficient cars. The parking lot is full of them. Some guy is six foot two and two hundred fifty pounds but he has to drive a Toyota Prius because he's a liberal. He can't breathe. The steering wheel is breaking his ribs. His knees are squashed against the dashboard and his feet are going numb, but he'll be damned if he'll break down and buy a full-sized car because what would all the other liberals say?"

"Bring a jacket, sweetness. They turn the air conditioning up so high."

"Oh, look," said Cindy as they entered the theater, "they've remodeled the lobby. Nice seats along the windows. And look at the nice photographs along the walls."

"Yeah," said Alexander as they walked the perimeter of the room. "Look at them. Just look at them. There's not a thing interesting about them. Not one sunset. Not one mountaintop, no pretty girls, no tropical fish. Pictures for liberals. We're not supposed to enjoy something so pedestrian as a view. We're too refined for that. We're supposed to want to think about things. Like this picture. It's a picture of a wooden door. Give me a break. And this one. Oh, they're a set. It's the same wooden door with milk bottles in front of it. And look at that one over there. It's an old twisted tree. Is that a commentary on the aging process? Because I gotta tell ya, to me it's just an old twisted tree, and it's ugly. I'm going to be old and twisted one day, and when that happens I guarantee you I'm gonna wanna look at pictures of pretty girls. Yeah. Pretty girls swimming with tropical fish."

"Perhaps you could make a polite suggestion to the theater's owner," said Cindy. They got in line for popcorn.

"And look at these kids behind the counter. Will you just look at them? Every one has multiple body piercings and tattoos and is dressed in black. You're telling me not one single cleancut kid ever applied for a job here? I have to buy food from a girl who has a metal stud driven through her tongue and a ring in her eyebrow. Not only does it take my appetite away, it makes me want to cry."

"I'll get us the popcorn, dear. I have faith your appetite will recover."

Inside the theater, the Rialto ran a slide show until the lights were turned down. The slides were the same kind of pictures as were hanging on the walls of the lobby.

"Here," said Cindy as she offered popcorn to her husband. "Don't look."

At 7:15 the lights in the theater were turned down, and fifty or sixty sensibly shod moviegoers settled in expecting to see *Black Swan,* but it was never shown. After a few minutes the lights came back on, and a kid wearing black appeared at the front of the theater and announced that the projector was broken and the movie would have to be canceled. He promised the movie fans they would get their money back. All they had to do was hand their ticket stubs over to the man in the ticket booth and he would issue a refund.

"Watch," Alexander grumbled to his wife as they got up to leave, "No one will complain. They'll all march out of here saying nothing. They're so reasonable I could scream."

"Please don't, honey. A girl can stand only so much fun."

A slow-moving line formed in front of the ticket booth, but two groups ahead of the Hammermills, it came to a stop. There was some commotion involving an old woman at the head of the line who was accompanied by two young girls.

"It's all right, Grandma," the kids were saying as they stood in front of the booth. They were stroking the old woman's arms as they spoke.

"I'm just so disappointed. The two of you are so busy. It'll be weeks before I can get together with you again."

"No, no, Grandma. This week. We'll come back in a few days."

"Excuse me," the young man in the ticket booth said. "Excuse me, ma'am. Your ticket stubs, please."

Distressed already, the old lady's face now sunk as if being pulled down by ropes, and Alexander thought he could see her hands shake.

"I . . . oh, no. Let's see." She began to look through her purse.

"I need the stubs, lady," said the kid inside the booth. He was about twenty-seven, skinny, with short, spiked hair and a ring in his nose. He wore a flowery shirt, open at the collar, underneath a black leather jacket. His eyeglasses had narrow lenses encased in a thick, black frame. To Alexander's ears the young man's tone made it sound as if the unplanned events of the evening had been the old woman's fault.

"I'm sorry. I just don't know what I did with them. I . . . ."

"Lady, no stubs, no refund."

"But . . . but that's thirty dollars. That's a lot of money to me." The woman's face was ashen, her voice had begun to crack.

"It's okay, Grandma," the teenagers were saying. "We'll treat next time. Come on. Let's go home."

"No! It's my treat and I'm not leaving without that money!" She was crying now, her voice breaking with emotion. "Young man, can't you see we must have been in the theater? What else would we be doing in this line?"

"Step aside, lady. I've got a line of people behind you."

"They'll wait." The voice was firm, masculine, and brooked of no dissent. Alexander had to do a scan of the lobby before identifying the source as a nondescript looking man who'd been in front of him all along. "And they'll be a lot happier while they're waiting if you start showing this woman a little respect."

The speaker stepped out of line, nudged ahead of the old woman and her granddaughters, and stood directly in front of the booth.

"Give her the money, young man. You know perfectly well this lady was in the theater."

"Gimme a break, buddy. Who are you, anyway—her Godfather?"

"I'm another customer without his ticket stub. That's who I am, k-kid, and I want m-m-m-my r-r-r-refund too!"

"You should've held on to the stubs. That's why we give them to you," said the kid, who looked beyond the stuttering man toward the people behind him, which seemed to make the man angrier still.

"Not g-g-good enough," said the man, who now slapped his hand down hard against the countertop. "G-g-get the owner."

"The owner's not here."

"G-g-get the m-manager."

"I am the manager."

"Then g-give me my refund. Me and this woman. Look, kid. How would we know to be in this line if we hadn't been in that theater ten minutes ago and heard your c-c-co-worker announce that the p-p-projector was broken?"

The man was yelling now, and several people in the line were mumbling quietly, "He's right. He's right."

The line was no longer much of a line but more like a throng, and it included people waiting for or coming out of the other movies. Everyone was watching what was happening at the ticket booth.

The manager stopped looking beyond the angry man and returned his gaze to the round hole in the glass that separated him from the customers, and through which he could see directly into the eyes of his antagonist.

"No stubs, no refund. It's company policy," he said, as if use of the phrase "company policy" was a rhetorical blow so powerful that no retort was possible. But while the manager's presumptuousness rankled Hammermill, it must have infuriated the old woman's champion, because his next move was to reach through the hole in the glass, grab the manager's shirt and pull back, plastering the side of the young man's face against the inside of the transparency.

The other worker in the booth, a young girl, screamed. The man holding on to the manager's neck, clearly now and with no stutter, eyes boring through the glass, yelled: "I, too, have a policy. It is my policy not to be abused by company policy!"

Inside the booth was mayhem. Four skinny, tattooed theater employees dressed in black, each with multiple body piercings, tried to get at the patron so as to pry his hand from their boss's neck, but Alexander had taken up a position next to the angry customer and would not be moved.

Several gray-haired people in mauve shirts and jackets began to applaud.

Finally, another moviegoer pushed through the crowd and approached the booth from the side opposite Alexander, flashed a badge, and said, "I'm a police detective. Please let go of him, sir, or I'll have to hurt you."

The man complied and the detective asked him to sit in the lobby, which he did. The theater manager staggered out of his booth, screaming, "Call the cops! I want his ass arrested! I'll sue his ass!"

"I take it that means you want to press charges," said the detective.

"Where is he? I want him!" the manager yelled as he pressed forward toward the lobby. But the detective held him where he stood with one hand placed on the man's chest and asked the girl in the ticket booth to call for a patrol car. The manager kept yelling as the girl made the call, and he didn't stop until the attacker got back up, clenched his right hand into a fist and started walking back toward the theater manager.

"Let him go," the assailant said to the detective. "Let's give him what he wants." It was the same powerful voice that had begun the conflict minutes earlier, and it still seemed to belong to anyone in the room other than its owner.

"Yeah," said the manager, but with not as much conviction as his adversary.

The detective, who had by this time identified himself as Detective Tony Zito of the Albany Police Department, looked hard at the man with the clenched fist as he continued to hold off the manager, seemingly now with little effort and, with a half smile and a slight shake of his head, turned to him and said, "You don't want me to let you go, kid. This guy is serious." Then, turning back to the rejuvenated combatant: "Take a seat again, please. We've had enough drama for tonight."

By the time the patrol car arrived fifteen minutes later, things had calmed down. The people who'd come for *Black Swan* had taken their refunds and gone home. The theater manager had stopped screaming and retreated to his office on the second floor. The man who'd grabbed him remained seated in the lobby along with his wife, the two of them holding hands.

The old lady and her granddaughters had disappeared without a trace. They never received a refund.

Cindy Hammermill drove home because Alexander was busy working his cell phone. By the time they got back, he'd tracked down his lawyer and had him run down to Albany City Police Court.

The name of the man who'd come to the grandmother's aid turned out to be Frank Rooney. He was charged with Assault in the Third Degree, a misdemeanor, and bail was set at $2,500. At the courthouse a man wearing jeans and a sweater told Rooney only that he was a lawyer who worked for Alexander Hammermill. He posted the bail and gave Rooney two cards, one each with his and Hammermill's name on it, Hammermill's being the same as the one given to Max Rodriguez at the vintage clothing store two days earlier.

Alexander also discovered, by the time he went to sleep, that Rooney was a chemistry professor at Rensselaer Polytechnic Institute in Troy, that he lived in Niskayuna, and that he'd never been arrested in his life.

"A regular Mr. Clean," Alexander muttered as he climbed into bed.

"Another insight, dearest?" said Cindy. "You know how I'd love to hear about it, but can it wait until morning so I can examine it in the light of day, as I'm sure it deserves?"

Chapter 9

Scott often checked the online version of the Albany *Times Union* newspaper to see if there was anything going on that might affect his mother. The Thursday after his adventure in the Berkshires, he saw the following notice:

FREE FRANK ROONEY!

Tuesday night, an honest citizen named Frank Rooney, while doing nothing more hostile than going to the movies, was arrested for the crime of defending an old woman. Frank Rooney was at the Rialto Theater, part of the Maiko Industries theater chain, when he was told, along with dozens of other theatergoers, that the projector was broken and the show would be canceled. Refunds were given to all except Frank and the elderly woman, who had lost their ticket stubs. And for protesting that injustice, what did Frank get? He got arrested. Everyone in line saw Frank and the woman come out of the theater. Everyone knew they had paid for their tickets. Why were they denied? Company Policy!

COMPANY POLICY KILLS! And it's killing us, every one of us.

Join us Saturday at 6:30 P.M. at a rally at the Rialto Theater to protest this injustice and demand that Maiko Industries drop the charges against Frank Rooney.

Paid for by T.U.L.P. Treat Us Like People!

Scott called his brother.

"She'll be there, don't you think?" he said.

"How do we know? Maybe she lives in Maine. Maybe she lives in Jersey. Maybe she doesn't read newspapers. It's a million to one shot."

"But it's worth the trip, don't you think?"

"No."

"That's some vote of confidence."

"You're chasing a chimera."

"I know."

"Not only that, but guess who never heard of a protest she didn't want to attend?"

"We'll go in disguise."

For Jane it was an old problem. She'd been setting off store alarms for years and no one knew why. It wasn't as if she had steel rods in her back or a plate in her skull. Yet anyone who knew to ask the right questions could always tell where she'd been.

She could cut a swath of malfunction yards wide just by walking down a sidewalk. Cell phones stopped working. Security systems failed. GPS devices got lost. Some items were safe. It seemed wire insulation provided protection from Jane's disruptive energy. But whatever the item was, it had to be wired from start to finish. So a computer that was plugged in and drawing its signal via cable was fine, but the moment it went wireless it lost its defenses. Walking into a Starbucks for Jane was like someone else yelling *fire!* in a crowded theater. Most household appliances worked, but the remote controls that might operate them did not. Radio transmission was out of the question.

Battery operation was a gray area. It depended, she thought, on her mood. The more confident she felt, the less likely a flashlight or video camera was to work. The more unsure, fire away. And on rare occasions, when she was feeling unusually chipper, even wired items like the town traffic signal in West Stockbridge were not safe.

"I hate malls," she would say, which was true. Her daughter learned to cover for her, as though her mom had Tourette's or some other kind of discomfort-producing disease.

Sometimes Jane would see it coming, like she had at the deli in West Stockbridge, but more often than not the alarms, with their laser beams and radio signals, would sing out on their own, and it would be her laughter that would save the day.

Olivia's Lookout had been shown to her by a man she'd once dated, a cad as it turned out, on a clear September night when the fireflies were lighting the way down to the lake.

"I arranged for them," he'd said. "I hope you like the show."

"Say what you will about cads," she'd laughed to her friends. "They know the best places."

Four days later, when she saw the ad about Frank Rooney, it was because her best friend, Serena, handed it to her as they ate breakfast on Jane's tiny patio in front of Jane's house in the village of Younger Lake. The three-bedroom Victorian was painted green and purple.

"I thought I'd try something restrained for this year," Jane had laughed to the man at the Sherwin-Williams paint store, who had laughed too. "And by the way, your alarm is about to go off."

"Isn't the Rialto Theater one of you-know-who's businesses?" Serena said.

"Oh, yeah," Jane laughed as she read the page, shaking her head. "Is it ever."

Jane knew all about Maiko Industries, Inc. It owned fifty-four movie theaters in six states, ten apartment complexes of varying sizes and shapes, a medical imaging company that did MRIs, X-rays and the like, and a bowling alley. The bowling alley was the only part of the Maiko empire that did not turn a profit, but its owner and CEO didn't care.

"Sarah, honey, come down and look at this," Jane yelled upstairs to her daughter.

A skinny fourteen-year-old, taller than her mother, with straight blond hair, large brown eyes, and in most aspects the look of a spider in sneakers walked slowly down the stairs.

"What?" she said.

Jane handed her the newspaper.

"Oh. My. God."

"Maybe you should give your father a call, sweetheart."

"Ohmigod."

The child pulled a cell phone out of a pocket of her denim shorts, threw it down on the kitchen table with a roll of her eyes, and grabbed the landline phone from the wall and dialed. "Daddy," she said, "did you read the *Times Union* this morning?"

There was a brief pause.

"Did you read all of it? Is there a newspaper at the bowling alley? Go get it. Read page B10, in the local news section. It's an advertisement, kind of. Just read it and call me back."

She didn't get a call back, which didn't surprise her mother. Jane could just see the big BMW 740I with the CHAZ license plate and a muscular, red-faced man behind the wheel tearing out of the Carefree Lanes parking lot.

Chapter 10

The only people in Wheaton who didn't see the T.U.L.P. ad in the paper that morning were the ones who were out of town, and they included Frank and Laura Rooney. Frank had woken at 5:30 A.M. with a burning desire to go for a hike in the woods, and he wanted his wife to go with him.

Laura looked at her husband with something more than uncertainty. He sat down on the side of the bed and took hold of her hand.

"Don't be frightened," he said. "I haven't lost my mind. I just have a sense that it's the thing to do. Come with me. We'll pack a lunch or something. It'll be a great day."

"Frank," she said as though trying to soothe a distraught child, "did you think grabbing that young man in the movie theater was also the right thing to do?"

"You know, I've been thinking about that ever since, and I must tell you I cannot find one bit of doubt or remorse in my heart for what I did. So, yes, I do think it was the right thing to do."

"Okay," she said. "Maybe if we go on a long enough hike you can explain it to me."

"Thank you, honey."

They were heading up the Northway toward Lake George when their paperboy threw the day's *Times Union* at their door. They were halfway to the top of Prospect Mountain when Charlie Remlinger pulled his BMW out of the parking lot of Carefree Lanes. And they were standing at the summit, arm in arm, looking out at a glorious view when Irena Poppadapoulos managed to get through on the phone to Alexander Hammermill.

"I know what you're gonna say, and it's a long story so I hope you're on an extended break there at the big airline phone bank in the sky," Hammermill said.

"Wow. Someone's in a good mood."

He told her about Frank Rooney, the old lady, and the theater manager.

"It does sound like our kind of thing," she said. "But you've committed our whole organization without consulting a single other member. I think you have a lot of explaining to do. What if the membership doesn't want to take up this protest?"

"They will. They must. Irena, I have to tell you this is the best thing I've done in years. I feel like a sergeant who was told by his commander to stay behind with his squad and guard the mess hall and suddenly he realizes the enemy general is just yards away on the other side of the hill. The sergeant can capture him and win the whole battle, but he's got to take the initiative."

"I still don't . . ."

"Irena, it couldn't wait. In two days no one would have cared. Right now, the whole town is buzzing. We've caught a wave. The local radio stations have picked it up. Everyone wants to know what TULP is."

"But how are we going to organize a rally on such short notice? How many members do we have out there?"

"I haven't figured that part out yet, but it doesn't matter. People will come out. College kids in the area will come. Professionals will come. I'm telling you, it just strikes a chord. They picked on a little old lady, Irena. People aren't going to stand for it, just like this Rooney character wouldn't stand for it. If they'd just thrown him out of the theater it would be different. But they arrested him. They've given us a target to shoot at."

"How does he feel about being in the middle of all this?"

"Don't know. I haven't spoken with him yet."

"You're kidding."

"Sorry, no."

"The old woman, then. What does she have to say?"

"No one's heard from her, and I don't know who she is."

"Alexander, you're just testing me, right?"

"Afraid not."

"Jesus, Alexander, have you lost your mind? What if he's some corporate type himself? What if he thinks what's wrong with America is we don't have *enough* corporate control? What if the woman is a scam artist who snuck into the theater through the back door? Alexander, this is reckless."

"Irena, this is perfect."

"Are you going to tell me you just feel it, so you're running with it? Is that it? Tell me you've got something more substantial than that."

"No, nothing. But that's pretty substantial."

"Alexander, who's going to deal with the press?"

"Our spokesperson. The rest of us will keep out of view. No trail. They'll imagine we've got millions of members."

"I'm not following you, Alexander, which is becoming a pattern."

"How many members do we have, Irena?"

"About fifteen hundred, more or less, probably less than more."

"And who knows that piece of information?"

"I do. You do. Three or four others. That's it."

"Correct. Now, would you be scared of an organization that only had fifteen hundred members nationwide?"

"That depends."

"Well, I can guarantee you Maiko Industries won't. Neither will any other big corporation. But if they think we number in the millions, if they think there are hundreds of thousands of us in every city in America, now that's something else entirely."

"So we're going to do this by stealth? We're going to con Maiko into corporate responsibility, is that right?"

"Something like that."

"And who's going to be the lead con man?"

"We only got our poster boy sixteen hours ago, Irena. Don't rush things."

All the way down the mountain and then in the car on the way home, poster boy Frank Rooney kept commenting on a strange light-headedness he was feeling.

"It's the thin air up there," said his wife. "You're not used to it."

"No, it's something else, honey."

"What, then?"

He didn't know, but when he turned off Vly Road in Wheaton and onto Phillips Street and saw the remote news vans of all three local TV stations parked in front of his house, he felt he had a good idea.

Chapter 11

Max's fingers trembled as he typed "treat us like people" into the Google search bar. He was already committed to the cause. His only regret was not starting the fight himself years ago in Madison.

It was during his junior year at Wisconsin. He'd bought a computer system from Comp America, which included a computer tower, keyboard, monitor, and printer, all for the sale price of six hundred ninety-nine dollars. It came with a six-month warranty. The computer worked for one month. Then it started shutting down. It would start up just fine, all the programs would operate correctly for about half an hour, after which it would simply turn off and would not reboot.

The people at Comp America in Madison were friendly. But, as Max would later explain, that was because everyone in Madison is friendly. They fixed his computer. He took it home. It shut down after half an hour and would not reboot.

"Did you let it run for a while after you fixed it?" he asked the nice people at the store.

"We always let the computers run after a repair. It's company policy."

"Yes, but for how long? You see, it doesn't shut down right away. It takes about half an hour."

"I'm sure we let it run for as long as it had to."

Max wondered how they knew how long it had to run and then considered pointing out they surely hadn't known because the problem remained. But they were so friendly and insisted they'd get it right this time, so he let it go. Three days later they called him to pick up his computer. He brought it home and turned it on. It ran for half an hour, shut down, and would not reboot.

"It's got to be the software," they said when he brought it back for the third time. "It's a software problem."

"So what does that mean?"

"We'll contact Sandstone, the manufacturer, for you and see what they suggest. Hopefully, they can help you."

Max felt a whole series of negative implications had been injected into the equation. "What do you mean, 'for me'? You said you'd contact them 'for me.' Aren't you contacting them for you? It's your warranty, right?"

"Oh, no. We warrant the computer. It's their operating system."

"But their operating system came with your computer. That's how you advertised it. You said, 'Ready to go, fully loaded, all you have to do is plug it in.' That's why I bought it."

"And it was fully loaded—with their operating system."

"Are you telling me I'm now on my own, that you're off the hook?"

"Oh, no. We'll help you. But it's not our fault."

"Not to be nasty or anything, but if it's the software and you don't do software, what were you doing with my computer the last two times I brought it in?"

"We didn't know it was the software then."

"Yes, so what were you doing with my computer?"

"We were following company procedures."

"But what did you fix?"

"Not the software. We don't do software. That's what we're trying to tell you."

Max took his machine home and went to the Sandstone website that Comp America had given him. They said he'd find the answers to his software problem there. The site had no menu choice for computers that shut off after half an hour and did not reboot. It did have a phone number. Max called and got a phone menu that did not list his problem. Then he punched the option that allowed him to talk to a person, but he had to wait for "the next available technician." Then a young man with an undecipherable accent came on and told Max to sit at the computer and the technician would guide him through the problem. Then the computer shut down and would not reboot.

Max called back the next day, stayed on the line for fifteen minutes, and turned on his machine only when he got a live technician at the other end. The technician had Max pointing and clicking and all the while the fellow was saying something that was either "Ya," or "Yes," or "Oh, brother." Then he told Max it was a hardware problem and he couldn't help. Then the computer shut down and would not reboot.

There was a student organization at the university that helped repair broken computers, but the kid behind the counter warned Max that once the computer was opened by someone other than Comp America, the warranty would be voided. If it couldn't be fixed, Max would be screwed. A phone call to Comp America led to a service representative who was delighted to confirm that fact.

Max returned to Comp America three more times. Eventually, he got them to take back the machine and send it to their repair center. If the problem could be reproduced, he'd get a new one.

"And if it can't?"

"Then there's nothing we can do. It's company policy."

The T.U.L.P. website contained a big sign in the middle of the home page that said, "We're under construction. Please try again soon." It was 9:30 Thursday morning. Max decided to head down to the Rialto Theater and check things out. He wasn't alone. About three dozen people, unable to get information about T.U.L.P. on their computers, had abandoned their mouse pads and taken to the street, and more were arriving every few minutes. Each new arrival took out his cell phone and called someone or texted something and minutes later more people appeared on the sidewalk.

The crowd was clustered around five utility poles in front of the theater on which someone had stapled large oak tag posters with these words: Banking, Computers, Insurance Companies, Automated Phone Systems, Everything Else.

Max strolled through the growing crowd listening to bits and pieces of emotional, highly animated conversations. People were saying things like:

". . . and she told me I couldn't get any information about my account without my pin number, including my pin number. So I said, 'Listen, for the love of God, my pin number is what I'm trying to get . . .'" And:

"The choices were to dial your party's extension if you knew your party's extension or dial 0 for the operator. But when I dialed 0, the recording said it couldn't connect me to that extension. And the person who'd sent me the letter hadn't put his extension in the letter, so I never got to talk to him. So they thought I hadn't responded to their letter and they canceled my account." And:

"They said they couldn't take it back because I didn't have the receipt. But it was a special offer and it had the company name and logo stamped right on the package. I couldn't have gotten it anywhere else. They said if they let me do it they'd have to let everyone do it and I said if everyone has one with your company name and logo on the package, you *should* let everybody do it."

Total strangers were hugging one another. Older people were in high demand, as they could be heard discussing something called civil disobedience, which the younger people in the crowd seemed eager to hear about.

A reporter named Meagan Swoboda showed up hoping to get something exciting on the air for her employer, WTXY local news— "First and Fair." And Charlie Remlinger showed up, both fists clenched, veins popping from his neck and forehead, shoving his way through the crowd to his office inside the theater.

Chapter 12

"Can't I shoot them?" Charlie asked his attorney. "It's my property. A man has a right to protect his own property, doesn't he?"

"No," the lawyer had told him, "you can't shoot them. That's *can NOT*. You got that, Charlie? First off, the sidewalk is public property. Second, they're outside your theater, not inside. Third, the theater is only a business, it's not your home, and fourth, they're demonstrating peacefully."

"What kind of kiss-ass rule is that?" Remlinger said. "They're fucking with me. That's all I know. And it's going to stop."

In kindergarten, Charlie Remlinger had punched a boy for obstructing his view out the classroom window. For Chaz, not much had changed since.

In the summer between his sophomore and junior years in high school, Chaz started a landscaping business. By August, he had four other kids working half days, two each in the morning and afternoon, while he worked all day long. As Chaz and Co. were without wheels, their sphere of influence extended no farther than they could roll the three hand-pushed gas mowers Chaz had purchased with money borrowed from his parents. What he found unfair about that situation was competition, particularly if it came from professionals, which meant anyone with a truck. Bad enough they could mow the whole god damned world if they wanted to. Why did they need to horn in on his neighborhood?

His business plan for meeting this challenge was a two-pronged attack, a forerunner of things to come. He slashed the tires of his competitor's trucks and then appealed to the homeowners' sense of loyalty to "nice neighborhood kids" to steal the professionals' business.

Eventually, he got a truck of his own. This allowed him to muscle in on other neighborhoods, even other towns. That was how he met Jane Blake, a pretty, smart girl who read books like they were going out of style, but had had to drop out of school to take care of three younger siblings. He was eighteen. She was seventeen. They were married within a year.

After the wedding they returned to an apartment over Chaz's parents' garage and set up shop, gradually ridding themselves of electronic gadgetry such as alarm clocks, can openers, and coffee makers, and replacing them with the manual models.

Chaz was a business natural. Landscaping gave him connections to construction people, who introduced him to real estate developers. All the while, he remained true to the business ethic that garnered his first payday, which was, "Grab the other guy by the throat and squeeze."

He was so upset that he couldn't do just that to the people out in front of his movie theater that he took out his frustration by tearing down the signs they'd stapled to the light poles. To insure his feelings did not go unnoticed, he did this while loudly questioning the protesters' masculinity, sexuality, and humanity.

None of the protesters left, but people did back off wherever Chaz stormed, and the commotion caught Meagan Swoboda's eye. By the time she got her camera crew together, though, hurricane Chaz had swirled back inside the theater. Instead, she found an engaging young man with a big smile who introduced himself as Max and suggested that if she'd turn on her camera, he'd be glad to tell her what the protest was all about.

Chapter 13

Max once guessed he'd witnessed fifty protests while at Wisconsin. After giving it more thought he revised that number up to one hundred. It didn't matter what was happening on Spaceship Earth, somebody in Madison was upset about it. Once, a group of animal rights activists set up a mock graveyard of cardboard tombstones on Bascom Hill, each with the inscription, "Murdered Baby Seals." That lasted a few days. Then a different group inherited the site, and the inscriptions on the "stones" were changed to read "The Bill of Rights." A week later the stones cried out their sympathy for "Chinese Sweat Shop Workers."

The tombstones were a one-size-fits-all appeal to conscience that Max stopped paying attention to after a while, but never came to fully ignore. For six years he was always certain there was something he ought to be feeling bad about.

On one glorious day for free speech, Max saw a group of gay rights advocates on Library Mall last only an hour before a larger group of anti-gay Christians pushed them away only to be swept aside by a furious, spontaneously assembled mob of anti-anti-gays—and it was still not yet time for lunch.

Max learned that TV reporters, shuttled as they were from story to story as fast as their vans could move, didn't know much about what they were covering. The tone of any protest was therefore set by the first person to get in front of a camera and explain what was going on—well or poorly, it didn't matter.

Still, it wasn't memories of Madison that made him tap Meagan Swoboda on the shoulder. It was memories of Mom. And the best memory of Nancy Rodriguez Max had, the one he had conjured up over and over during those black weeks and months following her death, had been created during a soccer match when he was a kid.

Max was a terrific ball handler. He used both feet equally well and controlled the ball with such authority that the other kids could never take it from him. They'd just wait for him to give it up which he did—freely, voluntarily, and with a smile—much to the horror of the coach, his dad and every other team parent but one. When Max was nine, his team was playing the only other undefeated team in the league. It was a scoreless tie late in the game when Max got his foot on the ball and took off on a journey from sideline to sideline and back again. In the process he dribbled around, behind, and through every kid on the opposing team, some more than once, while never advancing the ball one inch toward the goal. The parents screamed and howled, "To the goal, Max. To the goal!" But the little boy with the dancing feet was having none of it. Finally, the boys on the other team cornered him in a semi-circle with Max's back pinned to the sideline. None of them made a move for the ball. They just closed ranks and waited. Max sized up the situation, broke into his biggest grin yet, and tapped the ball to his nearest opponent as if to say: Here, now let's see what you can do with it.

The coach lectured him on his responsibility to his teammates, who wanted so to win. His father lectured him on the competitive spirit and what a shame it was to waste such talent. His mother told him it was the greatest thing she'd ever seen.

"You mean, in soccer?" he asked.

"No. Ever."

"Why?"

"Because it was beautiful. It was pure. It was just what you wanted to do. I could tell. You have a gift, Max, and I'm not talking about soccer."

"What does that mean, I have a gift?"

"I'm not sure yet. But you'll be sure of it someday. Things will come to you, and you'll know just what to do, just like you did today. They may seem odd to everyone else but they'll feel right to you. And you'll just have to do them. Promise me that, Max. You'll do what you know is right."

Young Max, sensing an ice cream in his future despite his father's disapproval, promised. Hijacking the press coverage of the protest at the Rialto Theater was nothing more than being true to his word. When he saw the reporter in search of a subject, he knew exactly what to do.

"What is this protest about?" said Meagan Swoboda into her microphone.

Max faced the camera.

"When corporations first appeared centuries ago, people feared they would be soulless and amoral because there was no single owner to hold responsible for the entity's actions. Later on, they feared corporations had become so powerful that they would control our lives not just economically, but socially and morally. They were right, but it has taken all this time for those fears to be fully realized. Now we see that the potential for harm is worse than anyone dreamed. Corporations—cold, unfeeling, and inhumane—dominate American life. But we, the people are fighting back. We're insisting on humane treatment, starting right here. Maiko Industries will either act like a good citizen—a good neighbor—or it will disappear, which is as it should be."

Meagan Swoboda held the microphone in front of Max an extra beat to make sure he was done. Then she said, "What is your name?"

"Max Rodriguez."

"Are you affiliated with T.U.L.P.? Can you tell us what it is?"

"T.U.L.P. is a grassroots movement of plain ordinary people who think corporations ought to learn right from wrong just like the rest of us. We're talking corporate morality here. Think of it, Meagan. Think of corporations doing the right thing. It's so unheard of, just the idea is shocking. But why? They're so much a part of our lives. Shouldn't they be good citizens too?"

Meagan stared into Max's green eyes with an expression that gave him the feeling she was not thinking about corporate morality. She turned to the camera and said.

"Meagan Swoboda for WTXY News."

Alexander Hammermill had seen Swoboda and her crew the moment they arrived. He'd been making his way slowly toward them, figuring his unique combination of size and knowledge would single him out as the man to be interviewed. That's why he'd been close enough to overhear Max's brief oration, which fell upon his ears like a song.

"Watch the WTXY local news at six," he told his wife on his cell phone. "We've found our spokesman."

Chapter 14

When Jane was not there, her TV hummed with two hundred digitally transmitted channels that her daughter surfed at lightning speed. With Jane within "destructo-distance," as the girl called it, the family returned to the ancient tradition of changing channels by touching the TV set. Jane didn't watch much, her favorite show being Trading Places, a BBC offering about interior decoration and home repair.

It was Thursday, and Thursdays were Chazzie nights, but Sarah called for early rescue whenever her father's temper and/or girlfriend accompanied him home from the office. Jane had a feeling there'd be an early call tonight.

She opened the downstairs windows so as to be able to hear the landline ring and went outside to water Aunt Gertie. Jane wondered why she bothered doing anything for her. It wasn't like the old girl might die. She couldn't even be wounded.

When Aunt Gertie was younger, she got packed in a plastic bag and shipped in a moving van from Guilderland to Clifton Park, a drive of about thirty minutes. The bag was then left untouched, forgotten and sealed in Jane and Chazzie's new backyard for the entire summer. When Jane finally opened it, there the plant was, bigger and greener than ever. She was even redolent, which philodendrons aren't, but Aunt Gertie had managed to produce the scent of roses.

The old girl's prior incarnation had been as Jane's aunt, her mother's older sister. Short, round, and volcanic, Gertie had blond hair that frizzed out to double the width of her head and in which was hidden, so she insisted, a fully grown attack ferret. Her clothing was a chaotic union of house dresses, scarves, vests, and hats, none of which ever rested where she wanted them to, which caused her to be forever adjusting and shifting her outfits as she rambled about her apartment. Aunt Gertie most resembled a churning, fast-flowing river of color in sneakers.

It was to her house Jane and her own older sister would go when their mom needed a break.

The first Aunt Gertie lived in downtown Newburgh, New York, where police and fire sirens blared throughout the night, frightening the girls. "Don't be ninnies," Gertie would holler at her terrified nieces. The girls would wait for an explanation as to why they shouldn't be ninnies, since the bedlam surrounding their aunt's apartment seemed reason enough, but their aunt said nothing further.

Being low to the ground, Aunt Gertie felt all things should be similarly sized. She held down nine-year-old Jane and cut her shoulder-length hair to within an inch of the child's scalp. The girl's fingernails met a similar fate, several times. Fortunately, the child had a small nose.

Aunt Gertie made money reading Irish cards, which were regular playing cards expertly interpreted. For a change of pace, she read tea leaves. Jane recognized repeating patterns in her aunt's predictions, applicable to nearly everyone if the reader had a little imagination. Gertie said the child had a real future.

The old woman once had a vision that became part of Jane's destiny. It happened when Jane was fifteen. The teenager was skinny and shy and certain she would never be kissed. Her older sister already had, so she said, and was just as certain it was the best thing ever. Overhearing them discussing the matter in the adjoining bedroom late one night, Gertie opened their door and shouted inside, seemingly to both girls, "You'll get any man you want, but then you won't be able to get rid of him. I see it."

That sounded good to the two girls. A decade later, Jane started referring to Aunt Gertie's vision as a curse. Men fell in love with her in supermarkets, at PTA meetings, on the bike path. Then they wouldn't go away. Nothing put them off, neither wedding ring nor child.

She was certainly pretty, with clear white skin, large blue eyes, and thick lips she referred to as "the kissable variety." And her figure had an hourglass shape with a high waist, long legs, and breasts slightly too large for her frame. Yet, her hair was stringy and unkempt all the time, revealing ears that stood out a little too far from her head, and her nose, while narrow and small, had bumps and turns she called "moguls." An attractive woman, but less so than others who did not receive a fraction of the male attention that came her way.

She had three unusual things going for her. The first was the insistence of every garment she owned, whether outer or underwear, to shift downward and reveal more cleavage than was intended. Blouses and dresses that provided full coverage in the store fell asleep on the job once she got them home. Bras showed an even more pronounced tendency, and bathing suits were downright rebellious.

The second thing was her impulse to laugh at the attention brought about by her untamed clothing, as though her breasts were telling one-liners and she couldn't resist them any more than the men who were listening so intently.

The combined effect of the cleavage and the laughter was to produce in men a complete absence of shame. For the first time in their lives they were gawking without guilt, and it gave them a sense of relief so profound, they treated Jane as if she were a woman wise in the ways of the heart, deserving of a respectful yet indulgent awe.

The third part of the triad was the song, "If I Loved You," from the musical *Carousel*. Had the hundreds of men who adored her gotten together and compared notes, they'd have discovered they'd all begun hearing the tune the moment they first saw her., and they'd each mistaken it for the sound of Jane's heart, declaring her passion for them and only them if they would but love her. Then they all began humming Rogers and Hammerstein.

"Some curse," said Jane's sister, who turned out not to have been in the old woman's vision even a little bit.

When Aunt Gertie died, the two women went over to the apartment to clean it out. The only thing they thought worth taking was a small, cut-leaf philodendron. On their drive home, streetlights flickered above them.

"Guess who?" said Jane.

A black BMW slowly turned the corner and stopped between Jane's house and the one across the street. Expecting trouble, Jane had been carrying her cell phone around with her, not that it would have worked.

Not only were the houses in Younger Lake scarcely large enough for people, the roads were barely wide enough for cars. Chaz called the place "Toy Town" in a tone Jane and Sarah knew well. Sarah got out of the car and turned her back to the big sedan as it rambled away.

"Was it really bad?" Jane said, and thought how much the child combined the traits of both parents. She was taller than Jane by a lot, with a strong chin and black eyes, like her dad. Her blond hair and thin "ski jump" nose came from her mom.

"So bad he didn't even want to talk about it. He just came home, told me to get in the car, and drove over here. I didn't even dare call. He was gripping the steering wheel so hard I thought it would break."

"Well, now that you're here maybe we'll see it on the news."

"Yeah. My friends all texted. It was already on the six o'clock."

"Has he seen it?"

"I don't think so. How's Aunt Gertie?" The plant was almost as big as her mom.

"Expanding."

Jane and daughter walked arm in arm into their home. "I think they're right, Mom. Why shouldn't this guy get his money back? Everybody knows he was in the theater. It's unfair."

"The newspaper said he grabbed the manager by the throat. Isn't that unfair?"

"No way."

"Well, don't let your father know how you feel. He'll short circuit or something."

"I'm going upstairs. I'll be down for the news."

"Don't you want dinner?"

"No. Ate at Dad's."

That meant there was so much texting to be done, there wasn't time to eat.

At eleven, Jane assumed her position on the kitchen side of the door separating that room from the living room. Normally, with Sarah there to operate it, the TV behaved well and Jane could watch from inside the living room. But at times of extreme psychic disturbance, nothing was certain and Jane and Sarah didn't want to miss the broadcast.

It was the lead story. After a brief intro by the anchors, the screen flashed pictures of throngs of people in front of the Rialto, with Meagan Swoboda providing the narration.

"An eclectic crowd of young and old, scruffy and well-heeled, black, white, Asian—just about any kind of person you can think of—descended on the Rialto Theater today to protest the arrest of Frank Rooney." As she spoke, the camera dutifully focused on the various types described in the voice-over. "Scruffy," was a nice looking guy who looked vaguely familiar to Jane. "Old," however, was unmistakable to them both. A gray-haired lady was shown directing the placement of a sign on a light pole. She turned and waved warmly at the camera.

"Oh, my God!" shouted Sarah. "It's Mrs. Gezunterman!"

Mrs. Gezunterman had learned about Frank Rooney's arrest just an hour after it happened. Her neighbor, Rose Pearlman, along with Rose's son, had been among the people at *Black Swan*. When Rose's son returned his mother to The Meadows, the assisted living complex where Mrs. Gezunterman and Rose lived, Mrs. Gezunterman was in the lobby, reading. This was Mrs. Gezunterman's favorite reading spot because it allowed her to speak to every resident who came and went.

"So? It was so bad you couldn't stay for the ending?"

"No, Flo," said Rose, and proceeded to tell her what happened. When she saw the paper the following Thursday, Florence Gezunterman knew what she was going to do that day. But first, she'd have to reschedule that afternoon's fitting.

At her sewing machine was a calendar with the names and phone numbers of her customers, for whom she did alterations and tailoring. It was a select group, as they were the ones who'd yet to hear her say things like, "Honey, I'm a seamstress, not a magician."

She dialed, and as she did her eyes caught the blue platform shoes under the table left behind by that Remlinger girl. It must be nice to be able to forget expensive things. She decided to give the shoes away if the girl didn't call for them by the end of the week. She felt three phone messages had more than discharged her responsibility. To be sure, though, she would call her son the Director and see what he thought about it.

"Flo," said Rose the morning after the protest, at breakfast, "I saw you on the TV last night. You were down at the protest giving orders. A regular organizer you are."

"What then? I should wait for someone else to get things going?"

"Of course not."

"If no one takes charge, nothing gets done."

"Sure, Flo."

"Are you telling me you think I should sit back and wait for some know-nothing to start giving me orders when I know better? Let me tell you something, Rose. It'll be a cold day in July before that happens."

"That's just what I told my daughter on the phone this morning, Flo. A cold day in July."

Chapter 15

"What's the downside?" said Alexander Hammermill. It was Friday morning, and he was in Patrick Monahan's office at Stuyvesant Plaza on Western Avenue in Albany. Alexander liked seeing Monahan there because the Plaza stores included a French restaurant ("Snooty as hell but they sure can cook.") and a bakery, where he'd stop and fill a bag with goodies to take to Monahan's staff. ("You're welcome! Join you? Why, don't mind if I do.")

Monahan did general legal work for Alexander. He was the attorney who'd bailed Frank Rooney out of jail. He wore white, button-down shirts, a solid blue or red tie, wingtip shoes, and a dark suit every day without fail. He was smart, efficient, and wholly without humor. Alexander called him "Sunshine."

"The downside is a misdemeanor conviction, a thousand-dollar fine and a year in the county jail," Monahan said.

"Oh, come on."

"Really. He's charged with an A misdemeanor. That's what the maximum sentence is. There are no guarantees. Just because you think the case is bogus doesn't mean a judge and jury will agree."

"Yeah, but for one quick grab? That's all it was."

"From what I hear, your boy would still have his hands around the guy's neck if that detective hadn't pried them loose. And then he went after him again. At least that's what the manager says."

"Was the manager1 even hurt? I was right there, you know. I saw his face get pulled into the glass. No bones were broken. There was no blood. Don't you have to show some injury?"

"You do, and I don't know about that yet. The guy went to the hospital and was released, but that could mean anything. Serious injuries do not necessarily manifest right away. Maybe he's seen some doctors afterward. We'll have to find out."

"Well, I don't see a judge throwing this guy in jail for this. I gotta tell you. The guy's a regular Mister Rogers."

"It's not your call, Alexander. You can't make him do this. And if you hire a hot-shot criminal defense lawyer to represent him, that lawyer's first responsibility will be to his client, not you. If Frank Rooney wants to make some deal just to get this thing over with, which is what most people do, you can't stop him, nor should you."

Alexander stood up and walked to the fourth-floor window and looked out at the stores below, wondering what time the French place opened for lunch.

"You wanna tell me again how you got your nickname?"

That afternoon, the Hammermills pulled up to 1440 Northumberland Drive in Niskayuna in their Ford Crown Victoria and stopped. Frank and Laura Rooney lived at 1436, but Frank had suggested over the phone that Alexander nose around a bit before coming in. The press deluge had been just the one afternoon so far, but the professor wanted to be extra careful.

Frank Rooney's home was an older version of the ones that surrounded Alexander's island retreat. It was a split-level with a large Hemlock tree in the front yard and shrubs lining the sidewalk that connected the front door to the driveway. The bottom level was done in brick, the upper in aluminum siding. There was a small porch, with just enough room for two people to sit. Double doors led the way inside to a tiny foyer and a staircase to the bedrooms. A wooden fence hugged the building on both sides. The backyard included a pool.

A day earlier, when a returning Frank Rooney had guessed that going out of town was the best thing he could have done, he hadn't known how right he'd been. Even before his car came to a halt in the tiny space the reporters had left in his driveway, they were yelling questions. He'd had no idea what they were talking about.

"Are you a member of T.U.L.P.?"

"Who wrote the ad that appeared in the paper?"

"What did you think of the protest at the Rialto today?"

Frank and Laura could only repeat a series of "I don't knows" as they fought their way to the front door. Frank did stop, just once, when he heard, "What are you going to do about the assault charge?" His face had taken on that faraway yet determined look that Laura recognized from the night before, as they'd sat in the lobby waiting for the police to arrive.

"I'm going to fight it," he'd said, as he'd shielded the open front door from reporters and cameramen long enough for Laura to escape inside.

"What do you mean 'you'll fight it' Laura had said as she finished pulling down the shades and checking the locks on the doors.

"I don't know. It just rolled off my tongue. But since Tuesday night, I feel like fighting."

"Not with me, I hope."

"No, honey." He'd put his arm around her with one hand and held up the paper he'd recovered from the front stoop with the other. Laura had held open a Venetian blind and peeked through. The press was packing up to go.

"Do we have any wine?" she'd said.

They'd sat on the high chairs at the kitchen counter. He'd popped a cork. She'd put out some cheese and crackers and they'd opened the newspaper.

The Rooneys had an unlisted number. Nonetheless, a call accompanied by a voice they'd never heard before was made to them later that night, and Frank knew right away who it was. He'd agreed to do nothing about his case until he met with the Hammermills the next evening.

Since being released by the City Court judge and before beginning to collect his thoughts so he could explain to his wife just why he'd done what he did, Frank Rooney had searched his memory for a time during their twenty-five years of marriage when he'd ever had to explain any bizarre or strange actions to his wife. He was still searching.

Frank Rooney was the kind of man who got swallowed up by the smallest of spaces. Average build. Average height. Straight, thin, sandy-brown hair and soft brown eyes. His taste in clothing ran to jeans, khakis, button-down work shirts, flannels, and hiking shoes.

He'd gone to a couple of anti-war marches as a kid, but that was only because he'd heard they were good places to meet girls. His one comment about politicians was a joke he'd stolen from Mark Twain. Every Election Day, he'd wait for his students to ask if he had voted yet and he'd say, "I never vote. It only encourages them." But half the kids had never heard of Mark Twain and all of them were so shocked that Professor Rooney was attempting humor, the joke laid an egg every time.

Laura's personality was so similar, people often took them for siblings. Also a Ph.D.—she taught biology at the State University at Albany—the two of them could fade into any background, which was just as they liked it.

Frank held a doctorate in chemistry from Cornell and had achieved tenure at RPI by the age of thirty-two, but he felt his greatest accomplishment was to conquer a debilitating stutter. He'd confided to a seventh-grade teacher that her job appealed to him and she'd used that information as a wedge to inspire the shy and talented child. "You'll never teach a day in your life if you don't beat that stutter," she'd told him. "And it's beatable."

So Frank read how-to books on the topic and talked his parents into paying for speech therapy. With the teacher's help, he tracked down famous people who spoke for a living, like actors and sportscasters who'd been stutterers themselves, and wrote to them begging for advice. Now, his stutter was undetectable except when he was highly agitated, and before one night ago, he couldn't remember the last time that was.

He liked movies: foreign or American, he didn't care. If it got a decent review, he'd see it. He liked his job, loved his wife, and adored his two bright, well-behaved teenage girls. There wasn't much in Frank Rooney's world to generate a fuss and he liked that most of all.

Recently, though, say over the last half-dozen years, he'd been muttering every once in a while at the TV. Commercials by oil companies about their efforts to preserve the environment caused him to mumble things like, "You've been telling us for years that the environmentalists were maniacs. Now you're one of them?"

A story on *Frontline* about predatory lending made him unable to sleep for several nights. It highlighted a bank policy of deliberately making loan documents so obtuse that most people couldn't, or wouldn't, read them. Then, ignorant of what their credit card or loan agreements called for, customers found themselves facing draconian penalties and late fees, which was the banks' design all along.

"Evil," he'd muttered at the flickering screen while Laura was preparing a meal.

"Frank? Are you talking to someone?"

"No, no. Just . . . hey, that smells good. Ready yet?"

"What does he look like?" Frank said. Laura was looking out at the front door from the dining room window.

"Like what I hoped he wouldn't look like—large, hairy, and radical."

"Radical? Honey, we're college professors. We're supposed to be used to hairy, odd-looking people."

"I know we are, but this one is in his fifties and he's the size of two or three of my students put together, and I don't know . . . I'm frightened about all this, Frank."

"I'm a little concerned too, but I think we'll be all right. I do."

Frank Rooney gave his wife's shoulder a squeeze and walked to the door.

Cindy Hammermill began speaking immediately after the couple entered the house. Frank got the impression it was a practiced approach to easing the tension her husband's presence might create. The man trailing after her was as much bursting with energy as he was enormous.

"When we were first married, I used to say, 'Don't worry, he grows on you,'" she said, reaching up as high as she could to tap her husband on the shoulder. "But somehow that didn't seem to be what people wanted to hear. So now I have him promise to let me do the talking for the first few minutes. It makes things easier. Believe me, once he gets going, he'll have plenty to say. Isn't that right, dear?"

Alexander reached down and took his wife's hand in his.

The foursome sat around a glass-topped coffee table in the living room. There was a brick fireplace that had a wood mantel and wrought iron grate that Frank and Laura had restored after buying the place from its original owner. The large couch, two chairs—each with an ottoman— and area rug had all been acquired over the course of their two decades in the house through patient, meticulous attention to sales. All the furniture reflected a vaguely Colonial style, not so much because of the Rooney's tastes or the style of their home, but because that's what stores sold in upstate New York. The room, along with all the others in the house, had the same cut-rate plainness that characterized all the discount furniture stores and therefore most of the other homes in the area, facts that the Rooneys were fully aware of and did not bother them one bit.

"You'll want to know who we are, why we're here, and what T.U.L.P. is all about," Cindy said. The Rooneys nodded in unison and off Cindy went. Ten minutes later, she was done.

"Isn't this kind of . . . radical?" said Laura Rooney. The word was spoken as it had been when she first saw the Hammermills, with great fear.

"Not at all," said Alexander. "We're just ordinary people, just like you and Frank. We are plumbers, teachers, builders, college kids, you name it. But since you did use the word 'radical,' don't you think you've done something radical here? Something radical and courageous?" He was gesticulating as he spoke, both hands waving in the air and his large body looking as though it was ready to lift off the couch. All the while, he was looking at Frank.

"You've recognized how big this issue is and you've decided to fight back. The twenty bucks it cost to go to the movies isn't the point. We're talking quality of life here. We're dealing with our humanity."

"I'd have gone away if they'd have given me my twenty bucks back," said Frank Rooney. "Mine and the old lady's."

Alexander nodded slightly.

"It's cheaper for corporations to ignore us," he said. "That's why they have automated phones and endless levels of bureaucracy. If no one is responsible to you, if nobody hears your complaints, you don't exist. It's so much easier for them that way, and they can't lose you as a customer because all the other companies will treat you the same way. You have no choice but to take it."

Frank noticed neither he nor his wife had yet to offer coffee to their guests, and he knew it was because, like him, Laura didn't feel their guests were in need of stimulation.

"Just what is it you want me to do?" he said.

"We want you to fight it."

Frank looked at Laura, but his wife would not make eye contact.

"We'll hire the lawyer, a hot-shot criminal attorney—someone you couldn't afford. It'll be a celebrity type who wouldn't otherwise deal with a misdemeanor case, but he'll take this one because of the publicity.

You won't have to pay for a thing. In fact, you won't have to do a thing. We'd like it if you spoke out, of course, but it's not necessary. If you want, you can just sit there and ride it out."

"Unless you lose," said Cindy, putting up her hands as she spoke, as if to hold back Alexander long enough for her to get a few words in. Laura Rooney's head turned toward Mrs. Hammermill. "The risk is all yours. You have to understand that. You're charged with Assault in the Third Degree. The maximum penalty is one year in the county jail or one thousand dollars or both. You have no criminal record, I assume. It doesn't seem he was badly hurt. The chances of jail are slight, but they're there. And if you lose and the judge thinks you should go to jail, you're the one going, not Alexander and not me."

"You want me to take one for the cause. Is that it?" said Frank.

Cindy's hand was still up, but Alexander jumped back in. "Not take one, hopefully, but represent us. Yes, we want you to refuse any plea bargain that's offered. We want you to insist the charges be unconditionally dropped. In other words, we want you to back them into a corner and force a trial. The trial will be our soapbox. We'll fill the courtroom with supporters. We'll have the case in all the papers."

"But he did grab that boy," said Laura.

"He was provoked," said Alexander.

"Yes," said Frank, who now felt his wife looking at him with the same kind of uncertain gaze that characterized much of their previous 48 hours. "I was provoked. Cindy, Alexander, how about some coffee?"

Chapter 16

The Rialto had survived for many years in an old neighborhood of two-family wood homes interspersed with restaurants—some of them new, a bakery, a gourmet grocery store, a tailor shop, a pharmacy, an elementary school, a few bars, and an ice cream shop. The buildings were worn but not neglected, and the street on which the theater stood had a confidence about it, as if though it might not be as important as it used to be, it counted nonetheless.

People started congregating on Saturday afternoon at about five. Some seemed sheepish, some expectant. Alexander and Cindy Hammermill showed up at 6:15 in an SUV with a half- dozen picket signs in the back and passed them out to the group that by then numbered about ninety. The signs read, "Let Frank Go" and "Arrest Maiko."

Scott and Keith showed up a few minutes later and took up a position on the curb across from the theater and watched. By then, the rally had morphed into a protest march, and its numbers were growing, But there was only one marcher whose presence had caught the brothers' attention.

"If we stand here long enough, she'll see us," said Scott.

"I know."

"She might not pick us out, though."

"Right."

"I don't know about you, but I can't move. It's overwhelming."

"Yeah."

"Well, she was always political." They stood quietly for a while, hands in pockets.

"Shall we?" Keith said. "The laughing lady might still show up."

"How about you join Mom, and I patrol the neighborhood looking for the Pathfinder?"

"I don't think so. If she's coming, she'll be in the protest."

Crossing the street, they joined in the march. Their mother was surprised, but not surprised enough to stop walking or chanting, so she confined the questioning of her sons to the off beats between "Maiko" and "Let." It went like this: "Let Frank go! Arrest Maiko. So are you seeing anyone?" And, to her other son, "Let Frank go! Arrest Maiko! So who's watching the kids?" Family Gezunterman was still moving to the beat of this syncopated interrogation when all activity on the street was preempted by the appearance of a TV crew. Stepping into the camera lights was a young man in his mid-twenties whom Scott did not recognize. A female reporter interviewed him, after which the protest lost its steam. Then the brothers took Florence Gezunterman home.

They felt like taking a ride, so why not come on up and see her, is what they said. They told her they'd read about the protest and had a feeling she'd be there.

Had it been anyone else telling so transparent a lie, she'd have seen right through it. But telling Flo Gezunterman that her sons found her so wonderful they'd come to see her even though they'd been there the previous Sunday supplied sounds so sweet, she decided it was perfectly reasonable. They stayed a couple of hours. Keith hugged his mother good-bye, Scott did not, and they left.

The next afternoon Mrs. Gezunterman was still thinking about her boys, the single one in particular, when Jane finally stopped by to pick up her daughter's shoes. Even so, Mrs. Gezunterman did not say, "Have I got a boy for you," the moment the woman entered the apartment, though the words were right at the tip of her tongue.

The old woman could tell that this beautiful woman who laughed even as she introduced herself was a real catch and that her son would thank her for the rest of his days—which he should be doing all the time anyway—if his mother fixed them up. This was obviously a woman who had more suitors than she could handle, a woman whose friends probably made matches for her all the time.

Mrs. Gezunterman thought Jane would appreciate a little friendly conversation without the pressure of being set up. Besides, her son the drug counselor had once told her, "Mom, sometimes you come on a bit too strong," which she vaguely suspected but thought no one else had noticed.

"So," she said, taking Jane's extended right hand while looking at the woman's ring-less left, "you're single?"

"Yes."

"Have I got a boy for you."

Jane grew up in a neighborhood of modest split-levels and ranch houses in Colonie, New York. Her father was a welder at an armory nearby, a job Jane guessed was good but not good enough because her parents talked about money, or the lack of it, all the time.

All the window screens in her house had holes. There wasn't a single door that closed properly. The building needed a paint job, and the family referred to their driveway as "the obstacle course."

She had ocean-blue eyes and a big smile and everyone liked her. Her sister Anna had dull brown eyes and an always forlorn look and if anyone other than her roommate, Jane, liked her, they hid it well.

There were four other children in the home, all boys, and the way they ate made Jane think their poor father could've owned the armory, and it still wouldn't have been enough.

Across the street was a church and Jane's parents, both atheists, sent Jane and her five siblings there every Sunday. Mr. and Mrs. Blake didn't know what denomination the church was. They just thought their kids should have some religion.

"Religion is nonsense," they'd say. "Go to church."

"If we'd lived opposite a synagogue," Jane says, "I'd be Jewish."

She did pray, mostly that her older brother, Larry, who beat her without mercy, would one day have vanished when she got back from school. The details were not her concern. She figured God would see to them. But Larry stayed put, the beatings continued, and so ended Jane's brief experience with prescribed religious belief.

To avoid Larry, she began hiding in the cemetery behind the church after getting off the bus. A sketchbook became her closest friend. She drew tombstones because "that's what you see in a cemetery," an explanation deemed inadequate by the guidance counselor who discovered the book in school one day and called in Jane's parents. She was eleven.

"I think we have a problem here," said the counselor.

"I agree," said Jane's dad. "The perspective on these drawings is all wrong. The tombstones look like they're wearing hats. But the trees are pretty good, don't you think?"

"Jane tells me she was hanging around the cemetery last night until eight. Did either of you know that?"

Her mother suspected as much, but knew she was safer there. Her father had no clue.

"There's a morbid quality to these sketches. Sketches of a graveyard. Everything is so dark," said the counselor.

"I'm sketching with a pencil," said Jane. "Black is the only color I've got."

"Quiet," hissed Jane's mom.

"Maybe the school psychologist ought to take a look at these things," the counselor said.

"Why?" said Jane's dad. "Does he draw?"

Mother, father, and child walked to the parking lot in silence.

"Religion is nonsense," Jane said when reaching the car, hoping a statement of common ground might help her situation. She needn't have worried. Her parents were apparently thinking of something else, as always, and nothing further was said about it.

By her junior year, visits to Aunt Gertie were history. Jane's parents suddenly discovered Jane's whereabouts because they decided they needed the girl to quit school and stay home to take care of her two youngest brothers. Larry was off to college by then, a place Jane would never go. Sadly, as far as Jane was concerned, he came home often.

"Don't worry about it," a sympathetic ex-teacher told her. "You're already smarter than most people." Jane had told the teacher about quitting school, but not the part about her brother.

"Then why should I have to quit school?"

"I can't answer that one. Just keep reading," the teacher said.

She did, and voraciously, the continuation of a habit that had helped her maintain an A average up until her formal education ended. She also continued to draw, but her parents continued to ignore her on both accounts.

One thing they did notice—her father anyway—was that Jane always hung around when he and his sons did repairs on the family cars. By the time she left home she could do tune-ups, oil changes, and a variety of minor repairs.

"You'll make some man a good husband," Mr. Blake said.

Jane was not amused.

Chapter 17

Cowboy Bob Sheridan hoped he'd get the call from the moment he caught the story on CNN, but he didn't get to be Cowboy Bob by hoping. "No, sir," he'd tell anyone who'd stand still long enough. "You can bet on it." He didn't get the alligator boots and the gold belt buckle and the big brown hat by dreaming about them. And he certainly didn't get the Aston-Martin convertible and the house in Vail and the sixty-five-foot cruiser now docked at Chelsea Piers in Manhattan by waiting for luck to find him.

It was Sunday night, but he called his publicist right away, gave the man ten minutes to deliver, and then called him back.

"I don't want to hear you can't find out how to reach this guy. I just watched him walk into his house on my TV. Somebody was standing there taking his picture. Unlisted number, my ass. And whaddayou mean this organization has no address? They gotta be somewhere.

"I tell you what, never mind about contacting them. Just get me on TV. That's right. Get me on the tube with a reporter asking me would I take the case if I was asked to. Hell, yeah, I'll come to New York. I gotta visit that boat of mine sometime, don't I? Upstate? Shoot, I didn't know New York *had* an upstate. How far? Listen, young fella, if they've got a courthouse, then it's my kind of place. You call me back today with some results. You got that?"

The publicist got the Cowboy on CNN the next evening, which was where Alexander Hammermill saw him. Alexander was on the phone to Pat Monahan the moment the interview ended.

"What about Bob Sheridan?" Hammermill said. "I just saw him on CNN."

"You mean Cowboy Bob?"

"Yeah."

"Good choice, actually. A real publicity hound, but a legitimate trial lawyer. Went to Yale or Stanford, I think. I actually went to a seminar of his years ago. It was called 'Never Lose A Case—Can't Miss Pointers From a Fella Who Never Has.' How's that for an ego? But it was good, I have to admit. The guy is the real thing, with or without his cowboy boots. Do you want me to contact him for you? He'll need local counsel to sponsor him. I don't think he's admitted in New York."

"Do it. Call me right back."

District Attorney Harold Bronstein had one word to say on Tuesday morning when he heard Bob Sheridan was going to defend Frank Rooney: "Shit."

Assigning more senior counsel would have been inappropriate, although Bronstein had thought about it. A prosecutor responds to the severity of the case, not the fame of defense counsel. For that very reason, he'd already decided he wasn't going to try the case himself. Press coverage aside, it was a simple assault charge, the kind of case young Assistant DAs handle themselves.

As a misdemeanor, the case would be heard in the local Justice Court, which meant some youngster had already been assigned to it. Bronstein checked his computer to see who it was. James Armstead. Jesus, was that the guy he'd hired less than a year ago? *Please tell me this won't be Armstead's first trial.*

"Lizette," he called through the open door to his office, "please give Jim Armstead a call and have him come pay me a visit."

Bronstein would help the kid all he could, but other than that it was going to be business as usual. The problem was, nothing about the Cowboy was usual. And by the time the Bob Sheridan road show rolled into town, it would be a circus.

Worse, Bronstein had already boxed himself into a corner by promising that obnoxious Remlinger fellow that the People of the State of New York would hold firm and not back down to the "deadbeats, gays, tree-huggers, and liberals" that Remlinger insisted were behind the whole thing.

"The guy's got a Ph.D. in chemistry, and he's married with two kids. I'm an avid environmentalist myself, and how do you know what his politics are?" Bronstein had said to the enraged businessman when they'd met the day before, the first business day after the protest at the theater.

"Don't be naïve. These guys hide it until they're pushed, then their true colors come out. Oh, and some fancy degree makes what he did okay? Well, pardon me. I only went to high school, but I don't go around assaulting people in movie theaters. Maybe if I'd gone to some hot-shot college I'd have learned how it's okay to do that."

"P-H-D." Remlinger had spat out the letters.

"My point was that he's hardly a . . . ."

"And he was there to see a French movie. Who goes to see French movies? What's wrong with American movies?"

"It was your theater."

"If these faggots want to put good money down to see this crap, who am I to stop them? But they're still faggots."

"Not that it matters, but why 'tree hugger'?"

"I heard the bastard went for a hike in the woods the day after it happened. My manager is in the hospital with a broken neck . . . "

"Cervical strain."

" . . . and this son of a bitch is hugging trees."

Bronstein had turned to Remlinger's attorney, Bill Copeland, who'd accompanied his client to the meeting.

"Bill?" the DA had said.

"Look, Harry, all we want is your assurance that you'll take this case seriously. We can't have our employees subjected to this kind of behavior. We may be facing some kind of mass movement against our business nationwide. There have already been protests in Buffalo, Chicago, Boston, Columbus. We want to know that if we're going to stand up to this kind of lawlessness, you're going to stand with us."

"Well, I'm certainly not going to condone assaulting a theater manager. I don't condone assaulting anyone. He'll be prosecuted."

"None of this adjournment in contemplation of dismissal stuff, either. That's what I really mean, Harry. No sweeping it under the rug just because it's difficult. He's gotta plead to something."

"Well, you know you're not officially the victim here. It's that manager of yours. In all fairness, we've got to see what the doctor says about his injury, and then we'll consider what he wants to do. Ultimately, of course, the decision is mine."

At that point Charlie Remlinger stood up, his neck and face bright red and turning redder. The DA thought he was about to be assaulted himself.

"Just tell me this, Bronstein. How'd you like to run for reelection against an opponent with unlimited financial backing? Theoretically, I mean. Sound like fun? You're term is up next year, right?"

The DA looked at Bill Copeland, who looked away.

"My people tell me it was close last time. You beat some guy named Peroni, right?"

"Patricelli."

"Oh, excuse me. I'll be sure to get his name right on the check I write for his next campaign."

The DA stood up and walked over to his window, not so much to gather his thoughts as to get the image of Charlie Remlinger's reddening face out of his mind. His view was of Route 787 and the Hudson River beyond. The river was not much to look at this far north. No one called it "majestic" or "beautiful" until at least an hour downstream. Here, the riverbanks were flat and dull and the water in between only a few yards wide.

Traffic on 787 was light.

"As I said, Bill," Bronstein sighed, still looking out the window, "I intend to take this case seriously."

"Thanks, Harry. That's all we can ask."

"You're perfectly welcome. Now, as far as your client's checkbook is concerned, tell him he can stick it where the sun don't shine. Then you can escort his ass out of my office. I don't want him back here again."

The Rooneys spent all day Wednesday in serious discussion about what the Hammermills wanted them to do. Early that afternoon, Alexander called them with the news about Bob Sheridan. They'd never heard of the Cowboy, but a quick Google search confirmed that their new friend hadn't been kidding when he'd promised a hot-shot attorney.

"Yes," Laura had said, "but did it have to be someone so flamboyant?"

"I don't think the reserved types go into trial law," said Frank. "Besides, he wins."

The next morning, Frank made up his mind. He decided he needed to talk about it some more. Laura, who had already concluded that the Hammermills were a bit nuts, felt she knew what her husband wanted to do even if he did not.

"You've always taken the conventional route," she said after brushing her teeth. "*We've* always taken the conventional route. It's been good to us. Now you want to change. Frank, I've given you all the reasons against it, which are many, but you're still not convinced. I think that tells you what you need to know."

"I'm not sure I understand."

"Yes, you do. You have to go with your gut." The sound of those words made her uneasy. Her tongue struggled to get them out of her mouth.

Frank and Laura Rooney had made every decision in their lives together and only after rational, detailed analysis. Pencil and paper were usually needed. The term "cost-benefit analysis" was often used. They cited pros and cons, gave them all values, created formulas. That's the way they'd decided where they'd live, for whom they would teach, when to have children and how many, whether and where to go on vacation, and which cars to buy.

Frank had never heard his wife use the word "gut." He wasn't sure she even knew it had a colloquial use other than what appeared in her biology texts, and now she was telling him to go with it down what seemed a perilous path.

"My instinct is to fight it like Hammermill wants me to," Frank said. Laura sat back down on the bed where Frank still lay and took hold of his hand.

"Yes," she said. "Instinct. That's so much a better word. I guess if we're going to act like lunatics, we're at least going to be educated about it. Not that it makes me feel any better, Frank, because it doesn't. The truth is I think you're nuts. I think the Hammermills are nuts. I think this whole thing is nuts, and you ought to reconsider. So, are you going to change your mind?"

"No."

Chuck Rodriguez could tell that the guys at GE Research and Development had not taken kindly to his son's TV debut. They said things like: "Saw your son on TV. Speaks well," or "That your kid? Independent thinker, I see," or "Nice looking boy. Your oldest, right?"

Nobody called the boy smart. No one said they agreed with him.

Chuck didn't agree with his son either, but he was so used to disagreeing with Max, he took it for granted. The only question was how forcefully he disagreed. Yet, he found himself watching the Tivo of the late-night news broadcast that Ben and Amanda had made over and over.

"I wish your mother could have seen this," he said as his younger kids hit PLAY for the tenth time. It was two nights now since the story had first been aired, and Max was not home. "Where is that boy, anyway?"

"Dunno," said Benjamin, "but the quest continues."

"Is that what he said?"

"Yup."

Chuck caught Amanda's eye and the two of them nodded. Max's quests had never progressed beyond start-up mode. The family didn't know if there *was* anything beyond start-up mode. And then, suddenly, it was—continuing.

"Wow," she said, and her father nodded once more.

"Don't talk like that," Chuck had told his wife after she'd brought up what only a short time before would have been unthinkable. "You're not going to die."

"Yes, I am, Chuck. I know it. The doctor knows it, and you know it." The two of them were walking hand in hand down Alameda Street, about three months after the diagnosis. Alameda had tall ash trees lining both sides of the road. The modest houses were all about the same size and quality and there was an egalitarian, we're-all-in-this-together feel that made it Nancy's favorite place to walk.

Over the previous few weeks, the neighbors had gotten used to the sight of this oddly matched couple out for a stroll. Initially, it was taken as a good sign. Nancy was upright, outdoors, moving. Then, as people realized how much weight she'd lost and how gray her skin had turned, they'd crossed their lawns and walked down their front steps not only to say hello but to breathe in the bittersweet aroma of a love about to end. After brief conversations, they'd kept watching as Nancy and Chuck walked away.

Nancy was tall and willowy with green eyes and red hair. She wore long, flowing skirts that cascaded around her knees as she moved, even toward the end, when she needed her husband's arm for support. Chuck, an inch shorter than his wife, was stocky and wide with a thick neck and black hair. His steps were plodding and deliberate, like a man testing his footing on ice.

"I know how proud you are of the children," she'd said. "But it would be good if you'd tell them that once in a while. That's the only advice I'll give you. I know they're in good hands."

"Nancy . . ."

"Well, maybe one more thing. You won't cry, I think. You won't cry when I go, and that's a mistake. You'll want to be tough for the kids. You'll want them to know they can lean on you. But it's okay for you to cry, and it's okay for them to see you crying. You'll lean on each other. That's how you'll all get through this. Think about it, Chuck. They're your kids. They're just as tough as you are."

Chuck Rodriguez, heartbroken beyond what he thought possible, shed not a tear at his wife's funeral although he did wonder, when Amanda refused to leave her room to witness her mother being placed in the ground, if a tear or two from the old man might have done the trick.

Part Two

Chapter 18

Jane left Chazzie the year their daughter completed grammar school. As soon as Jane had moved into her new home in Younger Lake, she threw herself a party. In addition to dozens of friends from the old neighborhood, the guests included two separate crews of men who'd helped her move, her lawyer's secretary, her ex-sister-in-law, the building inspector who'd checked out the house for the bank, an eighty-year-old woman who lived across the street and was trying to fix Jane up with her son, a childhood friend now born again and living in Arizona, and Jane's former therapist.

The therapist had begged Jane to continue her sessions even after conceding they did her more good than Jane. "You should be paying me," Jane laughed.

"How much do you want?" the therapist had said.

The movers ranged in ages from twenty-one to fifty-two. A couple of them brought their wives, but all four of the men were in love with their hostess. Jane had been overwhelmed by the tasks of packing up and getting out when the first crew arrived at the old house—"the palace," as Jane had called it. Charlie had just sped off after telling Jane, in a voice loud enough for the whole neighborhood to hear, that she'd never make it on her own, that she didn't have the ability to handle a move let alone manage her own place.

The palace was a mess. What needed to be packed hadn't been. Books and clothing clogged the staircase and halls. Paintings and posters clung to the walls. Jane was in tears.

After spending five minutes with the flustered woman, the first two-man crew swore to take care of everything. They bought her lunch. They worked overtime to get her stuff ready, but there wasn't enough time to do what was needed, so they came back on their day off, at no charge, to help her out.

The initial moving date had to be canceled because of a problem with the furnace at the new house, and the crew was committed elsewhere after that so Jane had to call another company. The new guys completed the move and came back also on their own time to help her arrange her kitchen and build shelves in Sarah's room.

Jane's lawyer's secretary was a young single mom who had lost all hope of meeting a nice man. "If a guy has a steady job and won't beat me, I'll take him," she'd told Jane. Jane didn't laugh at that. "How do you do it? Every guy you meet loves you. Smart ones, dumb ones. Rich, poor. Every single one."

"I don't know," Jane had laughed. "I just don't know. But there's nothing attractive in despair. I know that." Jane was trying to fix her up. "Here," she said when the girl came in, grabbing one of the single guys from the crews, "let me introduce you to a real mover."

The old lady, Ellen, had, in the space of the two months since Jane moved to Younger Lake, become dependent. Jane had fixed her screen door, replaced her car battery, and helped decipher her Medicare paperwork. "I want you to marry my son," Ellen told her new best friend, "but you may be too good for him."

An antique dealer who promised a discount for Jane and anyone who came into his store with her—provided Jane wore "those jeans I like so much"—was there. So was the accountant who had done the taxes for her and Charlie when they were a couple.

The kitchen and living room of the small house, both reconfigured and repainted since Jane moved in, were packed shoulder to shoulder with people. Every few minutes someone would raise their glass and shout "To the ELF!" and everyone else would shout "To the ELF!" and down a drink.

Most of the guests were huddled around a couple of platters of cold cuts when Ellen arrived, and they made way for her and her walker to get through. When she finally got to a chair and eased herself into it, she took a breath, looked up and said softly, "To the ELF."

"The ELF!"

"His ex-wife calls him the ELF," Bill Copeland was saying that Friday to his secretary. "It stands for Exasperating Little Fuck."

The phone rang. They both knew who it was. Fourth time in the last hour.

"Bill, why I didn't think of this sooner, I don't know. It's so obvious. This guy works for RPI, right?"

"Right."

"Then that's where the pressure should come from. They don't want some candy-ass protester corrupting their students, do they? There must be some kind of fund I can contribute to over there. I'll write someone a check and ask to see the university president for a chat. It's that simple."

"And what will you tell him?"

"I'll tell him to tell that guy to plead guilty or else."

"I don't think so, Charlie."

"Why not? Why not this one, hot shot? I've had four ideas in the last hour and you've nixed every one. What's wrong with this one?"

"For one, he's a tenured professor. They can't force him to do anything, and they certainly can't fire him for not pleading guilty. In fact, a criminal conviction may be one of the few things that can cost a tenured professor his job, so that makes it all the more likely he won't plead."

"Fucking tenure. Another liberal scam."

"Besides, he's got little to gain by pleading guilty. It's not likely he'll go to jail even if he is convicted, and with a jury trial, there's always the chance he'll be acquitted."

"Fucking juries. There's no damn justice."

"Yes, well, I can see you feel that way."

"So what's your idea, Bill? I'm still waiting. You know ticket sales are down fifty percent locally because of that jackass. I'm not sitting around and taking that kind of thing. Gimme an idea."

"Lay low. Be patient. Let the DA handle it. In another few days no one will remember this story. New movies will come out and people won't want to miss them and this will disappear."

"That's your idea? Do nothing?"

"That's my idea."

"That's not an idea. That's nothing. They can see new movies at some other guy's place. Tell you what, Mr. Legal, I'm going to go think of something to do to save my business. That's something, and it's what you should be doing too. I'll call you."

The next day, Alexander Hammermill was talking to Irena Poppadapoulos. The two were seated in his kitchen, Irena having flown in that morning for a TULP summit conference. Also at the table were Gus DeMauro along with Christina Clark, Lucy Goldstein, and Boris Petrovich, heads of the software, hardware, and HMO divisions, respectively.

"The worst thing that can happen for us is if they do nothing," said Irena.

"That's right," said Lucy Goldstein. "Think of all the great movements. Where would civil rights have been if Bull Connor hadn't used police dogs and fire hoses against the marchers in Selma?"

"Or the British hammering away at Gandhi's people in India," said Alexander.

"Or George-goddamned-Washington in the Revolutionary War." Gus DeMauro had decided to weigh in.

"I don't think George Washington followed the same pattern as Gandhi," said Lucy, softly.

"You're goddamned right he didn't. There is such a thing as action, you know. What they're doing is violent. No one's bleeding because it's being done subtly, incrementally and over time. But it's violence nonetheless. Guy goes to a movie theater, the whole world sees him go in and come out, and they won't give him his refund because he couldn't find his damned ticket stub? What if they wouldn't give him his refund because he had on a brown shirt instead of a green one? Banks, hospitals, businesses, retail shops, airlines. They do it and say 'It's policy' and everyone takes it and goes away. No more. That's why we started this organization, isn't it? I say we take action now. We don't need to wait for them to do something."

"Is both sides correct." Boris Petrovich still carried the heavy inflection that accompanied him out of Russia thirty years before. He was short and stout. His hair was gray, thinning and disheveled. He wore a goatee. To find his blue eyes, one had to peer through overgrown eyebrows into twin tunnels that bored deep into his skull. His voice came deep and slow. Everyone who met him assumed he was a novelist. He was not.

"In Russia," he would say, "I was engineer. In America, I am plumber."

Boris would smile at a homeowner while holding a broken faucet and give a lecture on hydraulics that ended with the words, "Not to worry. I fix."

Petrovich had become outraged, in his own way, when his HMO had denied him permission to have an out-of-town doctor perform surgery on his shoulder, and then told him an internal review was his only way to challenge their decision.

"Internal to cchhoom?" he had asked. "You mean own pipple? So you ask self if you are cchorrect? I shall hold breath acchwaiting decision.

"Is like Russia. One Party member says up is down. Second Party member says up is down. Up is down. Anyone says no is big trouble."

He reached for a cookie. "We make action, of cchhourse. Job is provoke response."

Cindy Hammermill picked up the plate and brought it closer to Boris. "He's right. We want a response that's out of proportion, but there's nothing to stop us from giving them a little encouragement. Gandhi was anything but passive." She passed the plate around. "By the way, where's our new spokesman? Don't you think he should be here?"

"I called him," said Alexander. "He said he'd be here. What do you think, Christina? You've been kind of quiet."

Christina Clark was in her early forties with hair so jet black it had to be dyed. She wore perfume, lipstick, and makeup, and Alexander Hammermill could not believe she was a member of the same

organization as Lucy Goldstein, whose appearance suggested to him a
lethal allergy to all those substances. Christina wore tight skirts and high
heels, and when she got out of the cab in the Hammermills' driveway,
Cindy had put a hand on her husband's elbow and said, "Please don't
faint, dear. You're too heavy for me to pick up."

"Boycott is the word that comes to my mind," said Christina.

Damn, thought Alexander, *her fingernails are painted.*

She continued, "It's the obvious thing. Boycott Maiko theaters until
they drop the charges. And the beauty of it is that no one has to give up
anything. People can see the same movies at other theaters. At worst,
they'll have to wait until the movies come out on DVD."

"So what do we do—call out the troops? Mobilize the membership?
It'll look pretty bad if we announce this and then can't muster the clout
to pull it off. You all know we don't have nearly the numbers for a
national boycott," said Irena.

"No, Irena." Gus DeMauro pounded the table with his fists as he
spoke, muscles rippling under his hairy forearms. "We take them on one
theater at a time, one city at a time. That way we can marshal our forces.
We pick cities with big college populations. We bus people around if
necessary. Besides, look at the action we've generated right here. Most
of those people out there today never heard of us before. And sign-ups.
We register new members right there on the sidewalks. By the time they
figure out how small we are, we won't be small anymore."

"That's not bad, Gus," said Lucy Goldstein. "Could it be you've
organized a protest or two before?"

"Berkeley. Class of '73. You name it, I protested it."

The whole table stared at DeMauro. Nothing about his bald head and
muscles said campus radical.

"Vut long strange trip has been," said Boris Petrovich.

"Yes, but with all due respect, I'm not sure we'll be doing sign-ups
this time around, Gus." It was Christina Clark. "We'll be texting and
tweeting. We'll have a Facebook page. We'll reach more people in
seconds than you were able to sign up in weeks."

Two hours into the meeting, Max Rodriquez made his way up the
long driveway to the Hammermills' island hideaway. The people inside
were distributing the labor around for the upcoming protests when he
knocked on the door.

"Ah, Max! Everyone, this is Max Rodriguez," Alexander announced
as the skinny young man entered the room, one shoulder dipping slightly
below the other. "Max, this is T.U.L.P., some of it anyway. We all
appreciate what you did in your TV interview. Couldn't have done better
ourselves."

Max sat. Cindy brought him his own plate of cookies and a tall glass of milk. Max took a swig, picked up a cookie, and realized the sound of his eating was the only sound in the room. He made eye contact with Boris Petrovich. "Cookie?" he asked, holding up the plate.

"Am full," said Boris. "Delicious, no?"

"Max?" It was Lucy. "How did you know about T.U.L.P.?"

"I didn't," the spokesperson said between gulps. "I took a wild guess. I figured if I said grass roots, anything that followed would sound at least half right."

"What do you do for a living?" Gus said.

"You might say I'm in transition. 'Course, you could also say I'm doing engine repair at a rest stop on the Thruway."

"Are you in school?"

"Just graduated. University of Wisconsin."

"Ah," said Gus. "Nice place."

"You'll pardon me for asking this, but if you're going to be our spokesman, I have to. Have you ever been arrested?" said Lucy.

"Me?"

"Yes. Even if you weren't convicted. Any arrest at all."

"I meant me as spokesman. Is that what you said? Are you saying I should be spokesman?"

"Yes, no one told you?" Gus again, now looking at Alexander.

"I figured we'd get to it once he arrived," said Alexander.

"Wow," said Max. "Spokesman." Max contemplated the cookies before him. "I think I can do that."

Max grabbed for the last cookie and polished off the milk.

"Yes. It feels right," he said.

"Actually, it's more complicated than it sounds. We have a strategy you'll be asked to effect. We want to make our organization sound bigger and more powerful than it is."

"Yes, it feels very right."

"More cookies," said Boris. "We're going to need."

To the great delight of Alexander Hammermill, one of Christina Clark's many skills was web page design. The T.U.L.P. website had to be ready to go ASAP, and Christina was going to construct it, build the Facebook page, and set up the Twitter account. Better yet, Christina had rejected Alexander's offer to put her up at the Residence Inn with all the computer equipment she'd need in favor of Cindy's offer of a room right there at the Hammermills'. Visions of shared pancake breakfasts with the perfumed, high-heeled Clark danced before his eyes. He could see her long, slender fingers with their painted nails reaching for the maple syrup as her dyed jet-black hair fell across her blue, mascara-rimmed eyes.

"So this is it," he said to Cindy. "Our island is to be mission control."

"Mission control and fashion central," said Cindy. The T.U.L.P. meeting was in recess, and Christina Clark had gone out to the foyer to get her luggage.

"Yes, an unfortunate development," said Alexander as his eyes followed Clark out the dining room door.

Gus DeMauro's thick hands were smothering a cup of coffee. "Things could be worse, believe me," he said. "Once, at Berkeley, we barricaded ourselves in the chemistry building to protest the university's acceptance of a research grant from Dow Chemical."

"Dow was maker of napalm, no?" said Boris Petrovich.

"Yes. We thought the symbolism added a nice touch. They cut off our power, shut off the water, and turned off the telephones. We lasted 24 hours."

"Was symbolic victory," said Boris.

"It's better this way," said DeMauro, waving his hand to encompass the surroundings of the Hammermill home. "Enough reminiscing. Come on, people. Let's get back to the table and see what we've got."

While the others broke for a quick stroll outside to get luggage from their cars or simply to chat, Max remained at the table. In his wallet, safely secured in one of the two inner compartments, was a dining hall pass from his mother's days at the State University of New York at Binghamton. He took it out and stared at it.

The pass included a picture of the then twenty-year-old Nancy Ketchum next to a calendar for the semester with the dates punched out, signifying Nancy had never missed a meal. He'd found the pass among her belongings after she died.

Nancy's hair was just a bit wavy, and it fell down over her left eye before disappearing behind her shoulder. Her green eyes glowed with the same easy, peaceful energy that Max remembered, her smile revealing a set of perfect white teeth far too large for her mouth. Her nose was narrow and a bit too long, with a slight change of direction at the bridge, as though it had been broken, which it had not. It was Amanda's face, and he could see bits and pieces of his brother's face in the picture as well as some of his own.

The word fetching came to mind. Max never used that word, but it jumped out from the picture every time he looked at it. He'd once asked his mom if she'd had to "fight off all the boys," which was his way of asking how she wound up with his dad.

"No," she'd said, "but I don't think some of the Jewish boys had ever seen a girl who looked like me before, and for some reason they seemed very impressed."

Those Jewish boys, who came by the hundreds from schools like Stuyvesant High School and the Bronx High School of Science and who left the campus deserted every Rosh Hashanah and Yom Kippur to return to their homes in Brooklyn and Queens, were more than impressed with Nancy Ketchum. They were wonderstruck. But they could never quite figure out what to do with her.

"You don't understand," they would tell her, one after the other, in hushed tones, as though revealing the secret code of their kind. "You're so . . . agreeable."

"Isn't that a good thing?"

"Of course, it's a good thing."

"You're agreeable."

"I know. But I'm the man."

"I don't understand."

"Yes, I know."

Eventually, it was Chuck Rodriguez, his brown corduroy pants ill-fitting, his plaid flannel shirt unpressed, and his thick black hair forever uncombed, who caught her eye on the city-bound train they shared daily during the year after her graduation. Nancy was living in Tarrytown and working as a fashion consultant at Macy's, and Chuck was in graduate school at NYU. She had to wait weeks for an opportunity to sit next to him and pretty much carried the first few conversations herself. But the young man realized his good fortune right away and committed himself to her from their very first meeting.

Max's new friends were closer to his mother's age than his, and he knew she'd have fit in well with them—their woolly host in particular—though he had been a bit surprised not to have heard the name Gezunterman when the introductions were made.

He left his mother's picture out of his wallet and on the table as the meeting recommenced.

"We'll start with the theater where it happened," said Gus. "We'll do one theater at a time. Alexander, can you get us another ad in the paper?"

"Done."

"And the website. We've got to get that up and running, pronto. Christina?"

"And the Facebook page. And the Twitter account. I'll start right after this meeting ends," Christina said.

"We'll need some legal work on this as well, Alexander. Will we need a march permit? If so, let's find out and get it. We want to picket. Now . . ."

"Cchold on, plis. Is too fast for Boris," said Boris. "Ccwe are march and picket cchwhen?"

"I say a week from Saturday. Enough time for this thing to percolate, but not enough time for it to die," said Gus. "Sound good to everyone?"

Apparently it did, there being no objection. Gus forged on.

"Christina, we'll set you up in a van across the street and funnel people to you for sign-ups. Maybe you can get a laptop going and we can put the new people into the database right away. I suggest we have the rest of us except Cindy walk among the picketers handing out flyers about T.U.L.P. and encouraging people to sign up. We'll just direct people to the van. Alexander, I think you should stay with Christina. We don't want to leave a woman alone in the middle of a protest. In fact, that's a rule from now on. No one is to be given a job out on the street alone."

"So I am backup to you on sidewalk by theater, yes?" said Boris.

"Yes, you and Lucy and Max, here. You'll all be with me on the sidewalk. Max, if that reporter shows up again, and I'm sure she will because we're going to call her, you talk to her. Tell her . . ."

"I'll tell her it's a spontaneous uprising, that TULP leadership from across the country hasn't even had a chance to organize a nationwide response to this outrage and this is just local people showing their displeasure. Why, that's why we have the sign-up van across the street. These people aren't even members. When the main body of members does get here, though, look out."

"Cchhan be good spokesman, I think," said Boris, nodding at Max. "Chave cchim say again just like that for Christina so she can put on media sites."

"Cindy will stay here and man the phones?" asked Lucy.

"What phones?" asked Cindy.

"The new phones you're going to order tomorrow. We'll need a couple of lines added, but no more than two. I want it to sound like we're inundated with callers. I want people to hear a busy signal or two before they get through," said Gus.

"I wouldn't put too much effort into phones," said Christina. "We'll get found on Facebook. When something good happens, we'll get it on YouTube. And as for getting the word out that we're planning something new, or that old plans have changed, that's what Twitter is for. That's where this thing is at, Gus."

There was an uncomfortable silence in the room as Gus and Christina looked at each other, looked away, then glared at each other for what seemed to Alexander like minutes.

"All well and good," said Gus, "but I couldn't find my nose on Facebook, I can't spell Twitter, and I'm telling you there are people out there by the boatload in their fifties, sixties, and beyond who remember what it was like to be treated decently when they, we, walked into a bank or a store. They'll support this thing, Christina. Don't freeze them out just because they haven't mastered technologies that aren't as old as their grandchildren."

"We forget focus, I think," said Boris Petrovich. "Focus is case against Frank Rooney, yes? Must work with big-shot attorney to organize protest at cchourthouse. And focus must be like laser. News of arrest is already eight days old, yes? Must make big fuss right here right now or whole think is goink novhere fast. Vhen is case be heard?"

"Boris is right," said Gus. "But we won't forget. We'll have to organize protests from the lists of people we recruit. And we'll put ads in the paper for the court appearances just like we will for the protests at the theaters. Maybe we'll be stretched too thin, maybe we'll have more people than we can handle. We're just throwing ourselves out there. Who knows?"

"And if it doesn't work?" said Cindy.

"If it doesn't work, it doesn't work," said Gus.

Suddenly, the room shook with the reverberation of Alexander's giant hand being slammed down on the hardwood kitchen table. The big man was nodding his head up and down.

"Yes!" he said. "It's gonna happen! We're gonna make this thing happen!"

There was silence, accompanied by a complete absence of movement.

"Don't you worry about Alexander," Cindy Hammermill said to the suddenly frozen group as she reached up and stroked her husband's shoulder. "He just realized he's going to be saving the world while stationed in a van with Ms. Clark and, well, there's only so much a good man can stand."

Chapter 19

At the core of the tension between Florence Gezunterman and her sons were conflicting views on the virtue of repetition. Mrs. Gezunterman, who'd delivered every sentence she'd ever spoken with the unshakable belief that no sentient person could disagree, thought it obvious that wisdom bore repetition. People didn't always do what she recommended—her sons were the worst offenders—but that was because they didn't want to face facts, an understandable but nevertheless undesirable human characteristic.

It was, therefore, not only her preference but her duty to remind her boys as often as possible of the mistakes they were about to make, had already made, and been saved from making on those rare occasions when they'd been smart enough to listen. This last category was "proof positive" that the other two categories would shrink to nonexistence if her sons would but accept what she told them as the wisdom it was. Why she still bothered she did not know—another point she made often—but against all odds, and for their own good, she repeated it once more, at the very least, each and every time she saw them.

Her sons' theory of repetition was that if it involved listening to their mother, once was already too much.

Forged when they were all much younger and entrenched in their minds by decades of warfare, these disparate views made debate the only mode of communication between the parties. Into that constantly fermenting mix, Mrs. Gezunterman was now injecting her latest piece of advice to her son the drug counselor.

The scene was her apartment, Saturday, a week after Mrs. G's appearance at the Rialto, where her oldest was visiting, Keith having drawn a by, and the question for the day was, Tell me why there is no Mrs. Gezunterman.

"Mom, aren't we too old for this?" Scott said.

"What, you're packing it in? You're not yet fifty."

"I meet women on my own, you know."

"I don't know. Maybe if you called once in a while I'd know, but you don't, so I don't. And if you meet so many women, why aren't you married?"

"Maybe I'm not married because I meet so many women."

"Very funny. A man your age should crawl into an empty bed every night. It's not natural."

"Actually . . ."

"Always an argument. Listen to me. I met this woman. She's perfect for you. Funny? You could die from it. Good looking. Sweet. Artistic, she is. Sews or designs things or something, I don't know what. Here, take her number."

"Okay. I'll take it."

"You'll call her?"

"No."

"Like a mule, you are. Did you know that? You get that from your father."

Scott often wondered when and how it happened. At some point in his family's past, a tributary trickling down some distant mountain had veered from its path and flowed unnoticed into River Gezunterman. There were many streams and tributaries in Germany and Poland, but did they carry the kind of water upon which an explanation of his unusual ways could float?

Maybe it happened generations earlier, when a black Moor, working his way into the good graces of a long-forgotten Gezunterman woman while the family was still in what would later become Spain, appeared on the scene. A union in Granada perhaps, made possible when the daughter of a Jewish artisan working on the Alhambra was bringing food to her father and met someone she should not have. Or a forbidden romance consummated in an alleyway of the Juderia in Cordoba, near where the statue of Maimonides now stands. Then, for generations thereafter, the seeds of its nature had remained hidden. Neither the Inquisition nor the long trek to Eastern Europe revealed it. The following centuries of isolation in the cold, snow-swept shtetl drove the coded message further underground, but not so far that it couldn't hop a train to the ship that led its immigrating carrier to the New World.

Whatever its source, the Scott code landed at Ellis Island as the twentieth century dawned and then, encouraged by the same freedom that had inspired its host to make the perilous trip, looked for a chance to make itself known.

It took two more generations to happen, a millisecond compared to the time it had remained dormant, but when Scott began bringing his own LP records home to play on the family hi-fi, his mother knew something was up. Not that some white kids weren't listening to black performers, but with Scott it was an exclusive thing. By the time the Temptations, the O'Jays, and Al Green became household names to the other kids, they were old news to Scott. Long before Sam Cooke became widely known for "Another Saturday Night," Scott had a complete collection of albums by a gospel group called the Soul Stirrers, for whom Cooke sang lead. Wilson Pickett was known to the boy as the lead singer for The Violinaires long before his friends ever heard of "Mustang Sally."

Blues singers like Blind Lemon Jefferson, Blind Willie Dixon, Cool Papa Bell, B.B. King, Buddy Guy, Mississippi John Hurt, Sonny Boy Williamson, Taj Mahal, Sonny Terry, and Brownee McGee made up about half of what the boy was listening to. (*Blind Lemon?* said Flo.)

The other half included singers with names like Mahalia Jackson, Bessie Smith, James Cleveland, and Andrae Crouch. One of Scott's favorite albums was by a group called the Mighty Clouds of Joy.

But it was his own singing that really shook the family. One day, as he was getting dressed for school, his mom heard this:

Go tell it on the mountain
Over the hills everywhere
Go tell it on the mountain
That Jesus Christ is born.

Mrs. Gezunterman had to admit it was a catchy tune, but she wondered where the boy had learned it. Had she followed him out of the house on Sunday mornings she'd have found out.

Scott Gezunterman's musical education was being supplemented by services at the First Baptist Church, a ten-minute walk from home. Scott stumbled past the building one day while walking his bicycle after getting a flat tire. The sounds of gospel coming from inside shook the wooden sides of the building until they hummed his name. He spent the next few Sunday mornings sitting on the front steps, listening. Only when an old man came outside one day for a smoke and nearly fell over him did the boy get through the front door.

It had been drizzling, but Scott had seen no reason to forgo his weekly fix. He'd been sitting there under his baseball cap for twenty minutes. The churchgoer, dressed in a suit and tie, looked down at the rain-soaked little boy.

"Holy Spirit find you anywhere," he said, "but at least it's dry inside."

"Well, actually, I just like the music."

"That the best part. Go on inside, boy. Nobody bite you in there. C'mon, I'll take you in."

With his escort by his side, Scott entered the church. His first reaction was: Color! It wasn't just the skin of the people in the pews, but the clothing on their backs. Yellows, reds, purples, shimmering blue, iridescent green. The women wore hats—hats with wide brims, hats with feathers—and their clothing continued the rainbow theme right down to their shoes. These people weren't just dressed up, they were *dressed up!*

The scene made his congregation at Ohave Shalom look like those old black and white movies that played on TV.

Then he heard the music, really heard the music, for the first time. Up close, without the buffer of walls and windows, it was clear and bright. It popped into his ears like the sound of crystal ornaments underneath a fancy chandelier, clicking and rattling as the fixture moved back and forth.

To Scott, a religious service meant a lugubrious slog through medieval tunes in minor keys. But these people weren't slogging. They weren't even praying, as far as he could tell, at least, not the in way he was used to.

They were celebrating.

Up front was a choir of six or seven people with a young, pretty woman in the lead. They were dressed in white robes, which Scott decided were needed to differentiate them from the rest of the crowd because everyone was doing exactly what the choir was doing, which was singing at the tops of their lungs and waving their arms in the air and dancing. The dancing was in place—people remained standing by their seats—but the movement was as unfamiliar to his eyes as everything else. They bopped heads or bent knees or turned shoulders. Some did all three. But without leaving their spots it seemed their movements served to punctuate the music, or perhaps to emphasize the message of the music, as if to offer a nonverbal uh-huh.

That was when he first heard *"Go Tell It On The Mountain."* The choir began slowly, with a soaring alto lead from the woman in front. Though the song was slowly sung, the audience had no trouble locating and keeping to its rhythm. Scott knew the crowd at his synagogue wouldn't know the piece *had* a beat, much less where it was, and that the only ones moving to it would have been he and his brother. But these people! Even the preacher was moving in sync.

They revved it up, the song doubling in speed. Yet everyone, one hundred percent of the congregation, kept their hands clapping and feet stomping in complete unison. The song went to a syncopated beat, with quick, staccato claps, two together—pause—one more—pause—two quick ones again. Everyone was into it right from the first bar of the change.

The little white kid who sat tapping his feet and clapping his hands in the rear pew was elated. *My people,* he thought.

Chapter 20

It was the T-shirts that reminded Frank Rooney of just how comfortable life had been for him as a shy man.

Reading about himself in the paper hadn't been so bad. People read papers and threw them away and forgot what they'd read in minutes. He hadn't been on TV, having refused all the interview requests that had come from the three local stations, as well as CNN, MSNBC, and Fox News. Initially, the Wheaton police had stepped up patrols around his house, but looking at a split-level in the suburbs didn't seem to interest many people, even if it did contain the famous chemistry professor. Three days into it, he was able to resume his after-dinner walks with Laura.

But the T-shirts were different. When they were on, they were on, and wherever the wearer went, whatever he did until he took the garment off, there Frank was, with a remotely serious but guarded look on his face. The photo had been taken as Frank had gotten out of his car the day after his hike in the Adirondacks.

His enlarged face was every bit as nondescript as the regular size: the fairly though not completely straight nose, a chin that looked like it wanted to recede even more than it did, cheekbones hidden away as if for safekeeping, flat, straight hair parted on the side, and glasses.

When he'd been a student, the heroic profile of the day had been Che Guevara's—handsome and dynamic, beret defiantly tilted to the side, face uplifted with eyes searching the horizon for the path to heroic liberation.

Frank felt ridiculous.

One student had purchased enough T-shirts for the entire class, and when Frank walked into the room the next morning, Friday, the day the T.U.L.P. leadership was first gathering at the Hammermills', twenty more Frank Rooneys had stood up and cheered.

"Oh, come on," was all their teacher could think to say.

Yet, he had to admit he had a self-satisfied feeling about what he was doing.

For the first time since high school, he remembered an English class where the teacher, a gruff, cynical guy named Mazzone, had shown a movie that had nothing to do with the book they were reading. English was not Frank's favorite subject, and he'd been happy for the chance to catch a few zzzs.

Frank half slept through the film, which seemed to be about a man bulldozing a section of woods, apparently for some kind of development, and all that was left was a single tree in which sat a young girl on the platform of her tree-house, arms folded in defiance. There may have been dialogue. He seemed to remember something about the man having a job to do and the tree facing certain destruction no matter what the little girl did. He remembered the guy being portrayed as sympathetic to the girl's plight. The film ended in a standoff with the man standing next to his machine, looking up into the tree. His arms were outstretched in frustration and the little girl was still in the tree-house, unmoved.

Mazzone seemed to resent the injustice of having to suffer dimwits like those seated before him. After turning the lights back on, he had ambled back to his desk and growled, "How many people here think that bulldozer operator has a choice?"

One lone hand had gone up. It was Jay Nussbaum, the kid who'd been the best student in the class until sometime in the eighth grade when something had happened, he never said what, but after which he came to school barefoot unless it had snowed, worn his hair in a ponytail, and read books relevant only to his own personally approved curriculum. Jay was immune to any put-down Feldman could issue.

Then, another hand. Felix Delhomme, whose idea of fun was to come to school with his pet snake wrapped round his neck. "Was it you or the snake who penned this drivel," Mazzone had once asked while handing back an essay. "You know, even mops and brooms come with written instructions."

Pigeons too easy for Mazzone to pick on, Frank had thought.

"Nussbaum and Delhomme," the teacher had snarled, shaking his head. "So be it. Well, better than nothing, I guess." Feldman had then stared down at the floor for a while, raised his head, and said, "I don't want anything to do with the rest of you. Class dismissed."

Professor Rooney took a seat on the edge of his desk and looked at his students. Twenty Frank Rooneys looked back at him, expectant. In all his years of teaching, he'd never so commanded a classroom.

"The bad part about teaching chemistry," he said, "is that you can't just take a day off and show a film."

The kids broke up.

"Call me Bob," the attorney announced upon entering the Rooneys' home, alone. "That Cowboy stuff is just for show."

"Are the Hammermills coming?" Laura asked.

"No. They're the publicity part, Mrs. Rooney. I'll deal with them later. Mr. Rooney, here, is my client, and I'm here to talk business with him. He's the person I represent, and I'll do what's in his best interests.

If that conforms to what the Hammermills want, that's fine, but Frank's the guy I'm working for. I want you both to understand that."

"Bob," said Laura, "Would you like a cup of coffee?"

They took seats where the Rooneys had sat with the Hammermills, while Laura flipped on the coffee maker and brought out some cake.

"Thank you, kindly," said Sheridan, taking a small piece. And if I could get just a half cup when it's ready, I'd appreciate it, Mrs. Rooney. Black, with no sugar, please."

"You're very welcome."

It was Monday, nearly two weeks after the incident at the theater.

The Cowboy told them the case was defensible. He'd already seen the medical records of the theater manager's treatment.

"The X-rays were negative. He has a sprain and strain of his cervical spine. They gave him a drug called Flexeril, which is a muscle relaxant, and told him to take it easy for a few days. He's been back to his doctor for one follow-up since then and had nothing new to report. Basically, it's a sore neck."

"Will that be enough?" said Frank.

"I don't think so. Nonetheless, I've got one investigator following him with a video camera and another one trying to get statements from the other workers at the theater, many of whom, we're told, are sympathetic to T.U.L.P. I brought an associate with me, and she's working with Mr. Monahan, the Hammermills' attorney here in Albany, on a trial memo for the judge wherein we'll argue the case should be dismissed for failure to show the requisite injury. We might call a doctor of our own to do a records review to explain to the jury just how minor an injury it is."

"Wow," said Frank.

"Pretty standard, Mr. Rooney."

"Frank."

"Frank. It's more than you'd normally see for a misdemeanor, but an unlimited budget will buy you a lot, and it'll all help."

"So, is there more?"

"Oh, yeah. Now comes the fun part. Frank, have you ever heard of juror nullification?"

"No," said the professor.

"I have," said Laura. "Isn't that when a jury is so sympathetic to one side that they vote that way even though all the proof favors the other guy?"

"Yes," said the Cowboy. "And that's actually a pretty good definition. How did you know that?"

"I took a course on the civil rights movement in college. During the sixties southern white juries wouldn't convict white men of crimes against blacks, even murder, no matter how strong the proof was. They just wouldn't do it."

"That's true. Those jurors were adhering to what they thought was a higher authority. Higher than the criminal law. Higher, even, than the Bible. For them, the higher authority was race hatred. But jury nullification goes back a long way and has a history not nearly as horrible as the sixties alone would suggest. William Penn was tried for the crime of being a Quaker, an "illegal religion" back in 1670 in London. He admitted it proudly but the jury acquitted him anyway because they thought it shouldn't be a crime. Here in America, people were prosecuted under the Fugitive Slave Laws during the 1800s and jurors often acquitted because they thought it shouldn't be a crime to help a runaway slave. There are many other examples.

"You have to understand the inherent issue, which is simple but technical. The law—in our case a statute in the Penal Law—defines a certain act as a crime. The lawyers offer evidence and argue whether the facts constitute proof of that crime. But what if the jury doesn't agree with the law or thinks the person charged should go free even if he did it? In other words, the jury gives a collective, *So what?*"

"They just nullify, or vote not guilty, right?" said Frank.

"Yes, that's right. That's because jurors cannot be questioned as to why they said *Not guilty*. They needn't explain themselves to anyone, and there's no appeal from a not guilty verdict. The case is over. Everyone goes home. So as a practical matter, they can flip a coin if they want; no one will ever know. But here's where it gets tricky, Frank, because the next question is, Can defense counsel ask them to nullify? And then, beyond that, Can the judge tell them they have that right?' And the answers to those questions are a bit bizarre.

"John Adams said it was not only a juror's right, but his duty to follow his conscience, even though in direct opposition to the direction of the court. The first Chief Justice of the United States Supreme Court, John Jay, said yes to both. He said both the law and the facts are up to a jury to decide, and they can say yes or no as they please and there shouldn't be anything secretive or mysterious about it, but those guys said those things over 200 years ago.

"Since then, things have changed. Prosecutors and politicians worried there'd be no order, no consistency to the justice system if every law was up for grabs in every trial. In the 1890s the Supreme Court said the trial court had no obligation to tell the jury it had the power to nullify. However, it didn't say they couldn't do it. After that, it's been downhill for nullification. Judges don't like it, and they don't want guys like me arguing it, at least not by name."

"But if the Supreme Court didn't say a jury could not nullify, doesn't that mean the jury can?" said Laura.

"Good point. And it does seem that way. Around 1969 or '70, a federal court said specifically that it could. But it also said the court could refuse to tell them so."

The Rooneys looked at each other.

"Helluva thing, I know. They have to promise they won't nullify but they can, provided the judge doesn't tell them they can."

By now, the coffee had been served. The Rooneys each reached for their cups and took long, confused sips.

"If that's not a corporate policy kind of muddle, I don't know what is," said Frank. "It makes refusing to give me my money back look reasonable. Anyway, what does all this matter to me?"

"To the extent your case is part of a social protest, it matters a lot. T.U.L.P. wants to argue, and I want to argue as well—because I think it'll work—that the injustice of Maiko's not refunding your money— yours and the old lady's—was so grave as to make your actions acceptable, even if technically illegal. I want to be able to stand there and say, 'Let's look at the big picture here. Corporate callousness is what's really on trial. Frank Rooney's response, under these circumstances, was nothing less than reasonable. He's a hero, not a criminal. The bad guy is Maiko even if Frank did grab that guy and yank his head into that glass partition."

Laura Rooney stood up and started collecting the coffee cups. Frank knew that to be the signal that she'd had enough. He also knew from the brusque and rapid manner in which she was piling dishes in her hands that while she liked Mr. Sheridan, her mind was made up, and not in the way their guest had hoped for.

Nonetheless, she stopped clearing dishes when she heard the words: "So we're going to stand up to the brutality of corporate policy. We're refusing to knuckle under."

Laura Rooney looked at her husband, from whose mouth those words had come. "Frank?"

Chapter 21

The last thing Johann Mathison did before leaving his home in Columbus, Ohio, was send a confirming email to Brian and Suzy Brindisi of Colonie, New York. It was Thursday, two days before the planned weekend of protests. "Leaving today," it read. "Be there late tomorrow. Thanks in advance for your hospitality."

He'd found the Brindisis on the newly updated T.U.L.P. website. They were among the people who'd volunteered to put up protesters from out of town. Fifty-seven families had signed up in the first hour after the new site went online. Five days later the hosts numbered in the hundreds, with more needed if beds were to be found for the thousands of out-of-towners expected to arrive by the weekend.

Mathison held a black belt in karate and taught at a dojo. He hoped to open his own shop someday. Two weeks before hearing about Frank Rooney he'd been out of town at a karate tournament in St. Louis and been surprised to see the following sign on the front desk in the lobby when he'd checked out:

To Our Guests:
Please be advised if you pay your bill with a credit or debit card, there will be a $25 hold placed on your card to cover against incidental charges. If there are no incidental charges, the hold will be lifted no later than 10 business days after checkout.

"What is this?" he'd asked the clerk as she'd prepared his bill.

"Oh, that's just if you used the phone or in-room snack bar."

"My room didn't have a snack bar, and don't you know if I use the phone the minute I pick up the receiver? I mean, it's all computerized, isn't it?"

"Yes, but just in case. It's nothing, really."

"Excuse me, but I don't think it's nothing. Do you mean you can't tell me right now, while I'm standing here, how much money I owe?"

"I guess not," she'd said, smiling. "But it's nothing."

"But I don't want a hold placed on my credit card. I don't think it's fair. Please check your records and make sure I don't owe anything else."

"Well, theoretically, there could be damage in your room. Not that there is, I'm sure."

"So can you please send someone up to check? I can wait."

"Oh, we can't do that."

"Why not?"

"It's hotel policy."

There'd been another man standing next to Johann, also checking out.

"Excuse me, sir," Johann had said to him. "Excuse me, but did you see this sign?"

"Oh, yeah. I travel a lot and all the big hotel chains are doing it."

"Doesn't it bother you?"

"Not really. They're all doing it."

"I don't mean to be pushy or anything, but that's an odd answer, don't you think? It's okay to be treated unfairly as long as it happens a lot?"

The man waved Johann off.

"What about this ten days business?" Johann returned his attention to the clerk. "Ten business days is two full weeks. At some point today a chambermaid is going to clean my room, so you'll have had your inspection, and you'll know for certain that there is no damage and I don't owe you any more money. Why can't the hold be lifted then?"

"Oh, that's between you and your bank."

"What do you mean, me and my bank? What happened to you?"

"It depends on the bank you have your credit card with. We'll let them know there's no further charge just as soon as we know, but some banks take longer than others to remove a hold. The longest is ten business days."

"But that's outrageous. My bank didn't stay in that room. And you're the one who placed the hold on my card."

"I know," the clerk had said in apparent agreement. "But there's nothing we can do about it."

"What do you mean, there's nothing you can do?"

"You see, your bank decides how long to keep the hold there. We've nothing to do with that."

With the word *nothing*, the clerk made a sweeping motion with the edge of her open hand, as if to emphasize to the distressed customer her employer's complete lack of blame for his predicament.

When Johann arrived at the Brindisis, he knocked on the door and the hosts came out. Brian and Suzy looked up at the man standing on their doorstep.

"Jesus," said Brian. "We're hosting a Viking."

Johann smiled down at them. His chiseled frame soared to a point even with the top of their front door and his head was topped by a full mane of nearly white hair that cascaded down around blond eyebrows and blue eyes stopping short of his straight nose and square jaw.

"I don't think we've got a bed big enough for him," said Suzy. She was talking to her husband as though Johann, perched way up high as he was, was too far away to hear her.

"That's okay," said the young man. "This happens to me all the time. You can put me anywhere, even the floor. I've got a sleeping bag in the car."

"Come on in," said Brian. "Most of our friends are having people too. Looks like quite the thing."

"Yeah. Quite the thing," said Johann.

Chapter 22

"Is perception problem," said Boris Petrovich. "We bring pipple from other places, perception is we meddle in local business. Use local pipple only, perception is we are small local group and no cchhompany will be afraid."

The scene was the same table around which the T.U.L.P. committee had first gathered in the Hammermill home, but other than the people at the table, little else was the same. The long driveway leading to Route 146 was lined with small cars and minivans. Tents surrounded the house and dotted the woods between the Hammermills' island and the neighboring subdivisions.

Alexander had brought in porta potties and had outdoor showers set up. Then he'd hired Fred's Bar-B-Q ("Our Ribs Will Stick To Yours") to supply food. It was Thursday, two weeks and two days since Frank Rooney's grab had started it all.

"Honey," his wife had said, "they don't expect to be fed. Look, they've brought food, clothing, and tents. If they need more supplies, there are three supermarkets nearby."

"And what'll they buy, Cindy? Organically grown vegetables and couscous? We've picked a fight here. You can't fight on veggies and whatever that other thing is."

"It's a starch, dear."

"They need meat. Ribs and chicken. Once they get a whiff of what Fred's cooking up, they'll strap on their arch-supporting sandals and line up for some real food. I'm telling you, Cindy, they'll eat like truck drivers."

Christina Clark said, "I do hope they provide silverware. Finger food is such a problem with my nails."

"Don't you worry," said Cindy. "Alexander will provide. Under that rough exterior lies the soul of a gentleman. Isn't that right, dear?"

By the time the group took up Boris's perception problem, a large American flag had been hung from an oak tree branch in the middle of the tent camp. It was a fifteen-footer, express mailed to Gus DeMauro from his business in Mountain View, California.

"I fly a flag outside my office on all national holidays," Gus said. "But I save this big one for my two favorites, the Fourth of July and Election Day."

"Election Day is not cchholiday," said Boris.

"Yeah, but it oughta be. It's the day we remind ourselves where the real power is."

Lucy Goldstein said, "If corporations like Maiko have their way, those elections won't mean a thing. That's the point here. We fit our lives into the boxes they design and when they need to change the shape of those boxes, we change too. It's policy."

"Is cchorrect, Lucy. So let's get to work."

Max was late to the meeting. He'd spent the day wandering around, talking to the new arrivals, waving as their cars and vans drove by. As the only recognizable face of T.U.L.P., he felt it his responsibility to be visible, and his gut, along with his eyes and ears, told him he was doing the right thing.

Just walking was an effort, though, because everyone he met wanted to hug him. It was like the time he'd scored the winning goal in the overtime of a high school playoff game. The next morning his name had been in the papers and all day long he'd accepted handshakes, back slaps, and hugs from the students and faculty. He couldn't get to his classes because he was too busy soaking up attention in the hallways and when he did show up, late, teachers and classmates burst into applause.

This was even better. *We've been waiting for you*, was the refrain he heard the most, along with *I thought I was the only one who felt that way*. He was offered food, wine, water, beer. *You're cuter in person* seemed to be a consensus sentiment among the women, whose faces he scanned, hoping for a glimpse of that TV reporter. He'd sit for a while at one campsite or another, and a crowd would gather, waiting to hear him speak. But that wasn't why he was doing the rounds.

"Tell me why you're here," he'd say, then direct his attention to responders in the group, and listen to their stories. He'd meant to stay for only a minute, but one story became three, three people around a campfire became fifteen, and his minutes became hours. Every story told was met with nods and choruses of *That's right! Me too*! and *I can't believe they're doing this to everyone!*

Max listened, growing aware that he was providing relief merely by allowing the complaints to find his ears, as if the simple act of unburdening to the Spokesman made the problems less severe. But before moving on to each new group, Max asked, "Is there anybody here named Gezunterman?"

Late that night a second flashpoint arose on the Hammermill island. As with Max, this one moved, picking up energy as it did. It was the news van for WTYX, and it contained Meagan Swoboda, who'd been the only reporter to put together vague reports of heavy traffic on Route 146 long after rush hour with the possibility that all those cars were connected to TULP.

Once her van entered the property, finding Max was not only easy, it was inevitable. People ran between the van, which stopped repeatedly to take video and allow Meagan to do interviews, to wherever Max's moving therapy session was located. Between the motion of the two attractions and that of the runners and onlookers, it was as though two weather systems were about to collide.

People seemed to want them to meet, as if to witness the moment something intensely personal yet somehow common went worldwide, as they were sure would happen. When Meagan and Max actually did meet, they were swept toward each other like potential lovers being introduced at long last by enthusiastic friends. Each of them had to lean back against the tide in order to avoid colliding. Only when Meagan produced her microphone and signaled for the van to come closer did the crowd back off.

"Are you the one behind all this?" she said. The guys in the van were not yet ready to film.

"No, and I'm not sure who is. Most likely you'll find it's a spontaneous demonstration. I'm just along for the ride."

"But they're all talking about you. It's as though they've been waiting for me to appear just so they could bring me to you."

She blushed a bit when she spoke those words, and Max could feel a strong gust of wind come up behind him.

"Would you say those words again?" he asked, and smiled.

She was momentarily silent. Then she pressed her hand to her earpiece.

"Hurry! We can still make the eleven o'clock. I told them to put a helicopter in the air, but no, they never listen to me."

"Fire away, Max said. We'll talk fast."

She gave him a half-smile. "Where is this *we* business coming from?" she said, looking at him with her head tilted, as if a different angle might reveal something new.

A man hopped out of the van and hoisted a camera onto his shoulder. A voice from inside the van said, "You're on."

"This is Meagan Swoboda reporting from some sort of staging area for tomorrow's expected demonstration by T.U..L.P., the organization that is demanding fair treatment by corporations. With me is Max Rodriguez, who has become a sort of unofficial spokesman for T.U.L.P. Max, what's going on here?"

"I'll be glad to tell you, Meagan, but first let me make an important correction. What we're looking for is to be treated like people. We want human treatment. You know, the United States Supreme Court says corporations have the right to free speech. Well, if they have that right, then don't they also have the obligations that go along with it? The big corporations that dominate our lives mistreat all their customers equally and claim they're being "fair" only because they abuse everyone the same way. That's not what we want. We want a level of civility, a degree of consciousness to be exhibited by corporate America. We want corporations to be good citizens."

"How many people are here, Max?"

"Thousands. And there are more on the way. Local people are putting up protesters in their homes all over the Capital Region. Plus, many people took hotel rooms. It's going to be a big demonstration."

"We seem to be out in the woods here. Do you know who owns this property? Does he support your organization?"

"Sure he does. His name is Alexander Hammermill. Why don't you follow me for a bit, and we'll see if we can find him."

Max began to walk with Meagan following, tethered to her van which moved with her. She continued the interview, the cameraman catching the commotion of dozens of people trying to maintain a circle around the moving target that was Meagan.

Max led her toward the giant American flag he had noticed over Swoboda's shoulder. Finding Alexander would be nice, but he wasn't going to worry about it. Directly beneath the Stars and Stripes he stopped walking. Meagan motioned to her cameraman to look up, but he was already framing the shot.

"We're a nation of people, not rules," said Max. "And certainly not corporate rules. We've spent over two centuries showing the world how to be free from government interference and government abuse, and we didn't go through all that just to trade government control for corporate control. If a government official treated Frank Rooney like Maiko Industries has, you wouldn't be asking me the questions you're asking. It would be obvious to you as an American that Frank was treated unfairly. Well, this protest is an American declaration of freedom for the 21st century. Corporations now have the power, just like the king of England did before our revolution. And just as the king had to be made to respect our inalienable rights, so does corporate America.

"What do you say, Meagan? Are you with us?"

The director in the truck spoke to her through her earpiece before she could answer. "That's enough of this guy," he barked. "I'd like to go home, Meagan."

Off went the camera lights and Meagan handed over her microphone.

"So what do you say?" Max said. As soon as the light went off, the crowd began to disperse.

"I say I'm a reporter. I'm not supposed to take sides."

"Ah, yes. Policy. But I wasn't talking about corporate America. I was talking about dinner. Say, sometime after the weekend. Do you like Indian?"

Fifteen minutes later Max was seated at the Hammermill dining room table, waiting for the ball to come his way.

"We're not as parochial as we used to be," said Christina Clark. "That concept of 'outsider' doesn't have the impact it did when the Freedom Riders were traveling though Mississippi. I'll bet there are a lot of people living in this area who weren't born and raised here. And even with the ones who were, how different are they from people from Ohio or Seattle or New Hampshire?"

Lucy Goldstein disagreed. "Never underestimate the desire of a human being to belong. I can just see some guy watching his TV and complaining about all those radicals from out of state coming into his town to tell him what to do, even if he himself just moved here from somewhere else. Why should he help take down a local business, put local people out of work, just to please somebody who'll be going back home to Illinois tomorrow? If we're gonna get that guy on our side, we're gonna have to show him some local faces, some faces from his own team."

Christina Clark responded, "But it's not that big an area. Face it, most of the people out there are from out of town. If we're going to make a big showing, we've got to use them. Or maybe we should divide our forces and send some people up to Buffalo. That's only five hours away. We could shut down Maiko's theater there while doing the same here. That would show we're not just a one-town phenomenon, and from this close a distance we could retain tight control of both operations."

"Is ambitious, maybe too much? Cchave we pipple to do it?" said Boris.

"Doesn't matter," said Max to a table full of people who'd forgotten he was there. "Excuse me," he said, raising his voice to be heard. "Excuse me, but it doesn't matter."

"Ah," said Boris, "Spokesman will finally speak. Cchwas cchwondering chwen chwould cchappen."

"This is a spontaneous uprising. We've tapped into a mother lode of energy, and we've no right to redirect it elsewhere. More to the point, we couldn't if we tried. These people are here because this is the flashpoint. We need to throw our full weight at Maiko right here, right now, confront them with overwhelming proof of our strength, and let the chips fall where they may. The best thing we can do is look like an organization on the rise. Better one big showing on Utah Avenue in Albany than a moderate or disappointing showing both here and in Buffalo.

"What we could do is pair up locals with out-of-towners, or just have the locals spread themselves around and tell them to be sure to step forward when they see a reporter or cameraman. That way we're doing what we can to keep the local flavor while not limiting our own progress.

And if a few guys from Portland get on TV, so what? Imagine what the *Wall Street Journal* types will be thinking of us if on our first time out, we're attracting support nationwide, however slight."

"Oh, my," said Christina Clark.

"Another thing. The work in Buffalo, Seattle, L.A., Austin, the work everywhere is already under way. I can feel it. Our job may be to simply put things in motion. Maybe some other organization will take over after that. Maybe not. We'll find out when it happens. But the cause is just, and we've got to take the first step. That's our obligation. If we discharge it well, the second step will take care of itself. Let's just win here."

"But where's the lawyer we hired?" said Alexander. Shouldn't he be here? We need to coordinate strategy."

"No, we don't," said Max. "He'll follow us. This is a social movement. The legal work is merely reactive to our efforts. Call him up and let him know what we're doing so he doesn't get caught by surprise, but that's all we need to do."

The protests were scheduled for Saturday and Sunday, in the hope that enough pressure could be brought on Maiko by ruining most of the weekend to make the corporation back down on Frank Rooney. Some last-minute details were tended too. Alexander called the State Police barracks just a few miles away to remind them there'd been threats of violence.

In fact, one man stopping for gas on his way down from Vermont had mentioned to the cashier that he was headed to Albany. "You one of those protesters?" the cashier had asked. When told yes, the man threw the change back at the customer's chest and said, "Protest, my ass."

Not exactly a death threat, but all Alexander wanted was a patrol car to come nosing around every once in a while, and the troopers promised that much. Plus, there was a volunteer security detail armed with cell phones and flashlights that would be walking the property all night.

The T.U.L.P. committee took one last stroll around the grounds before turning in. They stopped near Alexander's garage and looked out at a hundred campfires glittering under the spot-lit American flag.

Gus DeMauro lit up a big cigar and blew a mouthful of smoke into the air. "I feel like George Washington at Valley Forge," he said.

"Maybe so," said Boris, "but cchhee did not cchhave Fred to barbeque, or Alexander to give portable toilets."

The group stood silently, staring out at the flag fluttering in the breeze and at the fires that surrounded it.

"Thank God they don't make mauve-colored tents," said Alexander.

Chapter 23

"Can't we just rent a van that comes with all the stuff you need?" Keith said to his brother from the driver's seat. "You just push a button and the roof rises, the walls expand, and bingo—a fully stocked, one-bedroom apartment. I'll sleep on the couch. You can have the bed."

"I saw such a thing once on TV. They called it 'The Frontiersman.' The logo on the fender read, The Spirit That Made America Great. I think that's how George Jetson took his family camping."

"Yeah, but I bet he had more fun than we're gonna have."

"Well, there it is. Every hotel room in the area is booked. We've got a nice clean place to stay with dear old Mom, who's going to the same event we're going to, and I don't see what the big deal is. It's a natural fit."

"Right. Look in the CD case for a disc marked spirituals. There's a song by Ben Harper called "I Shall Not Walk Alone" that'll kill you. It's the last cut,

"The song begins with a solo piano introduction that is simple almost to the point of self-effacement, as if the pianist is apologetic for interjecting his sounds upon the listener. No other song I've ever heard creates this kind of mood right off the bat.

The music came on and both brothers were silent for a few bars.

"The lead singer begins. 'Battered and torn,' and his voice almost cracks with emotion. It's the voice of a beaten-down man whose need to rise up and tell the world of the Grace he's found is more powerful than the pain of his ordeal. Listen:

Battered and torn
still I can see the light.
Tattered and worn
but I must kneel to fight

"The theme is established in those first few words. What's yet to be established is the method by which this soul is to be saved, and that is the musical point of the song.

"Now here comes the help. It's The Blind Boys of Alabama singing the refrain in a harmony so rich it gives you chills. They're a musical cavalry summoned to action by the caller's belief and need.

When my legs no longer carry
and the warm wind chills my bones
I just reach for Mother Mary
and I shall not walk alone

"But Harper never completely joins the response of his friends. His lines are separate, his way apart from theirs, yet his strength is growing now that they've arrived, their arrival guaranteed by his belief that they would come—a perfect Circle of Faith in which the individual is saved by his own devotion.

"Harper sings the first two words of each line of the refrain the first time through and then stops, too weak to continue, but his friends pick up the lines and carry them to their ends. By the second refrain the lead singer, fortified by the unyielding support of his brothers, sings the full verse all the way through.

"From beginning to end the lead is emotional, unpredictable, needy, while the Blind Boys sing their refrain in a steady, almost fugue-like tone. Here's the message I hear, my brother: Go where you must. Fail where you may. Just remember that we are your rock, your constant rescue."

Scott hit the replay button.

"It's a great song," Keith said, "but at some point, we're going to get to Albany, and we're going to have to stop the car. Do we discuss it now or after we cross the city line?"

"One more listen. Then I'll be ready."

When Scott Gezunterman was in Hebrew school, he'd asked questions of his teachers like, "Come on, Mr. Finkelman, all the creatures fit on that ark? Every species? Then how did the giant turtles get back to the Galapagos Islands and the giraffes back to Africa and the alligators back to Louisiana after the ark landed? Come to think of it, how'd they get to wherever Noah was to begin with? Did he call them with a special whistle or something?"

He wasn't keen on the dogma of other religions, either. Immaculate conception, conversations with God. "Gimme a break," he would say.

Yet from a time that predated even that first Sunday morning in the church, there was a feeling he got that was always ignited by music that he'd come to regard as "spiritual." Not that he believed in a higher power. He didn't. What he did believe in was an inner spark, which he was sure existed, however buried, unacknowledged or denied, inside every one of the human kind. That spark ignited a light that shone the way to transcendence. It lifted the species above its daily routine, beyond the basic needs for food, clothing, and shelter, above even the heights attainable through reason. In that higher place a greater truth was revealed.

Those revelations were what art was created to bring us to, and the art form that communicated best to him was the one that spoke in rhythm. The types of music he heard clearest were as varied as the beliefs that inspired them. Gospel, American spirituals, Hebrew prayers, hymns, Gregorian chant. They were all the same to him as far as their potency was concerned, so the Hallelujah Chorus moved him just as much as Otis Redding's version of "Amen," and both let him see the world as if someone had just cleaned his windshield. He was certain if he knew anything about the music of India or Japan or Peru, he'd respond to them, too.

The music didn't have to be religious, at least not ostensibly. Motown, jazz, big band, blues, all had the ability to mark the moment, or, rather, hold the moment by stopping time from moving on. So did Irish folk music, Russian peasant songs, and Hungarian Gypsy tunes. He loved a marching band that played anything by Sousa, and would stand and cheer for a bagpipe and drum team, chills working their way up and down his spine.

When the moment occurred, it did so by chance—a note here, a phrase there—and no one source was a more likely point of inspiration than another. Suddenly, he would be somewhere else, and everything would have come to a stop—forced aside, or perhaps more accurately stated, held in place—by what he was hearing.

Gospel people call it being born again or getting happy or feeling the Spirit. When they're in the moment, they've transcended human experience and been touched by a Holy Joy.

He took license. Given his nondenominational view of spirituality, it was necessary. In the Blind Boys' tune he'd shared with his brother, the phrase "I shall not walk alone" is the second half of a sentence that begins with "I just reach for Mother Mary . . ." That Mother Mary meant nothing to him as a matter of religious doctrine was of no moment. Neither was it relevant that the Holy Joy felt by the gospel singers he so loved was the presence of Jesus Christ. Religion could attach its own labels to what he was feeling; that was mankind's weakness. It was mortal men who, in spite of themselves, created the words and the music that made those feelings happen. That was mankind's strength.

Soon after he began visiting the First Baptist Church, he glimpsed that strength in his synagogue. It came during the singing of two ubiquitous lines of a prayer known as ya-a-seh shalom, create peace. In Hebrew, they read: O-sey shalom bim-ro mah, hu ya-a-sey' shalom a-lei-nu, ve-al kol yis-ra-el ve-im-ru amen. He who creates peace in his celestial heights, may he create peace for us and for all Israel; and say, Amen.

The words appear in the Amidah, a meditation of devotion to God which is said four times during the Sabbath service, twice in silence and twice in song. They appear in the Mourner's Kaddish, also said twice each Sabbath as well as at funerals, and they appear in daily prayers. And they are sung at Sabbath dinners. He'd read them and sung them dozens of times, but it was not until he prayed at the graveside service for his Uncle Berel that it hit him.

There was no singing then, the words being quickly spoken by a somber rabbi. But the absence of song where he'd heard singing so many times before made the tune all the more present, and he found himself singing it out loud all the way back to his Aunt Shirley's house, where the eating and the mourning would begin, and he knew he had to take a closer look.

When the words are read in silence in the synagogue, they're accompanied by a ritualistic movement: three steps back, bow right, bow left, three steps forward. When sung, there is no such movement, but the tune initially hints at a musically pleasing sound, which is rare in the Sabbath service. That promise is redeemed when the congregation returns not to the beginning but to the middle of the sentence and sings, soaring in unison and an octave higher, ya-a-seh shalom, ya-a-sey shalom, shalom a-lei-nu ve, al kol yis-ra-el, create peace, may he create peace, peace for all of us and for all Israel.

The way Scott saw it, the congregation, at that point tired after nearly three hours of praying, sings those few lines with such fervor because the congregants have finally come round to the main point of their efforts. The bowing has been a preparatory exercise in humility. Not humility before God, in whom Scott did not believe even then, but humility before each other, humility before all others, inside the synagogue and out, humility before the entire world of mortals. We are all together. None better, none worse.

Having worked all morning to achieve that most unassuming perspective, the congregation is now concluding the service with its most human plea. Make peace. Make peace. Peace for all the world and for all Israel. Stripped of pretense and void of arrogance, what does the congregation pray for? Not for enemies to be vanquished or for nonbelievers to be made converts. Neither for wealth nor power nor glory. Simply, peace. And not just peace for Israel alone, but peace for all the world. That is why the congregants' faces are raised and everyone in the building sings loudest at that moment and the notes are scripted within an easily achieved range. It's why the same words appear and reappear so many times in the Sabbath service.

How did it come to be that this music was affixed to these words? Who decided on this particular combination of words and bowing that appears nowhere else in the service? What traditions were modified, incorporated from other cultures, or rejected entirely until they'd gotten it right? And how many changes in the order of service took place before these prayers appeared where they so perfectly belonged?

Other prayers might work this well given the right music. Other tunes might inspire as much if linked to the right words. Yet, through the centuries, those prayers, imperfectly matched with song, had slipped to insignificance while this one was burnished to perfection.

It was a human miracle, although he would not have called it such when he first experienced it. Now he would say it was a creation of the human variety, a manifestation of what we sometimes can be and an example of how easily we can fall short. What appears as a humble plea for peace by a small group of congregants in their tiny synagogue just before breaking for lunch is in fact the highest form of human endeavor: man-made experience that transcends the world of men.

Chapter 24

No one underestimated Charlie Remlinger anymore. These days, he was feared and reviled. He sparked anger and resentment. He'd even earned some grudging respect, along with a touch of deference. All worthless, as far as he was concerned. The times when adversaries called him punk or idiot had faded into memory, lost forever to a duller, less contented present.

It wasn't for lack of trying; he'd always been the hardest of workers, but the return on his effort just wasn't there. Even the insulting sendoff he'd gotten from the District Attorney had been lacking. Bronstein had known perfectly well what kind of man he was up against. That's why he'd been so conciliatory at first. Chaz had gone too far, of course. But the D.A. had responded like one important tough guy to another, a grudging acknowledgment of equal standing. It did not produce the warm sensation of blood rising to Remlinger's face and ears that had always accompanied a hard-earned insult. He couldn't remember the last time he'd had the kind of opportunity that came with a condescension-coated slur.

The blond in front of whom he now paced, his current blond and the one he'd mollified with a trip to Dr. Java's for a brownie the night they'd been overheard by Max Rodriguez, wasn't old enough to remember those days. If she was, she might have realized how much a simple "You're-in-over-your-head-Chazzie" would've done for his spirits. Not that it was a guarantee she'd have said it. Underestimating Chaz may have gone out of fashion, but helping him out was never in.

"Look at those candy asses!" he shouted, pointing at the TV. "Do you see them? They think they can push Chaz Remlinger around. Can you believe it? Who do these people think they're dealing with? I'm telling you they have no idea."

"That's not the impression I get, Chazzie. I think they know just what they're up against. That's why there are so many of them."

"You know, my damn lawyers don't know shit. Fancy educated candy asses. No fight in them. That's the problem. These people want a fight? They're gonna get one."

"Didn't your lawyer suggest just waiting it out? It's July already. Once the summer's over, they'll go back to their schools and jobs and this will all go away."

"Right. That's just how I got to be the big shot I am—by hiding in the corner and waiting for the bad man to go away. No way, kid."

"Well, what are you going to do?"

"I'm gonna call a cab to take you home. Then I've got some other phone calls to make. These wimps may think they're out for a walk in the park, but lemme tell you something: It's a park they're gonna wish they never entered. I guarantee it."

"Yes, I have faith in you, Chazzie. Call the cab."

He did, and when it arrived he walked her out, hand firmly supporting her elbow.

Several hours later there began to arrive at the Remlinger home a succession of pickup trucks and utility vans. Some contained two men but most just one. The oldest was Remlinger's age, the youngest barely twenty. To a one, they wore T-shirts, mostly white, stretched tight over broad shoulders and muscular chests, along with blue jeans, work boots, and angry looks. Inside they marched, exchanging hellos but otherwise saying little. Sixty minutes later, when they walked back out, the anger had been supplemented by purposeful looks and an air of grim determination. Now they said nothing at all.

Heavy truck doors popped open and slammed shut. Oversized engines roared and dust filled the air as pieces of gravel ricocheted off headlights and fenders, and then they were gone.

After his first day of the eighth grade, Max Rodriguez came home with the reading list and course syllabus for his honors English class. The list included *A Farewell to Arms, The Catcher in the Rye,* and *Stranger in a Strange Land.* In her course description, which both of Max's parents read, the teacher told the kids they "were going to learn to get used to ambiguity."

It was a word that gave Chuck a level of discomfort bordering on pain.

"Can she say that?" he asked his wife.

"Not only can she say it, but I couldn't be happier about it," said Nancy. "It's about time Max had a teacher who wanted to challenge the kids. These are real books, Chuck. No more pandering with those books for children. He's thirteen already. It's time. I think I'll bake that teacher a cake."

Back then Chuck saw no connection between ambiguity and adulthood. Now, as he watched his son once more on the late night news, he remembered that day. He knew if Nancy were still alive she'd be more than pleased with their son; she'd be ecstatic. More important, she'd be able to tell him why.

It hadn't occurred to him that some of the fellas at R and D were making a point of not talking to him about Max's rise to stardom. Then the story was picked up by the *New York Times* and CNN and FOX, and Chuck began to comprehend an unspoken truth: it was taking more effort to ignore the story than to acknowledge it. Yet his colleagues were making that effort.

To the extent that there was discussion about social and political issues, the people at work were nearly always in agreement. In fact, Chuck thought one of the reasons those subjects so rarely came up was that there was so little they disagreed about, until now. And now, they weren't even shy about showing it.

Or was he imagining the whole thing? Was it his own insecurities about what his son was up to? No one at the office had said a negative word to him. These weren't academics. There was nothing terribly subtle or devious about this crew. They were engineers, and one of them was learning to get used to ambiguity.

One of the many odd things about Younger Lake was that people still strolled about at night, and since the streets were so narrow and the houses so small, taking a walk was like window shopping for conversation. With postage-stamp sized yards and patios close to the road as they were, it was almost rude not to listen, so if something sounded good you just joined in. That's how Jane Blake learned about the hundreds of demonstrators gathering in the woods off Route 146 just a few miles away. She'd been sitting on her patio, a tiny square of bricks with barely enough space for a table and a couple of chairs, when Ava and Bartholomew from around the corner came strolling by, hand in hand, at about midnight.

Jane was fond of them, Bartholomew in particular, because as he liked to say, "It takes a real man to insist on being called Bartholomew."

"Heard about the big march?" Bartholomew said.

"If you guys are it, you're gonna need some help," she laughed.

"No, no. They're getting together somewhere off 146, hundreds of them according to the TV news, to march on the ELF's movie theater," said Ave. "You haven't heard?"

"Nah. I was just out here doing some stargazing."

"Looks like a little Woodstock over there," said Bartholomew.

"Oh, yeah? That'll sit well with Charlie," Jane laughed. Her neighbors said good night and moved on. Jane wondered what the ELF had in store for those poor, unsuspecting people.

Jane had been looking for more than stars. She'd been looking for a sign, and with the few house lights on the street quickly shutting off for the evening and her neighbors gone, her sign-searching could resume. She leaned back in the lawn chair and stared upward.

Mrs. Gezunterman had made her do it.

"This is Flo Gezunterman," the old lady had screamed into the phone a couple of days earlier.

"Yes," Jane had laughed. "I can tell."

"You're laughing already? I haven't said anything yet. Believe me, I'm not that funny."

"Oh, I believe you, Mrs. Gezunterman. I'm just in a good mood, that's all."

"You sound like this whenever I talk to you."

"Well, I'm almost always in a good mood." With that the phone went silent for a while. "Mrs. Gezunterman? Hello? Are you . . ."

"Yes, yes. I'm just trying to understand. Well, okay. I called because my son is up for the weekend. You remember my son?"

"The one you told me about, right?"

"Yeah. Sure. Who else? So he's up for the weekend, and I really want you should meet him."

"Mrs. Gezunterman, I . . ."

"I know. Everyone fixes you up. But with a man like this you've never been fixed up. If you were, you wouldn't be alone yet. He's artistic, like you. Plays music all the time. He's unusual."

"I don't know."

"So I'm giving him your number and telling him he can call you, right?"

"Well . . ."

"You won't regret it." Then she hung up.

Unusual. Such an odd way for a mother to describe her own child. So odd, thought Jane, it had to mean something good. Not handsome or smart or successful. Unusual.

She decided to wait for the stars to come out and look for a sign. She was still waiting an hour after Ava and her courageous husband departed when a pizza delivery car did the job. "Angelo's Pizza," the sign on the roof marquee said: "It's Unusually Good."

It wasn't so much that Frank Rooney couldn't sleep as he just didn't want the day to end. This business of having something exciting happen daily had gotten to him, although he'd done his best to hide the fact from his wife. The day had been quiet so far but he was hoping to get his fix from the late-night local news. He knew what was happening out at the Hammermill place, and he'd wanted to go out there, but his lawyer had vetoed the idea.

"Some cowboy," he'd said after hanging up the phone. Laura, at whose insistence the call had been made, had also been affected by all the excitement. She'd had her fill. By the time Meagan Swoboda and Max Rodriguez lit up her living room she'd been in bed for over an hour. Unable to sleep, she knew her husband was watching the news. What she didn't know was that he was more than watching, he was taking notes, and after the news was over and she finally had fallen asleep he'd written one more note, this one without the help of the TV. It read: "I had to go to the Hammermills to see what was going on. Couldn't help myself. Be back soon. Frank."

Twenty minutes later Frank parked his Acura in the first spot he saw along the Hammermills' driveway and began walking through the campsites. It was after midnight, but enough people were still awake to maintain the carnival atmosphere.

He'd worn a baseball cap and removed his glasses but he needn't have bothered. His was an irrepressible kind of nondescript. Fame couldn't touch it. TV exposure couldn't touch it. The only way he was going to be recognized was if he doubled up on himself and wore a Free Frank T-shirt.

Where a campfire was surrounded by people, he sat down and listened to the conversations. If two or three people had gathered to talk, he joined in.

He never heard his name. What the night sounded like was this:

"It was my fourth call to the service center and each time I got a different person and had to reexplain the whole problem. So I said, 'Can I have your personal line so I can call you back and not have to explain all this to someone else?'

"She said, 'I don't have a personal line.'

"So I said, 'No? Do you have kids?'

"And she said 'What's that got to do with this?'

"I said, 'Well, what number do they call when they have to speak to their mom?'

"She said, 'I can't tell you if I have kids.'

"I said, 'Okay, you have a mother, don't you? Don't tell me your mother never calls you at work. What number does she call?'

"She said, 'I can't tell you that.'

"I said, 'Tell you what. Give me your mother's number and when I have to call you, I'll call her and she'll call you and you can call me right back.'"

And this:

"Welcome to our automated answering system.

"How many times have we heard that? But stop and think about it for a minute.

Welcome? It's a computer! You're being welcomed by a machine! They don't even think you're worth being listened to by a human being, let alone be helped. It's like planning a trip to visit your sister and driving all the way across the country and finding a note on her door that says, "Welcome. I'm away on vacation. Go on inside and tell my furniture all about your life."

And this:

"My doctor's office has an automated phone system, but when I needed to make an appointment, I called and got a live answering service. The live person said they were closed for lunch.

"But why do they have you answering the phone? They have an automated phone system," I said.

"I don't know," she said. "Do you want to leave a message or not?"

"You mean I can talk to you and give you a message, and you'll write it down?"

"That's the idea."

"But you're only there when the office is closed."

"That's right."

"And if I call back after their lunch hour is over, you'll be gone and I'll get an answering machine?"

"Correct."

"So the only time I can actually talk to someone is when there's nobody there."

"I never thought of it that way."

"Catch-22."

"Now that you mention it . . ."

"You see what's happening? We're beyond irony. Satire is obsolete. Nothing is left but resistance."

He heard plans for the next day's march, but not a word about the man who'd started it all. When "the case" was mentioned it was almost in passing, as if that fellow in the movie theater was incidental to their purpose.

Whatever reservations he'd had about this cause were dissipated by the time he got home. At 2:30 in the morning, when he slipped into his bed and wrapped his arms around his sleeping wife, he was smiling.

Chapter 25

When Jane Blake heard the message, it was already too late. "Mom," it said, "I'm going to the protest with Maura and a bunch of other kids. Talk later."

A call to Maura's mom, who'd driven the carload of girls to Albany, provided details.

"She thinks it's going to be fun, just like the sixties," she'd said. "They've heard so much about those days. I think it's cute, don't you?"

"Sarah didn't say anything to you about her father, did she?"

"No. Why? Does he not like protests?"

"Oh. You could say that."

Jane could just see the TV reporter thrusting a microphone toward the giggling girls. They wouldn't be asked what their fathers did for a living; they wouldn't even think the situation ironic. But at least one of them would think it cool that their number included the daughter of the man against whom the protest was directed, and would point Sarah out, at which moment the young girl would become horrifyingly aware of the mistake she'd made. In order to spare her that insight, Jane would have to find her first.

As the Pathfinder headed south toward the Thruway, Jane thought traffic was heavy, even for a Saturday afternoon, and wondered if part of it was demonstration traffic. All doubts were removed when she found herself bumper to bumper on the Exit 23 off-ramp. Cars were backed up from Route 9, where a traffic cop had been stationed, back through the tollbooths. It took her a half-hour to find parking on Second Avenue and another twenty minutes to walk from that spot to Utah Street, and she had plenty of company.

Early radio news estimates of hundreds of protesters had been light. Utah Street was packed with people, although Jane's first impression was one of movement. As she fell in with the crowd she saw it was moving up and down in the same directions as cars would've moved, had there been any. Two columns of marchers, chanting songs and holding placards, were passing each other, smiling and high-fiving all the way, with people wearing bright yellow jogging reflector vests standing in the middle of the road keeping things moving and the columns separated. Jane couldn't decide whether the size of the crowd was good because her daughter's small group of friends was less likely to be noticed or bad because Jane was going to have a tough time finding her.

Opposing columns had been Boris Petrovich's idea.

"Is like vortex," he'd said. "Multiple purpose is served. First, cckeep pipple moving, crowd easier controlled, pipple keep energy, don't get bored. Next, protest grows from all direction. Is city street, accessible from ccheverywhere. Pipple come, is always room to join march because is always movement. Last, pipple from cchole march will pass Christina Clark and sign-up desk."

Joining Christina at the desk were Alexander, Lucy Goldstein, and Gus DeMauro, who'd decided some added security was called for. DeMauro also set up a video camera on a tripod and aimed it at the desk. Boris Petrovich sat in a van equipped with telephone, fax, computer, and a list of all the media outlets in the Capital District. Guaranteeing a constant stream of visitors was a refrigerator stocked with soda, milk, cookies, kosher salami, Hebrew National mustard, rye bread, and potato chips. The T.U.L.P. Spokesman stopped in twice in the first thirty minutes of the march alone.

When not eating, Max Rodriguez was out in the crowd shaking hands, accepting back slaps and reminding people to keep moving. Police would later estimate one to two thousand people took part in the protest, and the only dissenting voice Max heard came from the leader of a splinter group of about six senior citizens who were setting up lawn chairs on the sidewalk.

"Listen, sonny," said one old lady whose voice sounded familiar, "if you want to walk around in circles, be my guest. But unless you're going to carry us all, we're staying here."

Walking up Halsey Street toward Utah Street were Brian and Suzy Brindisi. Johann Mathison had popped into a bakery to grab a doughnut and told them he'd catch up. Moving down the same sidewalk but away from Utah Street were two muscular men in white T-shirts and jeans. As the twosomes passed each other, one of the T-shirted men turned a shoulder into Brian and leveled him.

"Oh, sorry," said the provocateur, but as he did so his buddy came over and drove a steel-toed boot into Brian's side.

"Maybe protesting ain't so good for your health," said the second man as a shocked Suzy Brindisi knelt by her husband, too stunned and frightened to cry out. "Why don't you be good little boys and girls now and go home."

They took nothing and did not touch the woman. She looked up at them, eyes wide with terror, hands spread out protectively over her husband. She was still staring at the attackers as they crossed Hurlbutt Street toward the bakery, where they were dropped to the pavement by two lighting blows from Johann Mathison. It looked like a kick to one and a punch to the other, but it happened so fast she wasn't sure.

"I want you boys to have a nice day," she heard Johann say, looking down, "but I want you to spend it somewhere else. Understand?"

They didn't seem to understand anything. Suzy wasn't sure they were still alive, movements from neither of them being detectable. But Johann bent over and whispered something else to them—she couldn't hear what—and they both attempted something like nodding motions with their heads.

Returning to his hosts, Johann helped Brian to his feet and asked if he wanted to call the police.

"No, and no ambulance either. Sirens wailing is just what those goons want. It'll disrupt the whole demonstration. Besides, I think I'm okay. I've broken ribs before and this isn't that bad. What did you do to them anyway?"

"I introduced them to a higher truth."

"Well, I'm going to spread the word," said Suzy, reaching for her cell phone. "Stay in large groups, be on the lookout for tough-looking guys wearing work boots and jeans and white T-shirts."

"Okay," said Johann, "stay close to me." The three of them walked slowly to Utah Street and melted into the moving crowd.

"That's odd." Suzy was looking down at her phone as they walked. "This phone was working just a minute ago."

Jane Blake was just then passing the bakery on Halsey Street. The two men who'd been leveled had managed to pull themselves upright and were leaning on the hood of a car, trying to get their own phones to work.

"You'll have to wait until I leave town," she laughed as she walked past. "They won't work until I do."

The men, who might have recognized her had they been able to look up, could not do so.

Unwarned, the remaining teams of Chazzie's boys stayed on the job. Two more marchers were assaulted before word of mouth tipped off most of the crowd. By then, the two who'd committed the additional assaults plus a couple more of Chazzie's teams had had conversations with Johann Mathison that convinced them their intentions had been misguided. Bruised and sore, they'd limped back to the Rialto.

Jane Blake fell in uneasily with the marching crowd. The numbers surprised her and she felt her chances of spotting her daughter before being recognized were not good. Her rolling blackout might subvert efforts to record or broadcast her presence but it did nothing to minimize the personal attention she always received, and attention was the last thing she needed, as she knew sneaking up on her child would be the only way to get the child out of there. She was therefore happy to fork over $10 to a young man who'd set up shop on the sidewalk and was selling baseball caps as fast as he could get them out of the boxes.

"I need a stealth system so I can find my daughter," she laughed.

"Okay," the hat man said, laughing, "you'll be almost invisible with this."

A block away, inside the Rialto Theater, Charlie Remlinger was on the phone with Romolo Ceriglio. Ceriglio, whose most recent act for the cause had been to plant his foot in Brian Brindisi's rib cage, was on his way to the Albany Medical Center for X-rays.

"I talked about unforeseen problems last night, Romo. You were there. I said use your cell phone and let me know if something comes up. Why am I hearing about this only now?"

"I tried before, boss. I . . ."

"I know all about that karate guy already, no thanks to you, Romo. The other guys are back at the theater, but at least they're here. Who is this guy? Superman?"

"Believe me, boss, you wouldn't want . . ."

"Don't tell me what I'd want. Why you guys can't use a simple cell phone is beyond me. The damn thing works now, doesn't it?"

"Boss, I swear I tried calling right after it happened. I kept calling as we drove away and it's only now I'm getting through. It's like the area around the theater was jammed."

Remlinger held his phone to his ear for a moment, saying nothing. Then he clicked it off, threw it at the wall, walked to a wall closet inside his office, and pulled out a pair of binoculars. "She's out there," he said to the wounded men in his office. One of them held a forearm gingerly by his side. Another was having trouble breathing and suspected fractured ribs. Two more held ice packs over bleeding noses.

Remlinger stood at his window and pointed the binoculars up Utah Street. Grouped in a bunch and moving slowly toward the theater from Hurlbutt Street was a group of marchers wearing matching bright green baseball hats. As one man turned around, the words Free Frank appeared in white block lettering on the back.

"I know she's out there," Charlie said. "Talk about ingratitude! Where does she think her mortgage check comes from?"

"Boss," said the man nursing the wounded forearm, "I think we've got some boys here who need to get to the hospital."

"Where are the rest of the guys?" Charlie spoke without removing the binoculars from his eyes. "Or did that big, bad man take care of all of you?"

He hadn't, but it didn't matter. Once word of Chazzie's two-man teams got to Boris Petrovich, he put out the word that no one, male or female, was to go anywhere without at least four men in their group. Those of Chazzie's teams fortunate enough not to have run into Johann Mathison were not finding couples or small groups to pick off. Nobody left the march for so much as a cup of coffee without full entourage.

"Is good discipline, no?" Petrovich said to Gus DeMauro over a black cherry soda inside the van.

"Yes it is. Too bad we didn't have that kind of discipline in '68. It's tough to get young people to be disciplined, though."

"Is true," said Boris, "especially ccwhen stoned, yes?"

"Is true, Boris. Hey, is there any of that salami left?"

When the Gezunterman brothers arrived, they fell in with the marchers just past the theater near a Vietnamese restaurant and were welcomed by a group brimming with euphoria. The march was a success.

"Where you fellas from?" said a middle-aged man in a green baseball cap.

"Downstate," said Keith.

"What do you know about this T.U.L.P. organization?" the man asked.

"Not a thing," said Keith.

"You're just here for Frank?"

"Who?"

"He's here for the women," said Keith. "We read about Frank Rooney on the net, but my brother is here to find a dazzling blond who laughs when she talks. Have you seen her?"

"There must be a thousand women here, fellas."

"You'd remember this one," said Scott.

"Well, good luck. I used to go to marches for the girls too, but that was decades ago."

Scott and Keith made the turn across Utah Street and started back the other way. Fifty yards ahead, Jane was approaching the Gezunterman redoubt opposite the Rialto. She spotted its commander and went over to say hello.

"With a face like that you wear a hat?"

"Hello, Mrs. Gezunterman," Jane laughed.

"Again with the laughing. How about you take off your hat and fix your hair? My son is here somewhere. Stay by me. I'll introduce you."

"I can only stay for a minute, Mrs. Gezunterman. I'm looking for my daughter."

"So? Maybe she'll come by. Wait. I think I see my boys."

But as Mrs. Gezunterman reached for Jane's elbow, Jane spotted her daughter among a group of girls eating ice cream on the sidewalk in front of the Jumping Bean Coffee Shop a block away.

"Gotta go," Jane laughed just before Mrs. Gezunterman could clamp down on her arm.

Less than sixty seconds later, an angry Florence Gezunterman greeted her sons. "Like two old men, you walk," she said.

"Hello, Mom," her sons said.

"Hello? That's all you can say?"

"Hello, Mom. How are you?" Scott said.

"You just missed that girl that I wanted you to meet, that's how I am," she said.

"Actually, Mom, looking for a woman is just what I'm doing here," he said.

"Not like this woman you're not. Slow poke."

Mrs. Gezunterman stepped slowly over the curb while trying to see through the crowd. Her sons milled about behind her, waiting for their first opportunity to make a break.

"I think I see her. Over there by that store with the yellow awning. What is that, an ice cream parlor? In the hat. Yeah. Quick, Scott, go over there."

"Mom, I'm not going over there."

"*Vey is meer.*"

"We're going over there," said Keith.

"What?" said Scott.

"Listen to your brother."

"We'll just rejoin the marchers," Keith said, more to his brother than his mom, and off they went.

"Her name is Jane," Mrs. Gezunterman called out after them.

One minute and half a block later Keith said, "Stubborn is too good a word for you."

"I wasn't concentrating."

"You weren't conscious."

"Yeah, fine. So you got us out of there. Thank you. Now keep a lookout for my woman."

"Oh? So she's your woman already?"

"She's not?"

"She's not even here, for all we know."

"She's here."

But they were too late. Jane had found her daughter and convinced her to come home. It had taken a bit of doing.

"Go away, Mom," Sarah had told her. "You're being silly."

"Do you remember what you gave Daddy for Father's Day this year?"

Sarah thought for a moment before putting her head down and mumbling, "Binoculars." Then she began walking back to the Pathfinder with her mother.

Outside the van Max Rodriguez leaned against a fender and looked down Utah Street, which was now almost shoulder to shoulder with people. Boris Petrovich, who'd been talking on his cell phone, came over.

"Is partly your doing. You are proud, no?"

"What? Oh, yeah. Nice job, Boris."

"Is on mind something, yes?"

"Huh? Hey, Boris, you haven't seen that girl reporter, have you?"

"Oh, yes. Meagan something, yes?

"Yeah. Swoboda. Have you?"

"I think TV truck is cchhere. Maybe on far side of protest."

Max began walking but Boris caught his arm. "Please to stay a moment. Cchave plans to make." And Boris gestured to the group across the street.

Christina Clark, Gus DeMauro, Lucy Goldstein, the Hammermills, and even Irena Poppadapoulos, just in that morning from Atlanta, were gathering at the sign-up table. Boris and Max joined them.

"This was the spark, Alexander. You were right. I never imagined there'd be this many people. The theater must be completely empty," said Irena.

"Completely," said Gus. "I've been watching the door for the last hour. It might as well be nailed shut."

"Not pour chwater on enthusiasm," said Boris, "but sparks not known for long life. Must now turn spark to fire. Cchapitalize on energy produced."

"I couldn't agree more," said Alexander, "and I think I've got just the right idea."

"Hey!" said Christina Clark, "Is that Cowboy Bob over there?"

The famous lawyer was dressed in jeans and a polo shirt but recognizable nonetheless. He'd attracted a crowd and seemed to be lecturing to them as they moved along, a cell of marchers with the Cowboy as its nucleus.

"Oh, yeah," said Alexander. "He called me early this morning and told me he'd be here. Frank Rooney was ordered to stay away. When Sheridan is finished being adored, he'll stop by and say hello."

"Dearest," said Cindy Hammermill, "we're all waiting to hear your idea. But I must tell you I draw the line at cheerleaders."

Alexander, who'd been preparing to attack a salami sandwich, put the food down and placed his hands in his overall pockets.

"We need a rally, a gathering. We need to be able to get these people in one spot so we can do a more complete job of organization. I see a lot of people walking by the signup table without stopping. Maybe they signed up on the net, maybe not. We need to know who all these people are so we can get them together for the next round. I know Christina will tell me I'm nuts, that it's about tweeting and texting and that's how you organize people, and maybe that works during a march or protest. The thing is, and maybe I'm just old, but I think we need more to sustain this.

"We're up against corporate forces here. They're organized from top to bottom. I think we caught Maiko by surprise today, but we can't count on that working the next time, or on the next Maiko. We need to talk to the people out here, and more important, have them talk to us. If we can't focus our energy where it's needed, if we can't draw all the creativity this large gathering can muster, we'll just be defeated next time out no matter how much grassroots support we have."

"He's right," said Max. "It's like Hannibal outfoxing the Romans at the Battle of Cannae or the British defeating the Spanish Armada in 1588. A smaller band of determined, organized fighters can beat a larger, less nimble force. But we have to stay a step ahead of them."

"Oh, my," said Christina Clark.

"Not bad," said Boris. "Is payoff for all money spent on tuition. Parents are proud, yes? But chwhere do we gather all these pipple together? We are in thousands, I think."

"Yes," said Alexander. "Good question, and I've got the answer to that one too. The Times Union Center downtown is dark tomorrow afternoon."

"Jesus, do you own that, too?" Max said.

"No, but I know the people who do. I've already made some calls, and I think we can do it."

"Do what?" said Lucy Goldstein. "Tomorrow afternoon is our last time to shine here. After that, these people are going home. It sounds like we're letting Maiko off the hook."

"No," said Gus. "Now is when a little division of forces is called for. With the press coverage we're getting we'll need only a couple hundred people here, tops, to shut this place down tomorrow. We'll ask for volunteers to miss the rally and come here, and the rest will go to the rally."

"A Confederate cavalryman, General Nathan Bedford Forrest did something like this at Parker's Cross Roads in 1862." said Max. "Surrounded by a superior force and about to be captured, he divided his troops in half and attacked in both directions. The move was so bold, he was able to escape."

"My, oh my," said Christina Clark.

"Maybe we ccan broadcast spiches from rally to pipple in street right cchhere," said Boris.

"Okay," said Gus. "Only we keep this under wraps for a while. We'll get the word out tonight over the net," nodding at Christina Clark, "and Twitter, and to the people camped at the Hammermills' place. It'll give that goon less time to organize something to stop us." He gestured with his head to the theater behind them.

"So we stay here today for how long?" said Max.

"I'd say until about eight or so," said Lucy. "By then the word will be out on TV and radio that there are thousands of people marching and people who want to go to the Rialto will forget about it. There's no need to stay until the late shows begin."

"Well, then, my work at this post is done," said Max. "I think I'll take a stroll."

Max joined the marchers and was immediately greeted with an ovation. Alexander and the others watched him go.

"Do you think maybe this has gone a bit to his head?" Alexander said.

"Cche is joking," said Boris. "Only pipple he wants see are ones on TV crew with cute reporter from last night."

"Oh, my," said Christina Clark.

Chapter 26

From her spot on the patio Jane heard her ex-husband's voice come over the TV. The muscles around her stomach tensed. *Maybe one more year, two at the most,* she thought, *and there'd be no more involuntary revulsion reflex when she heard that sound.*

"Business was brisk in spite of these hooligans," he was saying to a reporter. "I'd say we were at eighty-five to ninety percent of normal for a Saturday, which proves you can't bully good people."

Jane laughed. "Not bad for a man who has spent his whole life proving you can bully anyone," she said. Bartholomew and Ava had joined her at her patio table.

"Maybe more con-man than bully," said Ava. "That TV reporter Meagan Swoboda sent members of her crew into the theater a few times during the day, and she said on the air that the place was almost empty. I think your ex is losing the credibility war on this one."

"Wow. I can just imagine what Chaz is like right now," Jane laughed. "He gets so angry he can't speak, can't even move. It's like a hysterical reaction. It could last for minutes or even hours. Then he unwinds and oh, brother. I'm just glad I'm not there to see it."

"Word over at Little Woodstock is they're planning a diversionary move for tomorrow," said Bartholomew. "Protesters will begin showing up in buses just like today, but only a fraction. The rest will be at a rally at the TU Center downtown. What I'd like to know is where the money for this is coming from. This T.U.L.P. organization seems to have sprung up overnight and it's already got a website, a fleet of buses, food for hundreds, and now a gig at the TU Center."

"Anyone who takes on the ELF gets good karma," Jane laughed. "Maybe the money is just falling from the sky."

"Maybe. So, you wanna come with us to the TU? The ELF will be busy at the theater, I'm sure. He'll never know."

"I dunno," Jane laughed, "Stop by tomorrow on your way. I'll see how rebellious I feel."

The mood at the Hammermills' was buoyant. News of the plan for the next day's protests was greeted matter-of-factly by an army that had already decided it was unbeatable. There were even rumors of splinter groups planning to head out to yet more targets, an idea that quickly fizzled as people realized the next day was Sunday, which meant banks and insurance companies, the consensus favorite alternate targets, would be closed.

The ranks had swelled to several thousand, with Gus DeMauro estimating forty-five hundred people, including those in hotels and private housing, so it was decided they could spare four hundred people for the next day's march on the Rialto, with everyone else meeting at the arena.

Max got the word in a text message from Boris. The Spokesman was home, engaged in tense conversation with his father.

"All I'm saying is I work for one of the biggest corporations in the world, and the money they've paid me all these years has put food on our table, a roof over our heads, and you through college. And it's not like I spend my days stealing money from orphans. I help build turbines that bring power to people who have never seen a lightbulb. There are schools and hospitals that exist today because of the efforts of me and my co-workers and the company we work for. That's something I'm proud of."

"And you should be. I'm proud of you too, Dad. But this is the same company that polluted one of America's greatest rivers and now spends hundreds of millions of dollars fighting government efforts to get them to clean it up. How much of the Hudson could have been cleaned up with that money? And remember when Mom wanted that experimental treatment and they wouldn't pay for it?"

Nancy Rodriquez's cancer had already metastasized when it was discovered. Both her lungs and her liver were involved. A new, highly expensive medicine with promise for treating lung cancer patients was being developed by Merck, and volunteers for treatment were being sought. A phone call from Chuck had brought the cold, unyielding "No, we don't pay for experimental drugs" from the company health care administrator that Max was referring to. In the event the cancer turned out to have originated in the liver and Nancy was not a candidate for the test group.

"It never came to that," Chuck said.

"Yes, Dad. I know. But they'd have fought you. You know that. More importantly, how do we know someone else among all those thousands of employees didn't have the same exact issue with his wife? Look, your company provides important products and services, and it does those things well. That's why it makes so much money. That's fine. In fact, I admire that kind of success. But you wouldn't let me throw a gum wrapper in the Hudson. And if a mother of three was dying and you held the purse strings to money that might save her, would you be so cold as to say no? I don't think so. Your basic decency would prevail. So why is your company exempt from the requirement that it behave with the same decency?

"Is it okay for you to steal something tomorrow because you were honest yesterday, to behave dishonorably tomorrow because you're behaving well today? If I offered those rationalizations to you as excuses for thievery, you'd slap me. So why should a company be allowed to act like a brute now just because last year it turned a profit? And why shouldn't an entity that wields far more power than any of its employees be held at least to the same standard of behavior as they are?"

"They're not the enemy, son. A company that employs thousands of people and makes millions of useful products is a company that raises the quality of life."

"Dad, you and Mom raised the quality of life. Would either of you knowingly have hurt another human being?"

"You're not hearing me."

"Dad, how about coming to the rally tomorrow? We're meeting at the TU Center. You'll see what kinds of people are involved in this. Ordinary, everyday people. I'd really appreciate it if you came, Dad."

Whenever one of Chuck's children wanted to invoke the memory of their mother they demonstrated an uncanny ability to transform their face into hers. Just now Max's eyes looked so much like Nancy's that Chuck was forced to look away, but it didn't matter. He could still hear her voice telling him he wasn't giving their son a fair chance.

"Will there be TV cameras there?" said Chuck, stalling.

"I sure hope so. But you don't have to be on screen. You can sit in the back somewhere and just watch."

About one hour later Meagan Swoboda picked up a message on her voicemail at WTXY News: "This is Max. The real action tomorrow will be inside the TU Center starting at one, and the show will be just for you."

Chapter 27

Florence Gezunterman got the word from Ida Schwartz, whom she'd met at the Campbell Avenue redoubt the day before. Ida had heard it from her grandson Peter who was camped out at the Hammermills'.

"Flo? It's Ida. From the march."

"Of course."

"Of course, what?"

"Of course it's Ida."

"You knew?"

"You just told me."

"Listen, Flo, I have news."

"Of course."

"You know already?"

"When you tell me, I'll know."

"Of course."

"So?"

"So what?"

"So what's the news?"

"I didn't tell you?"

"Ida, you called me."

"Of course."

"*Oy, a clugg.*"

"So listen, Flo, I have news from my grandson. He tells me they're sending only a few marchers to the theater today. The rest are going to a rally at the Times Union Center in Albany."

"What time?"

"One o'clock."

"So, you're going?"

"Of course. And you?"

"Of course."

Florence dialed Jane Blake's number before hanging up the receiver.

"This is Mrs. Gezunterman," she said.

"Yes," Jane laughed. "I know."

"Of course you know. I just . . . never mind. Listen, are you by any chance going to downtown Albany this afternoon?"

"I don't know yet, Mrs. Gezunterman. Why? Are you going to the rally?"

"You know?"

"Of course."

"Well, I think I'm going with my boys—including the one I told you about."

"He's still here?" Jane laughed.

"Of course he's here. Where should he be?"

"I mean he hasn't gone home yet?"

"No, sweetheart. He's here for the weekend."

"If I go I'll look for you, Mrs. Gezunterman."

"Me I don't care about. It's him I want you should see."

"Okay, then," Jane laughed. "I'll look for you and your son."

"Of course."

Chuck and his three children hopped into the family sedan. Benjamin's iPod had just run out of juice, so he removed his earphones and took note of the outside world for the first time that day.

"I guess nobody gets dressed up for a protest rally," he said. Max was wearing a polo shirt over blue jeans. Chuck had on a button-down, short-sleeve shirt and khakis, and Amanda wore shorts and a sweatshirt emblazoned with New York Yankees, 2009 World Series Champions. She thought baseball was boring, but the color of the sweatshirt was blue, her favorite.

"Just what is it you're going to do at this rally anyway?" said Ben.

"I'm really not sure yet. I'll have to see how it plays out," said Max.

"But you must know something," said Amanda. "Like, are you going to give a speech? Are you going to be on the stage?"

"Too much organization stifles creativity," Max said.

Chuck looked into his rear-view mirror and caught Amanda's eye. They made disbelieving faces for each other.

"Right. You're telling us it's too much organization for you to know where you're going or what you're doing after you've stepped in the front door. You might wanna, like, flap your arms like a bird and fly around the arena while singing *On Wisconsin*. Or maybe you'll just forget about the whole thing and sell hot dogs from a concession stand. Come on, Max. You're gonna do something when we get there. What is it?"

Inside the car was silence, all eyes on Max. Even Chuck glanced over to see how Max was handling Ben's outburst.

"Little brother," Max began, left hand stroking his chin, eyes gazing out the passenger-side window, "that's the most creative thinking you've ever done and I'm proud of you."

Amanda giggled. Chuck and Ben shook their heads. Max placed his left hand gently on his lap and resumed stroking his chin with the right.

The first one hundred people who boarded the buses at the Hammermills' were designated as ushers. Half were assigned doorway and section entrances, where they handed out flyers containing the day's instructions, which were as follows:

There will be sign-up sheets both left and right of the stage. If you've not yet given us your name and email, please do so.
File in and sit as close to the stage as you can.
Sit next to the nearest person. Do not leave seats unoccupied.
There will be speakers on stage. There will be an opportunity for you to speak. If you choose to speak, please keep your comments brief, to the point, and polite.
Suggestion boxes have been provided at ten locations around the arena. If you wish, drop your written suggestions into one and include your name and email so that an appropriate response can be sent.
Treat Us Like People!

Meagan Swoboda was there with her film crew. She realized after hearing Max's message that parking her truck outside the arena would bring the other stations' trucks, so she had her producer take the crew in his unmarked minivan. Now she roamed the arena getting interviews with people as they streamed in.

She was struck once more by the breadth of the appeal of T.U.L.P.'s message. The first five people she spoke to included a black man in his twenties who drove a bus and took IT courses at night, a thirty-something housewife of Korean ancestry who wondered if a good education alone guaranteed her children success, a white man in his fifties whose house was now worth less than he owed on the mortgage, a Hispanic woman whose parents had brought her to America just after the Cuban missile crisis, and an old Jewish woman who'd told her: "If you don't speak up, dahlink, you get nothing. Of course."

There was a healthy percentage of boomers, but by no means were their numbers overwhelming. A group of white teenagers breathlessly informed the reporter that "the conspiracy goes way further than we thought " because they'd learned that not too long ago people pumped gas for you and you got to talk to a real live person when you called a company—even a big one.

The only thing missing from the group was the scruffy-looking Max Rodriguez, whom she hoped would appear soon. She didn't have long to wait. After depositing his family in seats high up and far from the action, Max had wandered toward the small stage set up in the middle of the building. There he found Gus, the Hammermills, Boris, Christina Clark, Lucy Goldstein, and Irena Poppadapoulos.

The group settled on Max, its most easily recognized member, as an emcee of sorts. He'd be followed by the team of Lucy and Gus, who'd outline the long-term strategy of isolating industries and individual companies so as to apply pressure in the most effective way. Cindy Hammermill would speak about the twenty-four hour hotline available to anyone whose "frustration, sense of despair, or rage against the system," threatened to spiral out of control.

"Is surprising turn of phrase for you," said Boris "Is phrase that used to go cchand in cchand with CCHRedical Chic, no?"

"Alexander wanted me to say it," said Cindy. "He thinks it will pump up the crowd."

"No doubt about that," said Alexander. "The foreign movie faithful are here. Did you see all the mini-cars in the parking lot? We need to remind these people about the good old days when they had a pulse. Otherwise they'll lock arms and start singing Kumbaya and we're finished."

"It's a touchy subject," Cindy whispered to Boris, as Max Rodriguez, microphone in hand, walked to the center of the stage.

The clamor caused by Max's appearance began with those closest to the stage, then surged all the way to the mezzanine where Max's family was seated. About 3,500 people—nearly one-fifth the arena's capacity—stood up and roared as they recognized their casual Spokesman.

"Isn't it amazing how much noise a small crowd of people can make without a corporate-sponsored scoreboard telling them to 'clap' or 'make some noise,'" Max said.

Riotous applause.

"This is the kind of energy we can generate when corporations treat us like people!"

More applause, more noise. Three pairs of eyes up in the mezzanine seemed more surprised by Max's handling of the crowd than anyone else in the building.

Down by the stage, Cindy Hammermill cupped her hands so as to make herself heard. "Look, honey," she said to her husband, "I see gray-haired people standing and cheering. I do hope they survive the experience."

"Watch a movie made in the forties, sixties, even the eighties, and pay close attention to any scene taking place in a bank or food market or gas station. Or any scene where a customer calls a store and wants to speak to the manager. What do you see? The graciousness is unreal. The level of service, the politeness, the solicitousness with which the companies always treated the customers. Imagine that, they actually were nice to their customers. What a concept.

"Now, you say, they didn't have computers so they couldn't have computerized phone systems, and today's corporations couldn't afford all the personnel for all that individualized service. Are you sure about that? Have you seen the numbers on corporate profits this year? They're higher than at any time since those numbers have been recorded. That's a period of sixty years. Is there anyone here who in all those sixty years can remember a corporation actually improving its service? So the worst service in sixty years equals the highest corporate profits in sixty years. Coincidence?

"You see what they've done? They've changed the societal norms. What was unacceptable sixty, thirty, even ten years ago is absolutely routine today. Of course, the new normal is always worse for us and better for them. Hence, their obscene profits and our ever more difficult, more expensive, and less gracious way of living.

"And who wouldn't mind waiting an extra few minutes on the phone in return for getting a human being—a polite, knowledgeable human being—to fix your problem.

"The words, 'It's corporate policy,' used to be three harmless little words. Now they're the sword with which the corporate world cuts down every person who attempts to stand up and say: Treat Us Like People!"

Cheering. The crowd was on its feet yelling, clapping, whistling.

"Corporations—faceless, soulless, and anonymous—create their own societal norms. Within their offices, otherwise decent and moral people are expected to leave everything they've learned behind and absorb the ersatz ethos of corporate culture in which common courtesy, basic fairness, and human compassion play no role. We know from painful history what happens when governments create societal norms outside the bounds of commonly accepted decency. People become unthinking cogs in an inhuman machine.

"How often do we hear from corporate functionaries, be they secretaries or CEOs, who tell us they have no say in the matter and that they're only implementing the instructions of their superiors? Yet no matter how doggedly you follow that trail of authority, it never leads to a single person who is responsible, which is exactly how those lines of authority are designed to work.

"Western civilization has a tragic history with the concept that obedience contains its own intrinsic value. What we've learned is that it does not. Sadly, we've had to learn and re-learn that lesson over and over again. The value of an order is derived from its moral underpinnings. Either it serves the cause of human decency or it does not. Following it does not relieve you of the obligation to make the inquiry.

"Corporate America is not herding you into cattle cars, but they are treating you like cattle by convincing their employees that they must blindly follow company policy.

"The military uses the word orders. The corporate world uses the word policy. The concepts are the same. The point is they want us to disavow the sense of right and wrong that we've learned from birth, and instead become cogs in their machine. And you're just as much a cog if you passively take what they dish out as if you're the one doing the dishing.

"But even the military recognizes the concept of an illegal order. And following one makes you morally and criminally liable for all that follows. It matters not if your abdication is offered up in the service of a military order or a company policy. Yet while the military acknowledges this, the corporate world does not.

"If something is wrong, if it is immoral or unjust, it is no less so simply because some company has made it 'policy.' It is still wrong and you should not do it. And you as the customer should not allow it to be done to you.

"Imagine their arrogance! You've spent your lifetimes, literally from the day you were born, learning from your parents, your aunts and uncles, your teachers, your clergy, teaching yourselves about truth and justice, good and evil, right and wrong, and some corporate functionary types out a memo with the word Policy stamped at the top and you're supposed to throw out all you've learned, all you believe in, and replace it with whatever this person has come up with. And if you dare question it, he acts like you're the one who's crazy!

"We need to be energized! We need to push back against every anti-human practice that the corporations dish out. They cannot make us buy their products if their policies are immoral. They cannot turn a profit if we do not buy their products. They cannot treat us like cattle if we insist they treat us like people!"

Max stepped down to raucous cheers and handed the microphone to Gus and Lucy. The plan was to target one company per industry—one bank, one supermarket chain, etc.—and amass all of T.U.L.P.'s power to bring concessions. Hopefully, the other corporations in the industry would see the light without more pressure having to be brought. Boris called it the Rolling Boycott. "Is like rolling thunder, but not so romantic." For the present, they'd finish out the weekend with Maiko and determine from the sign-ups whether to expand the protest to Maiko theaters in other cities or stay in Albany. The biggest protest, should it come that far, would take place when Frank Rooney went to trial.

When Max returned to his family, Amanda was standing and clapping, Ben was standing with hands outstretched and both thumbs up. Chuck, still seated, shook his son's hand.

"You're pretty good at this," Chuck said. "You're even standing up straight. But do you see any future in warming up the crowd at T.U.L.P. rallies?"

Max held on to his father's hand and laughed.

"I'm serious," said Chuck.

"I know you are, Dad, and I do," said Max. "Don't ask me how because I don't know yet, but I do. Anyway, thanks for coming, Dad."

On the other side of the stage, sitting between their mother and Ida Schwartz, were Keith and Scott Gezunterman. Both women were waiting for their chance at the microphone but the line was long. The first story came from a white woman in her fifties.

"I went online at my office to get the phone number of the nearest branch of a local credit union. I wanted to ask a few questions. But they don't put phone numbers on line because they don't want you calling. So I called the numbers they listed, which are an 800 number that's answered by a computer and a number for the corporate office, also answered by a computer. Neither one can give you the phone number of any local branch. I stuck with this for about twenty-five minutes without success. Then I remembered passing a new branch that was going up where an old Jiffy Lube had been, so I got in my car, drove over there, and walked into the bank. I spoke to a customer rep who answered my questions, and then I drove back to my office. It took twenty minutes and I bet you I could've ridden a bicycle instead of a car and still done better the old-fashioned way than with the computer."

Another man grabbed the microphone. He was black, about thirty-five, and spoke with the broad "a" of a midwesterner.

"Has anyone here ever tried to cancel their account with BAY OL?"

A small but vociferous group erupted in applause.

"I see a few of us have. To the rest, let me tell you what it's like. After wading through the automated answering system, you finally get to speak to a person. That person is in India. His English, which is pretty good when he first gets on the line, becomes terrible once he hears you say the word "cancel." He pretends not to know what you're talking about. You use all the synonyms you can think of but he claims not to understand a one. When you ask for a supervisor, he claims not to understand that word either. If you do get to talk to someone else, he wants to know why you want to cancel. You tell him what's the difference? He persists. You tell him it's none of his business and that it doesn't matter anyway. He gets angry. You argue. Finally, he tells you he has no authority to cancel your account—which makes you wonder why he was asking all those questions in the first place—but he'll transfer you to someone who does. You wait around a while and the new person asks the same questions. You give the same answers and after a while he tells you you're once again talking to someone who is not authorized to cancel your account. They put you on hold, longer this time. If you're still there when they come back, they give you to someone else. Nobody has the power to cancel your account, but they've got all day to try to convince you not to do it.

"No one has the authority. But just see how fast you get someone with authority when you call them to pay your bill!"

More stories followed, each one bringing a small smattering of applause from those similarly abused. Ten minutes went by. Then twenty. It seemed everyone had some complaint that needed airing.

A din began welling up in the arena, not of enthusiasm, but restlessness.

"They haven't got a plan for ending it," Scott said. "The energy in here is slipping away." His leg was bouncing up and down and he began shifting his gaze from side to side as if he was searching for something.

"What are you talking? Someone will get up and say it's over and home we'll go and that's the end of it," said Flo.

"No. It doesn't work that way. They started off with a bang. But they've got to end on a high note. You start strong and end strong. If you end on a low note, that's what the people will remember and it'll sap their enthusiasm."

"This you know from being a drug counselor?"

"Yes, Mom, this I know."

"*Azoi*?" (Is that so?)

Reverend William Walker and his wife Ethel were seated opposite the stage from the Gezuntermans. The Reverend had heard the rising din even before Scott.

"It's like a big ship in here, Mother," he'd whispered to his wife, "a ship that's dead in the water." The Reverend, a large, bald man with a deep, rich voice that carried and carried no matter how softly he spoke, always whispered when seated in an audience, but to no avail. The nearest thirty or forty people always heard him anyway.

Ethel was known as Mother Ethel to their flock at the Albany Mount Calvary Holy Church. Her voice occupied a higher register than her husband's and it carried nearly as far, but she wasted little energy on tamping it down.

"I know," she said. "That skinny white kid was good, but once he got them started, he didn't know where to take them. There's a good crowd here, Reverend, and they're just waiting for somebody to carry them home."

"I know I said they're dead in the water, Mother, but this isn't a religious meeting. They didn't come here to hear us preach."

"Is that so? Are we talking about people treating people with decency and respect or have I been daydreaming? If that's not Do Unto Others, I don't know what is."

"Well, you never did see a crowd that didn't need stirring."

With a playful slap at her husband's shoulder, Ethel rose up and headed for the stage only to hear the first words of a song she knew well, being poorly sung:

We are climbing Jacob's ladder
We are climbing Jacob's ladder.

The sound was more a cry for help than music. Ethel turned back toward her husband and winced, then kept moving.

The singer was a middle-aged man who now held the microphone. He'd said nothing by way of introduction, just taken the mike and started in.

By the time the man got to the last two lines of the verse, Mother Ethel was in full voice:

We are climbing Jacob's ladder.
We are brothers, sisters all.

Even without amplification, Ethel's voice found the man's ears, and his eyes seemed to pick her out as she made her way forward toward the stage. He soldiered on:

We are climbing Jacob's ladder
We are climbing Jacob's ladder
We are climbing Jacob's ladder
We are brothers, sisters all.

The myriad conversations that had formed the din vanished. People would later swear that a light had shone on Ethel, but there was no one manning the spots that day. She climbed the steps to the stage and took the microphone from the singing man as if the move had been choreographed. Then she held Scott Gezunterman's elbow to prevent him from leaving, and claimed the song for her own.

We are climbing Jacob's ladder
We are climbing Jacob's ladder
We are climbing Jacob's ladder
We are brothers, sisters all.

Ethel took to calling out the words between verses. By now, most of the audience was singing along with her. After leading them through one more rendition of the opening lines, she called out, "Another microphone, please." When Gus DeMauro handed the second mike to her she gestured to the Reverend and handed the mike to a person in the front row so it could be passed back. From his seat, Reverend William Walker's baritone boomed its echo to Ethel's next verse:
Every rung goes higher and higher

Every rung goes higher and higher
Every rung goes higher and higher
We are brothers, sisters all.

With the Reverend to help carry the load, Ethel was free not only to call out words but to lead the hand clapping.

"On the off beat," she pleaded. "Together, with me."

Every round a generation
Every round a generation
Every round a generation
We are brothers, sisters all.

The crowd stayed with those three verses for almost as long as Max's speech had taken. After a few minutes, so as to let Ethel break completely free of the refrain and soar where her voice would take her, the Reverend transported his great girth to the stage and held the rhythm steady under his command.

Reverend Walker wore a dark blue suit, red tie, white shirt with button-down collar and black wingtip shoes. Mother Ethel wore a two-piece emerald taffeta suit with ribbon embroidery, a matching hat, and emerald pumps. They were the only people in the arena so formally dressed, and the contrast between them and everyone else, their shabby Spokesman in particular, generated a feeling of inevitability among the protesters. A movement that could spread so easily from college grunge to gospel proper was a movement with legs.

Mother Ethel could feel the energy peaking. In the breaks between verses she called out, "Where's that skinny white boy? Get him down here!"

Max made his way back to the stage.

Way in the rear of the floor-level seats, Jane Blake stared at Scott Gezunterman, who was still standing and singing by Mother Ethel's side while clapping on the off-beat.

Florence Gezunterman leaned over to Keith and said, "All those records your brother sang along with and he still can't sing."

Toward the rear of the occupied seats, the Family Rodriguez was on its feet. Amanda was singing as loud as she could, her blond hair bouncing back and forth as she clapped. Benjamin was moving back and forth to the music, looking at his father as if waiting for a cue. Chuck Rodriguez, the slightest of slight smiles registering on his face, was silent.

On stage, Max reached into his pocket and gripped his mother's photo ID. Ethel and the Reverend brought the song to a conclusion and handed their microphones over to a waiting Gus DeMauro, who shouted,

"To the Rialto! The buses are waiting!"

Chapter 28

Meagan Swoboda's report was broadcast on the 7 P.M. news, just as the Rialto's last big showings of the weekend were starting to flicker before empty theaters. Watching the broadcast in the office with Charlie Remlinger was the same woman who'd been eating a fudge brownie the night Max Rodriguez overheard them in Dr. Java's Coffee Emporium. She noticed that the reporter never appeared on screen but instead narrated the action-packed sequence from off-camera, giving the T.U.L.P. stars Max, Lucy, Gus, and Reverend and Mother Williams the spotlight. The blond's name was JoAnne.

"She's boffing someone," snarled Chaz. "I'll bet it's that little Spokesman punk. Arrogant college shit. I can smell him all the way over here."

"Sure," said JoAnne. "Why else would an intelligent, attractive young woman be working as a television reporter?"

"Damn right. Hey, there he is, the little shit." On screen was the part of Max's speech where he was talking about people following orders that are immoral.

"Did you hear that? Can you believe this crap? I know what that son-of-a-bitch is saying. He's calling me a Nazi! I prosecute some guy for beating up my manager and I'm the Nazi? I'll sue his ass, that punk. That's gotta be defamation of character. Where's my lawyer?"

"Just a wild guess," said JoAnne, "but it's 7:15 on a Sunday evening. He's either home or out doing something with his family." This drew Chaz's attention away from the TV.

"Did I ask for your input?" he said. There were two other people in the room, a couple of Chaz's "assistants," who hadn't said a word for hours—JoAnne thought them incapable of speech—and somehow she didn't think Chaz was talking to them.

"Actually, I doubt it's defamatory. He didn't call you a Nazi. He was merely arguing that claiming someone else told you to do a thing does not save you from liability for doing the thing if it's a bad thing to do."

The two assistants started heading for the door but Chaz bellowed, "Did I tell you to leave?" so they stopped. "You wear that diamond bracelet on your arm, you drive a Mercedes that I bought you, and since you've been with me you've been to my place in Cancun five times. That's five. You wanna tell me what it is about all those goodies that makes you such a wise ass?" JoAnne said nothing and returned her attention to the TV screen. By the time the nine o'clock shows began, the protesters were gone. For the theater, the weekend had been a total washout.

The following Tuesday morning at around ten, Chaz got a phone call from the manager of his theater complex near Buffalo. The manager's wife worked reservations for the Hampton Inns. She'd mentioned to him that hotel rooms all around town were being snatched up for the following weekend at a terrific pace and was there anything going on she was unaware of? The manager thought there might be a connection.

Later that night two men approached the front door of the Rodriguez home. They had arrived in a pickup truck and were wearing white T-shirts and jeans. When they knocked, Chuck Rodriguez opened the door. Through the gap Max was visible as he stretched out on the family room couch.

"Is Max in?" said one.

"Who are you?" said Chuck.

"We wanna talk to Max. Is he in?" It was the other one now, and he was insistent. Chuck stepped outside and shut the door behind him.

"I asked who you are," said Chuck. "And I'd like an answer."

"We wanna volunteer for T.U.L.P.," said the first one. "They told us to come here." Chuck's eyes narrowed and his right hand began to form a fist.

"That's baloney" said Chuck. "They don't tell anybody to come here. Let me see some ID. Both of you."

"Look, old man . . ." said the more insistent one, but he never got the rest of his sentence out. Chuck buried his fist in the middle of the white T-shirt, and the man doubled over and fell to the ground. Then Chuck turned to face the other one but the man put up his hands with both palms open in a show of newly discovered peaceful intent, then leaned over to help his buddy up.

"We'll see you around," the lucky one said, holding up his friend. "You and the kid." The two made their way across the Rodriguez lawn to their pickup truck.

The door behind Chuck opened and Max came out. "Dad? What's going on?"

"You and I need to talk, son."

Chuck's face was flushed and his breathing was heavy. The boy's hand automatically reached out for his father's shoulder and held on, but before an explanation could be given, both men caught sight of Beatrice Lonergan, their across-the-street neighbor, rushing toward them.

The running joke on Alameda Street was that the signs warning it was "A Neighborhood Watch Community" meant that Beatrice Lonergan lived there. Beatrice, AKA Bee, AKA June Bug for reasons unknown even to old-time residents, took pride in the joke. It meant her job of obtaining and disseminating information about her neighbors was being done well. Now she was yelling to Chuck as she approached.

"I got the license number! I got it, Chuck! You were so brave! Two men! Chuck!"

"Dad?"

"Thank you, Bea," Chuck said as she reached them. "Maybe we should go in and call the police."

"I called already. They're on their way. I saw the whole thing! I just happened to be looking out the kitchen window. Good thing, right?"

"Yes, Bea. Good thing."

A grin was forming on Max's face. "Dad, have you been brawling again?"

Inside, waiting for the police to arrive, Max spoke softly to his father. "I know you'll want to handle this quietly, Dad, but my instinct is to call my people. I don't know why but I think they should know about this."

"Actually, Max, I agree. The more people who know about this, the safer you'll be. It'll be tough for them to send more goons over when everyone is watching." Chuck looked at Bea, who seemed a bit let down by that. "Not that our good neighbor, here, isn't vigilance enough, but a patrol car parked outside the house might carry a stronger message."

Bea smiled.

"So tell me, Dad, was it a jab or an uppercut?"

Forty-five minutes later, back in her living room, a breathless Bea Lonergan had all she could do to answer Meagan Swoboda's questions without passing out. The only thing keeping her going was Meagan's promise that if they wrapped the story up quickly, it might make it to the eleven o'clock news.

Across the street, Max and his father sat on a couch answering questions from a police detective. The two Rodriguez men had already decided they'd wait a day before talking to the press. They wanted to give the police a chance to run the plate, find out who the two men were, and talk to them. Bea was going to give all the details the press would need, and silence from Chuck and Max would fuel the suspicion that the men were Remlinger henchmen without running the risk of stating so and being wrong.

Max's picture was all over the TV screen that evening, and the T.U.L.P. website hummed with hits all night long. Also humming by night's end was Max Rodriguez, who had taken Meagan Swoboda for a walk around his neighborhood beneath the same ash trees that once stood watch over his strolling parents.

"I've done some research on T.U.L.P., Max. It was formed about two years ago. You were still at Wisconsin. As far as I can tell, T.U.L.P.

hasn't done much of anything since, until now. Their website sprang up almost overnight after Frank Rooney's arrest. It's as if they've been lying in wait for this moment. So who are they and how did you get involved with them?"

"You know more about their history than I do, Meagan. You might even know more about my history than I do. But do you know when corporations last wielded as much power in America as they do now? Never. Not during the Gilded Age, the time of the Robber Barons—the Rockefellers, Vanderbilts, and Morgans, which was their supposed heyday. Not during the Roaring Twenties, not during the high-tech boom of the eighties. Corporate America has never been as powerful as it is right now, yet it has never complained so bitterly. It owns both major political parties. Not influences, owns. We've just experienced the biggest stock market crash since 1929, which led to the biggest recession since the thirties, yet economists tell us the same systemic problems on Wall Street that caused this disaster are still here, and we can't get Washington to do a thing about it because Wall Street owns Washington."

"Actually, I know all those things. What I was really trying to find out about was you, Max."

The Spokesman stopped and turned to look at Meagan. Then he took a deep breath.

"Sorry. I got carried away. I guess I missed my cue."

"I guess so."

Max smiled and the two resumed walking.

"Something about these trees inspired my folks," Max said. "They had so little in common, but when they went on this walk, they looked as though nothing could ever separate them."

"Did you ever walk with them?"

"No, but sometimes I'd watch as they moved away from the house, or back toward it. It was one of the few things they did without the kids. And they always held hands when they walked, so if you're gonna walk with me, you have to hold my hand. It's a family tradition."

Meagan took his hand and said, "I'm so sorry about your mom. I saw her pictures in your living room. Your little sister looks just like her. What does your father do?"

"Well, he used to be an engineer but recently he's had a career change."

"Really? To what?"

"Apparently, boxing."

Part Three

Chapter 29

Jesse Armstead had no idea his paper on jury nullification would ever come in handy. He saved it because it was good, or so he thought, and he was proud of it and couldn't bring himself to throw it away. The Law Review editors at Albany Law School weren't as impressed. They told him it was more an outline than a completed piece, but that if he would "finish" the thing like it deserved to be finished, they'd consider it, and him, for the Law Review. He thought it was already finished, couldn't imagine doing even more work than he had already done, and declined the invitation.

Now that he was convinced he was going to need it for his next trial, he lamented not having given the thing a place of honor more prominent than somewhere in the small pile of memorabilia generated by the twenty-seven years of his life.

It probably wasn't in the scrapbook his parents kept of his schoolboy careers, but he took a quick look-see just in case. The book, which he retrieved from underneath his bed, was a photo album with bright blue and yellow flowers on the covers. The reason Jesse had it in his apartment was to show to a girl he'd once dated. His parents had made it clear the book was on temporary loan only.

There he was, in his Junior Warriors basketball uniform at age 8. Basketball was Jesse's favorite sport, but every year he was the shortest kid on the team. Even now, at 5' 9", he struggled against taller players of equal talent.

His best sport was tennis. Pictures showed him as captain of the junior varsity and later the varsity teams, dressed in the polo shirts and shorts that his friends called "Jesse's Black and Whites."

"What kind of black kid plays tennis?" teased his cousin Barry, who used to live just down their street. The album included a picture of Barry in his high tops, his arm draped over little cousin, decked out in tennis whites.

"My black kid," said Jesse's dad, Ed. End of discussion, until Jesse won a tennis scholarship to play at the University of Maryland, when Ed Armstead gave his nephew a call "just to stay in touch."

No jury nullification paper.

As he pushed the scrapbook back under his bed, he remembered the box he'd placed in his hall closet the day he moved in. It was a cardboard packing box labeled "miscellaneous papers," a catch-all phrase for *I don't know what to do with these things but they might be useful one day.* The top of the box was sealed by interlocking cardboard flaps that hadn't been opened since the day he'd left College Park.

He pulled the thing out, blew away some dust, and undid the flaps. The paper was at the top of the pile.

The earliest English juries were valued for their ability to efficiently resolve disputes while providing the Court and the Crown with a stamp of legitimacy, as in: "You see? Even your own neighbors think you should hang." Those juries tended to side with the Crown because they were packed with jurors who'd been bribed. There also the motivation of avoiding jail, because if a verdict was not to the Crown's liking, a second jury would be impaneled, the case retried, and, when the desired verdict was returned, the first jury would be locked up. Legitimacy was a highly malleable concept in those days. By the late 17th century, punishing juries for their verdicts was no longer allowed.

A century after that, men who regarded the untamed power of the state to be the single greatest threat to freedom founded the United States, and the idea of juries as guardians of democracy found its highest expression. Said Thomas Jefferson: "I consider trial by jury as the only anchor yet imagined by man by which a government can be held to the principles of its constitution."

The ultimate power held by any juror was the power to nullify; that is, to consider a case where the required elements of proof had been established, but to render a verdict contrary to that proof nonetheless for reasons that to him transcended the technical dictates of the law. Said John Adams of such a juror: "It is not only his right but also his duty . . . to find the verdict according to his own best understanding, judgment, and conscience, though in direct opposition to the direction of the court."

But people in power never recognize their own inner tyrant, so the State's displeasure with citizens daring to know better eventually held sway, and over time the power to nullify was driven underground. It still exists but only as the strange animal described by Bob Sheridan to the man Jesse Armstead was going to try: A jury can do it provided nobody tells them so.

The key at trial, as far as Armstead could tell, would be to prevent Sheridan from raising the issue at all. Given what Armstead had learned about local courts in his single year on the job, that was going to be difficult. He'd have to raise it as an issue before jury selection even began so the judge could make a pre-trial ruling.

But what kind of ruling? What if Sheridan wanted to say, "My client should not be convicted. Simple fairness demands he be found not guilty." No judge would ever prevent defense counsel from saying that. And with all the publicity this case was already getting, the jury would know what Sheridan was getting at.

He could play the safe streets card. Not overtly, of course. Stating it overtly was just as inappropriate as arguing jury nullification. Yet it was done all the time. What kind of world would it be, so the argument went, if this kind of behavior went unpunished?

Except he wouldn't say it just that way. He'd say, "Defendant wants to be able to grab someone by the neck and smash his head against a solid object without penalty. That's what he's asking you to endorse. Is that the message you want to send?" And then, just to remind them of their duty, "You took an oath to try this case on the law and the facts. If you're to honor that oath, you must find the defendant guilty."

He started to wonder just how great it would be if first-year nobody ADA Jesse Armstead beat big bad Bob Sheridan with the whole world watching. Before Jesse's first trial, an assault charge arising out of an argument between fathers at a Little League game, one of the older ADAs had told Jesse something he remembered now. The defense lawyer on that case had been a guy with a rep, too. A local rep but to a rookie, any rep is intimidating. The veteran's advice had been, "Look, he can't prevent you from trying your case. Maybe he'll be better than you, but he can't stop you from standing up and delivering an opening statement. He can't prevent you from calling witnesses and asking them questions. Trials are great levelers that way. So don't be so worried about him. Just prepare your case well and give it your best shot."

"Thanks," Jesse had said, "That helps."

"Any time. Just have a bottle of good whiskey at home in case he kicks your ass."

Chapter 30

"Look, punk"—Chaz was working the phone—"I don't give a crap about your company policy. It was less than two months ago. You're telling me that if the FBI ordered you to find those records, you couldn't? Yes, I'll hold. For one minute. One minute, kid, and then you're in deep shit."

"Charming," said JoAnne, half in the bag though it was only three in the afternoon. "You're spreading good cheer to people near and far."

"Can you believe this shit? I pay for our airline tickets to Cancun— that's our tickets, sweetheart—with my credit card, and now the airline tells me payment was never authorized by Visa and the reservation was canceled. I can rebook but the prices have gone up and it'll cost me an additional three hundred bucks and this little shit on the telephone tells me his records don't go back that far so there's nothing he can do."

"Really? By any chance, did he use the words, 'company policy'?"

"Yeah, actually, I think he did. So?"

"So it's not true what they say about irony."

"What?"

"I said, What exactly did he say?"

"He just said some crap about how it's company policy to save records only thirty days and there's nothing he can do for me and it's my fault in the first place for waiting so long to confirm the ticket."

"You mean . . ." She got up and wobbled over to a liquor cabinet opposite Chazzie's desk and unburdened a bottle of Scotch of its last few ounces. "You mean you didn't confirm the tickets like I suggested you do right after you made the reservations?"

"That's right, Einstein, I didn't confirm them two seconds after I made them. Sue me. I called to confirm a reasonable time thereafter."

"Obviously. So you asked for a supervisor?"

"What are you, listening in on the extension?"

"And he told you he'll get a supervisor, but the supervisor is going to tell you the same thing, right? You're just shit-out-of-luck. Chazzie, tell me when you start to see what's happening here."

"What I see is a drunk blond with a death wish. And an unappreciative one at that. Like all of them." Chazzie hung up the phone without reaching the supervisor and sat down. "She was there," he said in a barely audible voice.

"Who?"

"Jane. She was at the protest over the weekend."

"Someone saw her?"

"Nobody had to. The cell phones my boys were using stopped working, only they stopped at different times and in different places and then suddenly started working again. It was like a moving blackout. Only Jane can do that. I can even tell you what street she was on and when she was on it. She was there. And after all I've done for her."

"Well, maybe she doesn't see it that way, Charlie."

"Thanks. That's another thing I'd never have figured out without you."

Jane didn't see it that way, but not for lack of trying. On the day they were married she really did think Charlie Remlinger was the best man she'd ever met, which was both true and exactly the problem. By the time she turned twenty-one she was living better than her parents and feeling guilty about it, an emotion seized upon by her brother Ted the first Thanksgiving after her wedding. Jane had worn an expensive gold bracelet given her by Chaz for her birthday.

"Must've cost a bundle, that thing on your arm," he started. "Why don't you just end the suspense and show us the receipt. I'm sure you've got it floating around somewhere, like in your pocket." That was before the soup had been served, so it was already shaping up to be a long meal. Chaz had been sitting quietly, saying nothing and Jane knew he was already in a bad mood because he was going to miss the day's football games. There was a small TV in the dining room, but it drew its signal from an antenna, so it wouldn't work with Jane there.

Jane realized Ted's tirade was directed at her new husband. Ted seemed determined to reestablish himself as his little sister's tormentor-in-chief during a holiday meal so that his new brother-in-law understood who stood atop the pecking order. She hoped, prayed, Chaz didn't see it that way.

Another prayer unanswered.

"Come outside with me," Chaz said, looking directly at Ted.

"Nope. You can say what you want right here."

"I know that. But I can't kick your face in right here, so we'll have to go outside."

No one else in the room moved. Color draining from Ted's face, he stood up and headed for the front door. His last few steps were rushed after Chaz put a hand in the small of his back and shoved hard. The two disappeared from the house with the door slamming shut behind them.

Jane knew, even before the sounds of Ted being struck repeatedly came in through an open window, that she and her family had been held hostage for years by a coward, and that no tragedy is worse than one that could have been easily avoided.

Chaz had to half-carry Ted back inside the house, where the now-former terror was dumped into his seat, the prior frightened paleness of his face replaced with streaked brown dirt and bright red blood.

"I'm fucking hungry," Chaz announced as he crashed down in his own chair, face flushed and eyes beaming. He said nothing to his wife, did not squeeze her hand, touch her shoulder, or make eye contact. As to the others at the table, whose jaws all hung in amazement, he offered no acknowledgment. Slamming his open and bruised right hand down on the table, which made everyone jump, he shouted, "Let's get that damn turkey out here."

Jane didn't trust herself but couldn't help but act on instinct, so the man who sang "Jacob's Ladder" so compellingly out of tune was the man for her but, of course, what did she know? He had a softer look in his eyes than Chaz. And he was brave enough and intuitive enough to jump up on the podium and lead the crowd where it needed to go even though his voice was awful. In fact, with a voice like his, it was downright courageous.

She also knew she'd seen him before, somewhere.

She considered getting in her SUV and just driving, on the chance she'd somehow cross paths with him. Had Aunt Gertie been smaller, she'd have thrown the plant into the back seat and used it as a potted divining rod. She decided to speak to the old girl and see what she had to say.

"I found one," Jane said to the tangle of wide green leaves crawling up the wall in the dining room. "But there's a slight problem. I've got no name and no way to get one, unless you can think of something. I just saw him from far away and when I tried finding him later, he was gone."

The patio door flew open and Sarah burst inside.

"Mom. The trial's been set. It's gonna be one month from this coming Monday in City Court. People are saying there's gonna be all kinds of protests, just like this weekend. All those people who were in town are gonna be back. It's gonna be a zoo. Hi, Aunt Gertie."

The teenager walked past her mother and pulled open the refrigerator door and grabbed a Diet Coke. Jane reached for Aunt Gertie and placed a giant leaf in one hand and stroked it with the other.

"Talking to Gert again, Mom? So can I go to the trial? I'll sit with Daddy. He'll probably need the support. Okay?"

"Okay, Sarah. That's a great idea. I'll take you."

"Whoa. What happened to you?"

"That's hard to tell just yet."

Chapter 31

A week before the trial Judge Stuart Rheingold received two pre-trial motions and a trial brief. The brief was from the defense. It outlined the case law on physical injury in the context of the anticipated testimony from the theater manager as well as the doctor who treated him.

The prosecution was required to prove that the theater manager suffered "physical injury" at the hands of Frank Rooney. Physical injury was defined in the Penal Law as "impairment of physical condition or substantial pain." Attorney Bob Sheridan's argument was that the manager suffered neither, that at most he had a sore neck that healed within days if not hours, and that little pain, if any, was the result, as evidenced by the findings in the medical records as well as the fact that the manager was back to work the very next evening. In addition, Sheridan cited case law holding that "petty slaps, shoves, kicks and the like delivered out of hostility, meanness and similar motives are not within the definition of the statute."

The idea was to lay the groundwork for a motion to dismiss the assault count on the grounds that the manager's injuries were not serious enough to support a conviction as a matter of law. The motion would be made at the close of the prosecution's case. If granted, the case would end right there, before the jury got to decide a thing.

There being no need for a response brief from Assistant District Attorney Armstead, he did not submit one. Instead, he submitted a short letter stating the judge could not possibly rule on the issue until the evidence was heard, that medical testimony from the treating physician was expected to establish the requisite injury, and that medical records notwithstanding, pain was subjective and the jury could always reasonably conclude the manager had suffered it.

The motions, one from each side, were on the issue of jury nullification, one for and one against. Defense counsel's had been written by his associate, was fifteen pages long and quoted extensively from the Founding Fathers. It was compelling, patriotic, and best read while listening to "The Battle Hymn of the Republic."

ADA Armstead's motion was written by ADA Armstead and was, to Judge Rheingold's surprise, equally long and well researched. It cited case law the Founders' great-grandchildren might have read, extolled the virtues of law and order, and went best with Bach's Passacaglia and Fugue.

Judge Rheingold's historical ear heard neither piece of music. What he heard instead was opportunity knocking. Elections were scheduled later in the year for State Supreme Court judges, and he intended to use the publicity he hoped to receive from the trial as a springboard to the big time.

Deciding to allow or disallow specific arguments prior to trial was a good way to streamline the case, but "Stewy," as he was known to his buddies at the Capital Tennis Center, where his caginess as a doubles player was legendary, had no desire to end things before every last headline that included the words, "Judge Rheingold" had been published in the local papers.

He advised both sides that after carefully considering their arguments, he was of the opinion that no blanket ruling on the issue could be made before hearing the proof. He would rule on objections as they arose during the trial.

"Damn," said ADA Armstead when he got the judge's decision.

"Bingo," said Cowboy Bob.

"All I'm saying is there's a way out. A way out of a difficult situation." Chazzie's lawyer was on the phone with his most volatile client. "This nonsense has already cost you lots of money and will no doubt cost you more, and from what I can tell, it's a very close call as to whether there's physical injury here. If your manager had suffered the same injury by slipping and falling in his own bathtub, he probably would not have even seen a doctor. That means you're going to go through all this, you'll continue to lose money, and the guy may get acquitted anyway. What happened last weekend in Buffalo was not the end of it. I hear hotel rooms in Columbus, Ohio, are going like hotcakes. That's where they'll be next weekend."

"And that's where I'll be. Did you see the paper today? There's another three letters to the editor in my favor. That's three in the last two days. I'm telling you the tide is turning and you're too chicken-shit to see it."

The letters—from a bank teller, a customer representative for a credit card company, and the service manager for a car dealership—had been Chazzie's only positive news after a weekend that saw his Buffalo theaters run movies to empty houses for three solid days.

The bank teller had gone right at the professor: "Doesn't he have rules? Don't the kids in his classes have to behave a certain way, meet certain requirements, keep to certain schedules? Rules bring order to our lives. Who is this guy to go off on his own and expect things to be different for him than they are for everyone else and not only that, but get violent when he's told no, you don't get special treatment?"

The customer representative wrote: "You wouldn't believe the abuse I have to take from some people. They yell at me like I was the one who got them into debt, or like I was the one who set the interest rate they have to pay. When I tell them to read their credit card contract, they get furious, like I've said something awful. Hey, I didn't twist their arms. But whose neck can I grab? Nobody's. I just have to take it. Well, so does this guy."

According to the service manager: "We are a nation of laws. One of them is you can't assault people. That should be obvious to everyone, but I guess it isn't. He had recourse. He could've gone to small claims court to get his money back. I hear all this talk about company policy, like it's some sort of evil conspiracy. What crap! Try running a company without a policy on every little thing. It can't be done. If you tried it, you'd have every one of those joker protesters complaining they weren't treated like the others. I can hear them whining now: 'The guy who was here before me had his repair covered under warranty. Why not me? I know a guy who got a loaner vehicle without reserving it in advance. Why not me? You had fresh coffee for my Aunt Toby a month ago. Where's mine?' I hope they pick me for your jury, professor. I'd love to show you what my policy is on whiners like you."

Bill Copeland had seen the letters.

"Three letters. And how many thousands of people from several states have picketed and boycotted your theaters in two cities?"

"That's because the trouble-makers are making all the noise, and the good people are being cowed. Well, I'm not the type that gets cowed. The protesters have their Spokesman, that skinny shit. Fine. The rest of us have me."

"Jesus."

"Oh. You don't think I'm good enough to be a spokesman? Let me tell you something. I'm a man of the people. And so was Jesus, since you mentioned him."

"Christ."

"That's right, Jesus Christ. Born with nothing, spoke his mind, and changed the world."

"I guess you could look at it that way. But I think you'd have more people tell you he was the son of God and was therefore divinely inspired, led a rebellious life that put him squarely at odds with the rich and the powerful, like you, and sacrificed everything for the good of mankind."

Charlie looked at his attorney, shook his head slowly, and said, "No wonder you can't help me with this mess. You don't even understand the Bible."

It was possible Frank Rooney still felt light, as he'd told his wife not many days before. It was also possible he felt so burdened he could not move. It was the night before his trial, and he was so nervous he couldn't tell which.

Bob Sheridan had told him that trials were more like marathons than sprints.

"There'll be moments when you want to crawl under the table and then, when you least expect it, you'll hear something from the witness stand that makes you think you can't lose. The trick is to maintain an even keel. Don't show dejection when things go badly, and don't gloat when they go well."

But it hadn't helped. He'd decided to cook. It would give him something to occupy himself. Laura had to do the shopping. Rooney was actually famous enough for people to recognize now. He decided on scallops with zucchini and sun-dried tomatoes in a garlic and wine sauce. Lots of slicing and dicing and sautéing, all done in silence until his girls got home, after which he might as well have called a press conference.

"You can't really go to jail for this, Dad, can you? I mean, even if you're convicted, they wouldn't put you in jail, would they? Don't, like, even murderers get probation the first time?"

"No, not murderers. I'm told I would probably not get jail, but there's no guarantee."

"But how can you get convicted? What about all those protesters?"

"It all depends on the people in the jury, girls. They're the only ones who count."

"Are you scared?"

"Well, a little bit, I guess."

With that answer he stopped stirring the zucchini.

"It's really the first time I've ever had something to be frightened of," he said. "This is something that could do me harm or make me look foolish and over which I've no control." His wife and daughters gathered round him, six arms of reassurance.

"To tell you the truth, I'm only worried that I put myself in this position for a reason that wasn't good enough, that's all. If I did, then I'm a fool. But if it's worth it, then I guess I'm ready."

"It is worth it, it is." The six arms reached for better perches as three heads nuzzled his shoulders and chest.

"I appreciate the support, ladies, but the zucchini is getting limp."

They let him go after one last good squeeze each, then his oldest, Melissa, put a CD on the stereo—Beethoven's Violin Concerto, the recording by the New York Philharmonic with Itzhak Perlman as soloist. It was her father's favorite piece of music.

Favorite meal. Favorite music. Hugs from his wife and children. Frank Rooney didn't know if he was going to be tried for a misdemeanor or shot at sunrise.

Chapter 32

Clinton Street, where the Albany City Courthouse is located, runs uphill from Broadway. Just a few yards down from the courthouse is the Palace Theater, a vaudeville era venue with an electronic marquee that catches the eye of everyone who passes through the intersection. Continuing on Broadway toward the downtown are at least a dozen bars and restaurants.

"Is too good for true," said Boris when he first saw it. "Electronic protest sign, food and alchocchol all next door to cchourthouse. We make all cchracket we want and cchwee cchannot be stopped becchause we not step foot on cchourthouse property."

"I'll give you a million dollars if you can say that three times, fast," said Alexander.

On Sunday morning a full page ad in the *Times Union* read:

Imagine a world in which every corporation has a conscience.
We can make it happen.
Free Frank Rooney.
Treat Us Like People.
The trial begins tomorrow at the Albany City Courthouse on Clinton Street.

The ad also ran in the *New York Times,* the *Chicago Sun-Times,* the *LA Times,* and the *Boston Globe,* along with *The Daily Gazette* in Schenectady, *The Record* in Middletown, *The Daily Freeman* in Kingston, and a dozen other papers in the Hudson Valley and in Rochester, Buffalo, and Columbus, but mostly it was for show. T.U.L.P.'s nationwide email list now numbered in the tens of thousands, and there would be little problem getting enough people for a credible demonstration.

"We should protest every day of the trial," Gus DeMauro said. "We'll have five groups of people ready to go. The Monday group, the Tuesday group, so on. That way everyone only has to take one day off from work or school. It'll be more than enough."

"Is good," said Boris, "but must not lose sight of Grand Plan."

"Which is?" asked Irena.

"Which is target one cchompany in each industry, not to bite off more than can chew. One bank. One supermarket chain, et cetera. Bring all T.U.L.P. power on that cchompany to force concessions. That way, other cchompanies in industry make concessions without big fight. Is like rolling thunder, but not so romantic.

"Meanwhile, must make biggest protest possible here."

Boris's idea was to extend an enthusiastic invitation to the Reverend Walker and Mother Ethel, along with the use of a bus in case members of their choir were so inclined to make the trip. "Ask them ccome on first day best," he said. "And maybe again on day jury to decide cchase."

Boris, along with Max, Lucy, Christina, Gus, and Irena Poppadapoulos—just back from Atlanta—were at the Hammermill home and the mood was positive. Then Irena spoke again.

"He could lose," she said.

No one said a word.

"My brother does criminal law. He tells me that even if the sentiment on the street is for Frank, that doesn't necessarily mean the jury will acquit. The fact is Frank grabbed that guy. It'll depend on how independent the jurors are. If they're the type of people who like to go their own way, think for themselves, reach their own conclusions, we'll win. I mean, Frank will win. If they're the kind of people who feel obligated to put their heads down and follow the rules, the kind of people who love authority for its own sake, he'll lose. The wildcard is the level of that guy's injury. If he's really not hurt at all, that could make even the law and order types acquit because they'll feel they have no choice. My brother thinks it's a tough case because, as I said, Frank grabbed that guy."

Ballpoint pens clicked on and off. Christina Clark ran a pencil back and forth across a page, filling in a big empty space she had doodled. The refrigerator came on. Gus unfolded a piece of gum. Someone adjusted their chair on the kitchen's wooden floor. Max Rodriguez sat back and looked across the table to where Irena Poppadapoulos sat.

"Irena, do you believe in magic?" he said.

Chapter 33

"They lost because of you, but more important, you won because of you," Ed Armstead said. "You remember what it was like? All those fancy boys? Asian kids, Jewish kids, Indian kids, WASPS. All fresh from their private lessons with momma sitting in her Lexus SUV with the air-conditioning on because it was too hot for her sensitive constitution?"

"I think so," said Jesse, "but I don't remember it being so dramatic."

"Trust me. It was dramatic. You played competitive tennis from the time you were eight years old through your senior year of college. How many black kids did you play against? You didn't even know how odd that was. That was your advantage. You thought you belonged because you were good, but that was only one part of it. You were confident, cocky. I couldn't help you with private lessons or advice on how to play, so you had to do it all by yourself. And you were out there on the court all by yourself. No teammates to bail you out or pick you up when you were down. That's inner strength, son, like what a grown man has. Not like basketball, which is a sport for overgrown children. Seven-foot guy parades around like a peacock because he just dunked. Any taller and he could've done it while sitting down."

Jesse's father never did like basketball.

Jesse's mom used to call them the twins. Ed was the same height and same build, only thicker. His hair was graying, he wore glasses, and his hands were callused from a life of hammering, sawing, and building .

He had stopped by his boy's apartment unannounced, knowing his son would be hard at work on the trial. One thing his boy could not have too many of, Ed always thought, was pep talks.

"Basketball never did a thing for you or for your big-mouth cousin Barry. Didn't do a thing for the other kids you played with, either. All it teaches you is to compete against other kids with big mouths. And when you're having a bad day, you pass it to a teammate. You let someone else guard the hot player. Tell me where all those kids are today. Nowhere.

"Not like tennis. In tennis, it's just you. No one to turn to. Nobody else on that court to hand it off to. And that's what it's gonna be like tomorrow in that courtroom. It's gonna be just you at that table, and you're ready for it."

"I think so, Dad. But you know there's never any telling what a jury will do. You can try your best case and lose."

"Then walk into that courtroom and try your best case."
"I will, Dad. Hey, you can read about it in the papers."
"You bet. Goodnight, son."
"Goodnight, Dad."

Chapter 34

Jesse Armstead didn't sleep, which didn't worry him. By the time he was done showering, his system had pumped enough adrenaline to keep him alert for a week. He put on the outfit he'd selected the night before—gray suit with pinstripes, white button-down shirt, red tie—and slipped into the brown shoes he'd polished over the weekend.

"It's a misdemeanor assault, that's all," was what he said to himself as he walked out his front door. Then he got to the courthouse.

Mother Ethel and the Reverend stood shoulder to shoulder with their choir, the Sweet Honey Gospel Singers, just a few yards up the hill from the courthouse, and their twelve combined voices were rolling "Amazing Grace" down toward the Hall of Justice. They had on robes—white with black trim—and were arrayed in equal numbers on either side of their musical and spiritual directors, who, being of considerable girth and surrounded by their costumed choir, appeared anchored to their spots on the sidewalk like great oak trees.

Below the courthouse, along the sidewalk and in front of a couple of bars and grills that wouldn't open until lunch time, were two hundred or so protesters marching in a circle, chanting "Free Frank Rooney" and carrying signs that read the same.

Armstead heard both the choir and the marchers pump up the volume as he walked through the door of the courthouse. "Just a misdemeanor assault trial," he mumbled to himself.

Bob Sheridan arrived. A black Lincoln Towncar dropped him and his assistant, recent Columbia law school grad Valerie Whit, at the curb to wild cheering and sign waving. Color-wise, Sheridan's outfit was not much different from the ADA's. Price wise, it cost more than Armstead's entire wardrobe combined, and it looked it. Ms. Whit was eye-catching in a snug dark blue skirt that ended a pleasing distance above her knees, with a matching top pulled over a green blouse, the top two buttons unbuttoned.

Their client and his wife were with them, Frank in khakis, a blue shirt, blue blazer, and a gold and red tie and Laura brightly sporting a red and white dress with a flowery print under a white sweater. The four of them walked briskly inside the building—the lawyers confident, even eager, the Rooneys grim. Reporters and photographers from a half-dozen news agencies and TV stations barked questions and snapped pictures.

Sheridan said nothing, barely suppressing a smile. His assistant and the Rooneys stared straight ahead, acknowledging none of the commotion.

Having waited all morning for the Rooneys and their attorneys and receiving nothing for the effort, the media turned its attention to the choir.

"Reverend Walker!" Lou Boudreau was trying to get the Reverend to take a break from singing. Boudreau worked for the *Saratogian*, which hadn't endorsed a liberal or progressive candidate, according to the boast of its editor, "since that volcano buried Pompeii."

"Reverend Walker! Isn't it conceded that Frank Rooney grabbed the theater manager by the neck? What about the law?"

The Reverend lifted two huge arms in the air and the singing stopped. He turned to face his inquisitor.

"Son," he rumbled. "Even the law has a greater calling."

"Amen," said Mother Ethel, nodding her head.

"I said, 'Even the law has a greater calling!'" The Reverend's voice boomed up and down Clinton Street.

"Amen! Tell it! Tell it!" called out members of the choir. Hands in the air as they spoke, they seemed to know what was coming.

"And that greater calling, that greater good, that larger goal, my young friend, is Justice!"

"Amen, brother. Tell it! Tell it!"

"It's right in here," said the Reverend, holding up a Bible, "and it's available to reporters and anyone else who'll take the time to look. Justice, justice shall you pursue. Thus sayeth the Lord, your God. Now go home, son, and do some real research."

It was a synopsis of the same Bible lesson he'd given over the phone just three nights before to Cowboy Bob Sheridan.

Judge Rheingold had never been so happy. He'd had his robe dry-cleaned and had bought several new white shirts as part of his personal trial prep. Before even meeting with the lawyers or receiving a formal request, he'd informed the members of the press the trial would be open to the media. The only conditions he'd imposed were that the jury not be shown on camera, that none of the names of prospective or selected jurors be used until after the verdict, and then only with the jurors' permission, and that cameras not be brought into the courtroom until after the jury had been selected. He'd gotten those ideas from one of his tennis buddies, a federal court judge named Prendergast, who'd suggested that the personal information divulged during jury selection need not be aired on the nightly news and that the extra days it might take to get a jury with the cameras whirring would cost the city money it didn't need to spend.

His Honor was ebullient. He practically hugged ADA Armstead and Bob Sheridan after calling them into chambers.

"I take it you'll accept nothing other than an outright dismissal?" His Honor said hopefully to Sheridan."

"Nothing but, Your Honor."

"And you're not inclined to make such an offer, are you, Mr. Armstead?"

"No sir, Your Honor."

"Okay, then. We'll have a spirited and keenly fought trial, but no nasty stuff. Can we agree on that, gentlemen?"

"Of course, Your Honor," they said.

"State the grounds for your objections clearly and concisely. No speeches. If I want to hear more, I'll ask."

"Understood, Your Honor," they said.

"And when I make a ruling, you say *Yes, Your Honor* and sit down. No *But Your Honor,* or *If I could just be heard on that . . ..* Understood?"

"Yes, Your Honor."

"Good enough. Let's go pick a jury."

Before either attorney had had a chance to stand up and begin his voir dire, Judge Rheignold's preliminary questioning of the sixty prospective jurors led to disqualifications of twenty, the first fifteen of whom indicated they'd heard and read about the case and thought Frank Rooney should never have been arrested in the first place.

From where the prospective jurors sat, the defense table was furthest away, with Cowboy Bob seated closest to them. The line-up after him consisted of Frank and Laura Rooney and Ms. Whit, in that order. Closest to the jury box was the prosecutor's table at which sat Jessie Armstead, alone.

Laura Rooney, whose level of anxiety seemed to her husband to be in serious need of reduction, turned to Valerie Whit and raised her eyebrows in an expression of optimism. Whit said nothing, but scribbled a note on a pad she placed on her lap and showed it to Laura. It read: "Show no emotion! There's the other shoe yet to drop."

As Whit predicted, ten of the next twelve jurors to excuse themselves had already made up their minds that Frank was guilty.

It came in waves, a point not lost on the chemistry professor, whose recently discovered streak of independence was the reason for the trial about to start. *One guy says he can't be fair because he's with me, and the next eight or nine echo his view. Then one guy goes the other way, and the next group falls in behind him. Is that really what this country is about?*

By 10:45 the jury box contained eight potential jurors—six for the jury and two for alternates—and ADA Armstead rose to speak his first words of the trial.

"We're here for the trial of a criminal complaint," he said.

Frank Rooney thought he detected a hint of unease, a slight tremor in the ADA's voice, but it dissipated so quickly, the professor was not sure he'd heard right.

"All the hoopla aside, including the singing from the choir outside, it's a simple assault charge that should not take long to try. My name is Jesse Armstead. I'm an Assistant District Attorney and I'll be presenting the People's case to you. Mr. Franklin, you're juror number 1, or at least that's the seat you're in. Do you feel you can follow the judge's instructions in this case?"

"I think so."

"Do you feel you can apply the law to this case as the judge explains it to you?"

"I'll do my best."

"Now, unless you're an attorney yourself, chances are you don't know what the law of assault is. Am I right about that?"

"Yeah."

"So you're going to need the judge to explain that law to you and define each element of it, agreed?"

"Agreed."

"Will you promise me you'll apply the law as the judge gives it to you and in no other way?"

"Yeah."

"Can you and I agree this is not an exercise in creativity?"

"I guess so."

"You'll follow the rules that the judge gives you to follow. Right?"

"Right."

For the next hour, the eight people in the box were barraged with statements on the sanctity of the law, each one disguised by Armstead as a question. Yes, they would follow the law, the judge's instructions on the law, and his definitions of the law. Yes, they would uphold their oaths to do so. No, there would be no ad-libbing, no improvisation, no invention, and no novel interpretation of concepts that the courts of New York State have spent centuries refining. And then, to the last series of questions Armstead asked, they promised yes, if the case looked open and shut, they'd say so with a no muss, no fuss verdict of guilty as charged.

Armstead was careful to elicit verbal responses to his questions from each individual juror. The mass nodding of heads wouldn't do. Each and every juror was asked to make an unyielding promise of obedience to the Penal Law of the State of New York.

Rooney glanced at his own attorney who, through all the ADA's questioning, maintained a bemused but polite look upon his face. Sheridan kept a blank legal pad on the table before him, on which was a pen that the Cowboy did not bother to so much as touch. He did not confer with his assistant or speak to his client. Neither did he look at his watch, tap his fingers on his desk, or move his body in his chair, except for an almost imperceptible shifting of his weight, which he did only twice. He just waited, apparently content to sit there, unmoving, all day if necessary.

After Armstead sat down, Judge Rheingold addressed defense counsel.

"Well, now. It's about 11:45, Mr. Sheridan, and you're just about the only person in the courtroom who hasn't yet had a chance to speak, so I'm going to give you a chance to stretch your vocal cords a bit. Perhaps you can ask a preliminary question or two and then we'll break for lunch at noon."

Sheridan stood up and thanked His Honor. Then he softly introduced himself to the jury, along with Ms. Whit, his client, and Laura Rooney, who, he informed the boxed eight, would not be at counsel table during the trial but would return to the audience after jury selection was finished.

He walked toward the man in seat number one, stopped, smiled somewhat, and said: "Mr. Franklin, I've but one question for you this morning. Do you believe in justice?"

Chapter 35

"Why are they so interested this case?" Bob Sheridan had asked his assistant when pictures of Reverend Walker and Mother Ethel appeared in the *Times Union* on the morning following the rally at the Times Union Center.

"For the same reason everyone else is. Corporate greed run amok, insensitivity to the basic tenets of civil behavior, adherence to form over substance in an increasingly impersonal world. . ."

"No. There's something else going on here. I can feel it. The guy Frank Rooney grabbed was just doing what he'd been told, and if there's one thing the church likes, it's a guy who does what he's been told. No institution in the course of human history has stood for rules and obedience like the church. When Franco rose to power in Spain in the 1930s, he did so with the support of the church. It's an institution that brooks of little change and tolerates no troublemakers. It forced Galileo to commit suicide, brought us the Inquisition, the pogroms of Eastern Europe, and the Crusades. It doesn't like wise guys, Val, and we're representing a guy who's being portrayed as a major wise guy. So why are this Reverend and his wife here?"

"Maybe some credit card company gave him some grief and he wants a little payback."

"Look at these two," Sheridan said, holding up the photograph. "Does it look to you like that's why they've put their reputations at risk to lead thirty-five hundred people into a state of anti-corporate frenzy? You may not be old enough to remember this, but during the Vietnam War a couple of brothers named Berrigan—one had been a priest—took to the streets to protest. It marked a sea change in the movement. If priests were fighting the established power, if men who once wore collars were taking to the streets, what must this government be doing over there? That's what many people started thinking."

"I know all about the Berrigans. Phillip, the ex-priest, was arrested several times for damaging government property and spent years of his life in jail. Is that what you . . ."

"There's something here I'm not getting and I need to know what it is."

She didn't bother looking at the photograph. "You want to talk to Reverend Walker, don't you?"

"Damn right I do."

"What brings you to me, Mr. Sheridan?" the Reverend asked. A meeting could not be arranged due to their schedules, so they spoke by phone. "I've been pondering that question ever since Ms. Whit called me. You know, I ask the question of everyone who comes to me and tells me they want to talk."

"Well, as you know, I represent Frank Rooney and I want to make sure I've not missed a view of the case that . . ."

"I didn't ask you that. I asked, What brings you to me?"

"Yes, I was saying . . ."

"You were avoiding my question is what you were doing. I'll ask you again. What brings you to me, Mr. Sheridan?"

Sheridan held the phone away from his ear for a few moments and looked out the window of his moving limousine. He was in New York City on his way to an interview with a reporter for *Newsweek* magazine for a feature story on the top criminal defense lawyers in the country. The car traveled half a block, then a few feet more.

"I need . . ."

"Yes. You have a need. That's a start, Mr. Sheridan. You've acknowledged a need. And with His help, I will endeavor to meet that need."

Another half block went by before Sheridan said, "Please, call me Bob." And then, to the driver: "Pull over and stop somewhere."

He knew at that point that he was going to miss the interview.

"What have you done, Bob? I mean, with your life. Oh, I know you're rich and famous. We preachers have the Internet too. But what have you done? Tell me."

"I've represented many people successfully. Tough cases. You heard about that millionaire CEO in Dallas who was charged with killing his wife over an affair? I won an acquittal for him."

"That one got you started, didn't it? I mean in the big time."

"Yes. And . . ."

"Someone else would have represented him."

"Excuse me?"

"I said, someone else would have represented him. He was a millionaire. He'd have found another top lawyer. Someone else would have done it."

"Okay, what about that high school principal in Omaha who was charged with killing the cheerleader? They had fingerprints, two eyewitnesses, a motive. What about that one?"

"What about it?"

"What do you mean, *What about it?* It was a great win."

"Yes, one in a series of great wins. But you've not answered my question, which is, *What have you done?* You don't understand me, do you? You're a brilliant attorney and you've used your education and skill to make fame and fortune yours. And the next person you represent will be lucky to have you. Mr. Rooney is lucky to have you. But you've been a lawyer for thirty years now. I looked it up. And all you've proved is that the rich and the powerful can always get off, while the poor and the downtrodden still suffer."

"Now wait a minute. I didn't charge that teacher in Omaha a cent."

"Yes, and the article I read said you received as much as eight million dollars in fees as a result of the publicity you received. Come on, Bob. What have you done?"

Sheridan was, at that point, staring at the back of his driver's head, his own head a muddle.

"I've done my best, Reverend."

"And yet you still have a need. A burning need. Isn't that so?"

"Yes, perhaps. I called you. I have to admit I had a feeling I should. But I'll be damned if I know why, if you'll excuse me."

"I'll excuse you, but I think now I need to tell you about Deuteronomy."

"Ah. That's the one with all the laws, right?"

"That's right. Deuteronomy and some Talmud. That'll give us some law, as well as commentaries on the law. You see, you're just coming to this now, but brilliant men have been contemplating what God had to say about just this kind of stuff for centuries. Deuteronomy, chapter 16, verses 18 to chapter 21, verse 9 contains one of the most-quoted phrases in the Bible. It says, *Justice, Justice shall you pursue.* But if you consider the whole phrase, it reveals a context that's central to Mr. Rooney's case. The entire section goes like this:

Judges and officers shall you appoint in all your gates, which the Lord your God gives you, throughout your tribes; and they shall judge the people with just judgment. You shall not pervert judgment; you shall not respect persons, nor take a bribe, for a bribe blinds the eyes of the wise, and perverts the words of the righteous: Justice, justice shall you pursue, that you may live, and inherit the land which the Lord your God gives you.

"Now tell me, Mr. Lawyer, what's the one word that is so conspicuous here for its absence?"

"Jesus, I don't . . . oh, damn, excuse me again. I'm not much on the Bible, Reverend. To tell you the truth, I didn't expect this kind of reception from you. I mean, you don't even know what I want."

"I asked what you wanted a couple of times and you couldn't tell me. I think I know, though. I think you want to know what's missing from the Bible verses I just read you."

"Okay, well . . ."

"I'll give you a hint. It's the thing you claim to have been doing your best to practice all these years but really have not come to understand, and understanding it like the Bible understands it is what you're needing right now."

"Man, I haven't had this kind of pressure since the Bar exam."

"Which tested you on . . ."

Sheridan had looked away from his driver's neck and spotted a pushcart vendor across the street selling ice cream. Sheridan was hungry.

"Law, Reverend. The passage never mentions the law."

"Yes. That's correct, my friend. Very good. But it does mention justice, and not once, but twice. And it also mentions judgment. And not just any judgment, but just judgment. You see, Mr. Sheridan, the law and justice are not synonymous. The former only serves the latter, nothing more. And the only judgment recognized by God is one that is just. A judgment that is technically correct but is unjust is not worth the paper it is written on.

"I'll tell you something else that may interest you. The ancient kings of Israel had the right to impose sentences outside the law. Remember, the Israelites were a heavily codified and rule-bound society, ruled directly by the Bible. But the kings could go outside the law to prevent a strict reading of the law from perverting the law's intent—in other words, to preserve the spirit of the law over the letters upon which that law was constructed.

"The law is a wonderful thing, Mr. Sheridan. It can give us order and safety and predictability. But it takes a back seat to justice."

Sheridan said: "Then what do you say to the Catholic who eats a cookie and sips some wine and insists it's the body and the blood of Christ, or the Jew who'll eat beef but not pork or the Hindu who won't touch a cow when people all around him are starving to death? They're following religious laws, and to me those laws are plain silliness. Where's the justice there?"

"The law exists to help us worship God. That is how we relate to Him. And the law, with its many rituals, helps us find him. For those who understand that, laws and rituals are sources of comfort and inspiration. However, there are those in all religions, as well as those who are not religious at all, who are obsessed with laws for reasons having nothing to do with God or Justice. A man who is obsessed with law, religious or secular law, for no reason other than the law itself, is a zealot, and zealots are dangerous precisely because they do not understand that laws are pathways to God and justice, rather than holiness in and of themselves. In fact, these people do not seek God or justice. They seek compliance. Imagine that, Mr. Sheridan. Entire lifetimes devoted to so lowly a goal as compliance.

"The zealot does not use the law to help him worship God. Instead, he worships the law. To him, that's where faith ends. There is no higher goal. He can see no greater purpose. He is misguided and should be pitied. If possible, he should be helped, but under no circumstances should we attribute to him a greater understanding by virtue of his obsession.

"That's why Mother and I are supporting Mr. Rooney. He knows how dangerous this kind of thinking is. That's why he did what he did."

"And since I'm his lawyer . . ."

"Since you are his lawyer, you are standing at the crossroads of holiness and order. You know, Mr. Sheridan, according to Talmud, one who renders a true judgment, based upon truth, becomes, for that moment, a partner with God. Remember, it is the law that is judged by the truth, not the other way around. That's what you've got to get those jurors to understand."

"I think you're expecting a bit much from me, Reverend. When all is said and done, I'm just a guy with a briefcase. Maybe if I knew more, like you. Maybe someday in the future, after some study . . ."

"Study can bring you worldly knowledge, but that's not what I'm talking about. What I'm talking about is spiritual knowledge, a flash of insight after which you suddenly know all you need to know. It comes from outside your head. In the church we call it feeling the spirit, or feeling the fire. You can call it whatever you want. From what I've read, your client felt it just before he grabbed that theater manager. Maybe you should talk to him and ask him what it felt like. It's why you called me, and I think you know it."

"It's that simple?"

"Simple and wonderful. Mr. Rooney, a chemistry professor, a man of science, is already there. Join him. You'll make an unbeatable team."

Chapter 36

Back in court after the lunch break, Sheridan started in where he'd left off.

"There's a sign on the wall of United States Supreme Court Justice Ruth Bader Ginsberg's office that says, 'Justice, justice shall you pursue.' Can anyone tell me where that phrase comes from?"

Juror number 7 raised his hand. Sheridan looked down at his notes. Juror number 7, Alfred Schmidt, was a regional manager for Northeast Energy, a power company. Sheridan was planning to bump him, along with anyone else whose livelihood depended on a large corporation.

"Mr. Schmidt?"

"It's from Deuteronomy. chapter 18, I believe."

"You know your Bible, sir."

"I'm a deacon in the Mormon Church. I've studied the Bible nearly all my life."

The bemused grin that had shaped Cowboy Bob's face before lunch was now a warm glow. "Then you know about judging with just judgment, another phrase from that same part of Deuteronomy."

"I do, indeed."

"And is a just judgment on my client what you promise me you'll render, and nothing less than that?"

"Yes, I can make that promise."

"Your company is a big one, is it not?"

"Yes, very."

"There must be volumes and volumes of company policies you've got to follow, am I right?"

"Oh, yeah. On everything."

"Give me some examples, if you would."

"Oh, everything from how to climb a utility pole to what you can put on the walls of your office to when you can disconnect service."

"How long have you been with Northeast Energy?"

"Twenty years."

"In that time, Mr. Schmidt, have you ever been asked to carry out a company policy with which you disagreed?"

"Objection!" ADA Armstead was on his feet.

"Well," said His Honor, contemplating the point with great seriousness, his body tilted back in his chair, eyes gazing up at the ceiling, "I'm going to allow it. Go ahead, Mr. Schmidt. Answer the question."

"Only once, actually. But it was a big one."

"Can you tell us about that?"

"We were asked to do a disconnect on a building where it was suspected squatters or maybe even drug users or both were hanging around. There may have been animals inside as well. I don't remember exactly. But it was winter and I wanted the animal control people and the police to clear the place out. Then I wanted to get together a group of volunteers to board it up. I was afraid if people or animals returned, thinking it was still warm even though we'd pulled the plug, they'd freeze to death."

"Your superiors wanted you to do it?"

"Yes."

"They ordered you to do it?"

"Oh, yes."

"What did you do?"

"I told them I'd been a company man for years and hoped to continue being one, but that this was immoral and I wouldn't do it."

"Had you pulled the plug, as you say, would the disconnect have been in accordance with company policy?"

"Yes, they'd given all the right notices and such. It would have been legal."

"But not just, is that right?"

"Right."

"What happened?"

"They gave me one more day to do it my way, so I checked with the police and made sure the place was empty. Then I got some people from my church together and we went over there and boarded up the place and painted some signs telling people the heat and electricity were off."

"Thank you. Now what about you, Ms. Avery?" Juror number 6, seated next to Mr. Schmidt, was an accountant for the New York State Department of Tax and Finance. "Can you promise a fair judgment of my client?"

"Yes, but I'd have pulled the plug."

"Okay, fair enough, but . . . "

"I'd have pulled it in a minute. People nowadays think they can have something and not pay for it. It doesn't work that way. Somebody always gets the bill. Probably, in a roundabout way, the public wound up paying for that extra day of power. Besides, the people in there had no business being there. I'd have cut the power, no problem."

"Have you heard about this case, Ms. Avery?"

"Yes, on the local news. I've read an article or two about it too."

"Do you have a view, right now as you're sitting here, of what the correct judgment should be?"

"No, but it does sound odd."

"How so?"

"Oh, you know. A chemistry professor grabbing someone. Although I had a chemistry teacher once I'd have liked to take a poke at. Oh, I'm sorry. Am I allowed to say that?"

"No need to apologize. He did grab someone. We can't refute that. But since you brought it up, does the fact that it sounds odd to you suggest that there may be a lot more to this case than meets the eye?"

"Objection!" responded ADA Armstead, who'd been squirming through Sheridan's questions thus far.

"Sustained," said Judge Rheingold. "That's not a qualification for jury duty, Mr. Sheridan."

"Very well, Your Honor," said Sheridan, having made his point. "I'll move on."

The Cowboy was rolling, and not so much because he was getting good answers from every juror. He was not. Ms. Avery did not seem to be on his side, Neither did Mr. Santucci, an electrician who wondered why he had to miss time from work if Rooney was admitting he'd grabbed the manager, or Mr. Burke, a retired teacher who asked where someone on a professor's salary got the money to hire high-priced talent like the Cowboy. What made it feel to Frank Rooney like Sheridan was rolling was that the man never blinked, never stumbled, and seemed able to cut off and cut out the objectionable jurors without letting them get much traction, while at the same time propping up the favorable ones.

Sheridan questioned for about an hour. When he was done, Judge Rheingold asked the lawyers into chambers to exercise challenges, but ADA Armstead asked for "two more quick questions."

"I'm holding you to that," said the judge.

Armstead walked briskly up to the jury box and addressed the group. "Do you all strive to follow the law? I'm not talking about in your position here as jurors, but in your lives, outside this courtroom. Do you try to follow the law?"

Heads nodded.

"And does anyone here think it's unfair to expect others to follow it as well?"

Heads shook.

"That's about as evenhanded as it gets, don't you agree?"

"That's three, Mr. Armstead," said His Honor.

Armstead bumped Mr. Schmidt, and Sheridan excused Ms. Avery. Mr. Santucci was dismissed for cause—Sheridan was able to get him to admit, without much effort, that his mind was already made up. Since it was a misdemeanor case, the attorneys had only three peremptory challenges each and didn't want to use more than one on the first go round. Mr. Burke, the teacher who wondered where Sheridan's fee was coming from, had also agreed with Sheridan that it didn't matter and that his verdict would be based on the evidence.

That left Patrick Brennan, a mechanic, Mary Contempassis, who owned and operated her own dance studio, Anthony Malozzi, an inspector for the New York State Department of Environmental Conservation, Brian Anderson, a retired post office worker, and Sandi Commisky, a secretary with the New York State Attorney General's office. Six down, two to go. By 2 P.M. they had them. Completing the group were Matthew Salvadore, a probation officer, and Julia Phelan, a hairdresser.

Judge Rheingold told the lawyers they would go with unnamed alternates, which meant the two alternates would not be selected and removed from the box until the jury was about to deliberate.

The courtroom was cleared of the remaining jury pool and spectators were allowed in. Seated in the second row, behind a group of reporters including one each from the New York Times and the Washington Post, as well as Meagan Swoboda, was a man wearing a rayon shirt and two-tone shoes. An old woman accompanied by a younger man who looked a bit like her sat down in the next seat. The younger man had tried desperately to find a hotel room for the trial, but the Capital Region was booked solid, and the old woman, his mother, had insisted she'd need a ride to the courthouse, so why not just stay with her?

"I don't know why not," he'd said. "But if you give me a few minutes, something will come to me."

"Very funny you are," she'd said. "Like this you treat your mother. Protesters are coming from Timbuktu. A room you'll never find."

"I know," he'd groaned.

"So come stay by me. I'll cook."

"I know that, too."

The old woman had plopped down on her seat and turned to the man in rayon. She addressed him as though he was obligated to justify his presence in the courtroom.

"And you are?" she'd said.

"Mario Lambruzzo."

"You're for Frank or against?"

"For."

"Okay. I'm Flo Gezunterman. This is my son Scott."

Within minutes the entire gallery was full. Reverend Walker and Mother Ethel, along with their choir, were the most visible. Sarah Remlinger was there. Most of the T.U.L.P. leadership was not inside the courtroom because the Cowboy didn't know which of them he'd need as witnesses, and potential witnesses were not allowed to view prior witnesses' testimony. They sat outside in the hallway, waiting. Inside were Johann Mathison and Brian and Suzy Brindisi. Poking his head in and out of the courtroom so he could later report back to his client was Bill Copeland.

"I have a preliminary charge to give you before opening statements," said His Honor.

The preliminary charge had long been a focal point of Bob Sheridan's seminars. "It's impossible to understand," he would tell his audiences. "It includes lines like, 'You cannot infer a positive fact from a negative response,' and 'You must ignore evidence I rule inadmissible, even if you've already heard it.' Its only impact is to convince any jurors who may still have any doubt that they really are on their own and that their decision rests on their own good sense. As a practical matter, it throws ten centuries of common law jurisprudence out the window and paves the way for charming people like me and you to convince juries that they shouldn't convict our guys because they just shouldn't convict them. It's my favorite part of the trial."

ADA Armstead's opening was fifteen minutes long, in keeping with his theory of the case, which was that it was open and shut with nothing much to think about: Defendant Rooney, though unprovoked, had grabbed the innocent theater manager and smashed his face against the window, causing a physical injury. That's all there was to it.

Bob Sheridan spoke longer: "Seething just below the surface of my client's calm demeanor, in ways even he did not comprehend, was the same frustration and resentment we all feel when presented with an incorrect charge on a credit card or utility bill that we can't correct because we can't get through the automated phone system to speak to a human being, or the exasperation we feel at having the most reasonable of requests denied by a hotel clerk or store manager on the grounds of company policy. Or the helplessness we feel when our new health insurance company tells us it won't pay for medication our doctor has been prescribing for years, and then won't allow us to speak to the person who actually made that decision, again, because 'policy doesn't allow it.'

"What Frank Rooney comprehended, at the moment the theater manager refused to refund his ticket purchase, was that Frank, his wife, and indeed every single one of us has surrendered his independence, and with it his humanity, to any and every entity large enough to have something it calls a company policy.

"Company policy is not the law, and it is not God's word. It is arbitrary, it steamrolls over the basic principles of fairness that we were all taught as children, and it renders us weak and powerless cogs in someone else's big machine. Frank is not the one who acted unjustly by fighting back. It was Maiko Industries, Inc., that was unjust by inflicting its policy on Frank."

Sheridan sat down.

"Fine," said Judge Rheingold. "I think we'll have time for one witness before we break."

"The People call Detective Joseph Zito to the stand," said ADA Armstead.

Detective Zito, in a herringbone sport jacket, blue button-down shirt, blue tie, and gray slacks, walked over to the court clerk, placed his left hand on the Bible, raised his right, and took the oath. He was only about an inch or two taller than Armstead, slightly built, full head of thick, salt-and-pepper hair brushed straight back. He walked to the witness chair, sat down, and placed a pair of glasses upon his straight Roman nose.

Under confident, rapid questioning by Armstead, Zito told the jury about responding to the commotion at the ticket booth and finding Frank Rooney's right hand reaching through the window, holding the manager by the neck. The manager seemed to be trying to free himself, but Rooney had a good grip on him.

Armstead's direct examination took but a few minutes. Sheridan then stood up.

"Detective, do you remember a tall, heavy-set man with a beard standing next to Mr. Rooney at the ticket booth?"

Zito thought for a minute.

"Yes. As a matter of fact, I do."

Sheridan asked how long Zito had been on the force.

"Seventeen years."

"You must have seen a lot of fights in that time, am I right?"

"I'd say so."

"Did anything strike you as unusual about this one?"

"Actually, everything struck me as unusual."

"Tell us, Detective."

"Well, first of all, Mr. Rooney didn't look like the combative type. I learned later he was a professor over at RPI, and that's just what he looked like. And he was there with his wife, and she didn't look like a hell-raiser either."

"What else?"

"He seemed very calm throughout. I mean, he was holding on to that guy, but he wasn't screaming or yelling or trying to break the window to get at him. And when I identified myself as a police detective and told him to let go, he did."

"Did he tussle with you? Give you a hard time in any way?"

"No, not at all. I told him to go and sit in the lounge area and he did. Just sat there with his wife like they were waiting for a bus."

"Did he try to run away from you to avoid arrest?"

"No, he was as cooperative as he could be."

"What about the manager?"

"He was wild. He wanted to continue the fight. He wanted to get his hands on Rooney."

"Did the manager seem hurt to you?"

"Not much."

"Did he seem unable to carry on the fight?"

"No."

"Did you see any blood, scrapes, any signs of injury?"

"His neck was red."

"At any time while you were there, did he ask for medical help?"

"No."

"I take it you prevented further fighting, is that right?"

"Yeah, I did."

"What was Mr. Rooney's response to the manager's stated desire to continue the fight?"

"That was odd too. Basically, he stood up and said, in a very calm, quiet voice, 'Let him go,' as if to say, 'If he wants more, I'm ready.'"

"That surprised you too?"

"Yeah. I didn't peg the guy to be a brawler."

"Detective, have you had occasion to break up fights between people who were intoxicated or high?"

"Many times. That's what it is most of the time."

"Did you reach an opinion as to Mr. Rooney's state of sobriety that night?"

"Stone cold sober. That's one of the things I remember most clearly. I've seen people drunk, seen them stoned. He was neither. He was perfectly clear-headed. At least, that's how he seemed to me. He seemed calm, almost at ease, like he'd done something good and was pleased with himself."

"Thank you. That's all I have."

"Mr. Armstead? Redirect?" said Judge Rheingold.

"Detective, in spite of the unusual nature of Mr. Rooney's demeanor that night, did you have any doubt, based on what you saw and heard, that he should be arrested for assault?"

"No."

"And if I suggested that in your seventeen years on the force that you've seen a lot of unusual things, would I be right?"

"Oh, yeah."

"Thank you."

"Mr. Sheridan?"

"Thank you, Judge. Detective Zito, you told us you had no doubt an arrest for assault was warranted. But didn't you ask Mr. Connally if he wanted to press charges?"

"Yes, I did."

"Well, what if he'd told you he didn't? What would you have done?"

"Usually, case like this, no blood or broken bones, if the victim wants to forget it, I will too."

"So you'll exercise discretion, is that right?"

"Yes."

"In fact, as a law-enforcement officer, you exercise discretion all the time, do you not?"

"Oh, yeah. Goes with the territory."

"Who to arrest. Whether or not to arrest? What to charge people with? Is that right?"

"Sure."

"Do you consider yourself a good cop?"

"I do."

"A law-abiding citizen?"

"I hope so."

"So sometimes, the strict letter of the law is not what guides you, correct?"

"I guess you could say that."

"One more thing, Detective Zito. Do you believe in justice?"

The detective smiled at this. He tilted his head at Sheridan and said, "I better. I'm a cop."

"And that belief in justice, is that what drove you to become a cop?"

"I guess so. It's good work."

"Indeed, it is. But until you started your training to become an officer, you didn't know the Penal Law of the State of New York, did you?"

"No, not specifically. Not before."

"But you did know right from wrong, didn't you?"

"I had strict parents, and I was an alter boy, if that's what you mean."

"That's exactly what I mean. Thank you. No further questions."

"Mr. Armstead?" said His Honor.

The young ADA popped right up again.

"But in this case, after evaluating the facts and circumstances at the theater that night, you did make the arrest, didn't you, Detective?"

"Yes, I did."

"So you must have felt it was the right thing to do, am I right?"

"Yes."

"Thank you."

"Tomorrow morning, then, ladies and gentlemen," said the judge. "Same place, 9:30 A.M. See you then."

By the time the jurors left the building, Max, Boris, Alexander, Irena, and Gus had made their way down to the corner of Clinton and Pearl and joined the waiting protesters. Three of the jurors—Ms. Phelan, the hairdresser, Mr. Brennan, the mechanic, and Ms. Commisky, the secretary—made a point of walking past the protesters to try to get a look at the face of T.U.L.P. It wasn't hard. Max had joined the Sweet Honey Gospel Singers as they began to sing *I Believe* while the rest of the TULP people began walking in a circle around them.

Jesse Armstead went home wondering who the big man with the beard was, what that man had to do with the case, and why he was hearing about him now for the first time.

Chapter 37

The loud hello shouted by Beatrice to Max and Meagan as they walked hand in hand past her house on Alameda Street would've been enough for Max, but Bea thought some follow-up was required.

"How are you, Max?" she called as she bounded out her front door. "And that brave father of yours. How is he?"

"We're both fine, Bea. How are you tonight?"

"Oh, I'm just great. Were you at that trial, Max? Are you going to testify? It's so exciting. And who is this lovely . . .You're Meagan Swoboda! Why, Max, you didn't tell me you two were a couple. You know, Meagan, Max's father and mother used to walk just like you and Max are walking now, right past my window. I used to watch them night after night."

"I'm sure you did, Bea."

"I miss her, I really do. Oh, look who I'm telling I miss poor Nancy." With that, Bea started to sob. Max reached toward her to put an arm around her shoulder, but she waved him off and ran back to her kitchen lookout, a worn tissue in one hand as she dabbed at her eyes.

"Our night watchman—woman," Max said.

"I have a feeling the neighborhood would be devastated if she ever left."

"No doubt."

"Max, what's all this about a mysterious large man with a beard? Everyone's buzzing about it."

"Am I now—what do they call it—deep background or something?"

"I guess so."

"Apparently, there was a woman, an elderly woman, in line right in front of Frank Rooney, and she didn't have her ticket stub either. They wouldn't give her her refund, and worse than that, she'd taken her two grandchildren to the movies with her so they screwed her out of the price of three tickets. I'm told she was very upset, almost weepy, and Frank watched this whole thing unfold. Finally, he couldn't take it anymore, and that's when he stepped in and grabbed the manager. Now, as luck would have it, the guy behind Frank was Alexander Hammermill."

"No. The guy on whose property the protesters camped out?"

"The very same."

"So he's the big man with the beard. But where's the little old lady with the grandchildren?"

"That's just it. We can't find her. Alexander hired a private investigator. We've plastered senior citizen homes with flyers. We considered putting an ad in the paper, but we thought the DA might find her first. We think she's afraid, and that's why she hasn't come forward."

"So why hasn't Sheridan told the jury about her?"

"Because if he promises a witness and then doesn't deliver, it looks bad. It could get Frank convicted. On the other hand, Alexander heard the whole thing and he was angry about it too, so when Frank grabbed the manager, Alexander stepped up beside him to fend off any attempt by others in the line to help the guy behind the window. What Sheridan was doing today was laying the groundwork for Alexander's testimony later in the trial. Now that the detective has admitted there was a large man with a beard, there's no fear that the jury will think Alexander is just some nut who's making her up."

"So Alexander will just testify about them refusing to refund her tickets, right?"

"Maybe."

"Why only maybe?"

"Because that's as much as I understand. Sheridan told me the jury might not hear it. I don't know why. Something about hearsay."

"Why not just ask the theater manager?"

"Because we don't know what he'll say. Maybe he'll remember the old lady, maybe he won't. Maybe he will remember but will lie about it."

"This trial business is like a chess game or some super complicated puzzle. Doesn't it make you want to go to . . ."

"No."

" . . . law school? Not even a little?"

"Meagan, in college I took a psych class and I learned about our ability to perceive spatial relationships. They do this test where they take an ordinary shape, like a triangle, that's been divided into various different smaller shapes—a square, a circle, a half moon—and then they ask the subject to arrange the smaller shapes so that they reassemble the triangle. Really little kids, like three and four year olds, do it easily. But a year or two later those same kids can't do it at all. What's happened in the interim?"

"I don't know."

"They've learned to read. Once that happens, the wiring in their brains changes, and the magic they were capable of is no longer possible. Or, to put it another way, it's been lassoed—corralled and broken. Law school, Meagan, is the ultimate lasso. I watched it happen while I was at Wisconsin. They take in people with the light of wonder still in their eyes and over the next three years something very strange happens to them. When their law school education is finished, so are they."

Chapter 38

Boris Petrovich was worried the protests might be seen as outside interference by the jurors, even though local news outlets had correctly reported large numbers of local people had marched in support of Frank Rooney from the start.

"Is like ccwhite people from north going south during civil rights cchera and cchaving southerners say, 'Cchwe don't need you down cchere.'"

"You know," said Christina Clark, "Cche's right."

Emails were sent out Monday night to encourage the locals to come out with signs and team T-shirts and jackets identifying their towns. On Tuesday the throng downhill from the courthouse looked like an all-sports Section Two tournament staging area. Niskayuna Silver Warrior soccer shirts marched with Bethlehem Girls' swim warm-ups and Shenendahowa football jackets. There were signs reading, "Delmartians say Free Frank," and "Albany High supports Frank," and "BSpa–BH is with Frank."

The Sweet Honey Gospel Singers stayed home, but the Reverend and Mother Ethel were there. So too were Florence Gezunterman, her son Scott, Mario Lambruzzo, Johann Mathison, and the Brindisis. Many of the marchers came inside to watch the trial. Meagan Swoboda was there, notebook in hand. Max and the rest of T.U.L.P.'s leadership waited outside.

"Let's see if we can wrap this up today, shall we?" said Judge Rheingold as he took the bench. In reality, he didn't think there was a prayer of finishing without a third day of testimony. He just felt that looking like he was trying to move things along was a good thing.

"The People call Harrison Connally to the stand."

It was the theater manager, and a collective rumble loud enough to make His Honor strike his gavel on the bench rose up from the crowd.

Jim Armstead's heart sank as he watched his star witness approach the stand. Armstead had met with Connally to prep for trial but hadn't thought to tell him what to wear. He'd worn tight black pants that might have been jeans and a black T-shirt underneath a black sport jacket. His hair was gelled and spiked. He brought with him an earring in one ear and a nose ring in the nostril on the opposite side. *At least his piercings are symmetrical,* thought the ADA. Compared to the cleancut family man Armstead was prosecuting, as well as every juror in the box, Connally looked like Sid Vicious.

Connally recounted the events of that night. The projector wasn't working. Customers who had ticket stubs would get refunds. Those who hadn't, wouldn't. That's what Mr. Remlinger had told him when he'd taken the job a year before.

"Then this guy starts hassling me because he didn't have his stub, like it was my fault. He wanted his refund and he was a jerk. A real jerk."

"How long did this go on?" said Armstead.

"Not long. Only a minute or two."

"What happened next?"

"He reached inside the hole in the window and grabbed my neck real hard and yanked me forward and crushed my head against the window."

"What did it feel like to you?"

"I was scared, I gotta tell ya. It felt like I was choking. He had a damn hard grip on my neck, and I couldn't get him to let go."

"What happened next?"

"Some other people came to help me, but they couldn't get his hands off me either. Then that detective guy came up, flashed his badge, and the guy let go."

"Now, before Mr. Rooney grabbed you, had you threatened him in any way?"

"No."

"Had you touched him or tried to touch him?"

"No."

"Where did you go after the detective arrested Mr. Rooney?"

"Home, but I went to the hospital the next day."

"Why didn't you go to the hospital that night?"

"It hurt right away but not as bad as it did the next morning."

"What complaints did you have at the hospital that next morning?"

"Pain in my jaw. I was worried the guy had broken my jaw. Plus, pain in my shoulders and pain shooting down my left arm and into my left hand. Plus, pain in my neck."

"What treatment did they give you?"

"They did X-rays and set me up for physical therapy."

"Now, did you miss any work because of this injury?"

"Yeah, about three days."

"Did you return to the hospital for further testing?"

"Yeah, I had an MRI that showed a herniated disc in my neck."

"How long after this incident was that diagnosis?"

"About a week."

And after the MRI, did they give you any devices or medication to help with the pain?"

"Yeah, painkillers, muscle relaxants, and a script for a neck brace."

"How do you feel now?"

"I still have pain. I have it every day. It got worse the week after the accident. It's a bit better now, but it's still there."

"Thank you. No further questions."

Sheridan waited for the Assistant DA to take his seat and rose slowly to his feet. He walked to a spot about six feet in front of the witness box, set his feet, pushed back the lapels of his jacket, and placed his hands in his pants pockets. To Frank Rooney, it looked like Sheridan was planning to take root there.

"Mr. Connally, this neck injury must have been quite a blow to you, am I right?"

"Yeah, and I still haven't recovered from it."

"I notice that neck brace you mentioned isn't with you today, is it?"

"No, I'll probably need it tonight, though."

"Those braces must be expensive, am I right?"

"I guess so."

"You don't know?"

"Well, insurance paid for it."

"So you bought it after this incident and sent the bill to your health insurance carrier. Is that right?"

"Something like that."

"Well, Mr. Connally, it was only about two months ago. You don't remember?"

"Yeah, that's what happened."

"Where did you buy the neck brace?"

"I got it from a store."

"What store?"

"What's the difference what store?"

"Please answer the question, sir. What was the name of the store?"

"I don't remember."

"Where was the store?"

"Objection," said the ADA. "Relevance."

"Overruled," said His Honor.

"Look, I really don't remember. I wasn't feeling well. A store in Albany somewhere."

"You've told us about how you had pain in your shoulder and arm. Did you also have weakness in those areas?"

"Yeah, very weak?"

"And in your elbow? Was your elbow on that same side feeling weak?"

"Yeah, that too. Very weak."

"Okay, back to the brace. When did you buy it?"

"When?"

"Yes, when?"

"After they told me I had a herniated disc."

"That was a week later, correct?"

"Yes," At this, the manager sighed and squirmed in his seat, as though answering the questions of a dim-witted child.

"You're sure about that?"

"Yeah." More sighing. "I'm sure."

Sheridan moved to the table at which the court clerk was sitting and picked up a thin stack of paper.

"I have in my hand Exhibit 1, which has been stipulated into evidence by both Mr. Armstead and myself. Exhibit 1 is the hospital record of your visit to St. Peter's Hospital in Albany for the MRI. I'll represent to the court that the date is indeed about a week later, as you say, eight days to be exact, and that you were indeed advised in the discharge summary that a neck brace might give you some relief. Does all this ring a bell for you?"

"Yes, it's what I've been telling you." Connally seemed agitated now.

"And it wasn't until the people at St. Peter's suggested the neck brace that you bought one, correct?"

"That's the way it went."

"Then if you were wearing a neck brace only three days after the incident, that would have nothing to do with the injury you claim to have suffered at the hands of Mr. Rooney, is that right, Mr. Connally?"

There was no answer from the witness, only the sound of his body shifting in its chair.

"Isn't it a fact, Mr. Connally, that when you returned to work three days after this incident, you were already wearing a neck brace?"

"Yeah, so? I guess it hurt worse than I remember."

"But you hadn't yet received the script for it from a doctor because you hadn't yet had your MRI, isn't that right?"

"Yeah, so?"

"So you don't remember where you got the brace, you don't remember when you got the brace, and you don't remember how much it cost, correct?"

"Like that makes a difference."

"It makes a difference, Mr. Connally, because you already had a neck brace from a car crash you were involved in three years ago, isn't that correct?"

No answer.

"Will Your Honor please instruct the witness to answer the question?"

"Please answer the question, Mr. Connally," said the judge.

"Yeah."

"And in that car crash, you injured the very same disc in your neck that you're now claiming was injured by Mr. Rooney, isn't that right?"

"I don't remember what the injury was. I'm not a doctor."

"You brought a lawsuit over that injury, didn't you, Mr. Connally?"

"Yeah."

"And in that lawsuit, you claimed you suffered a herniated disc in your neck and that the injury was permanent, isn't that right?"

"It was all legal mumbo-jumbo. I don't know what the attorneys said."

"Mr. Connally, when you told us just a few minutes ago that you'd gotten a neck brace because the doctor at St. Peter's had recommended it, and that you'd purchased it from a store here in Albany, and that you'd done so only after having your MRI eight days after the accident and, finally, that your insurance had paid for it, that sworn testimony was all —" here Sheridan paused, as though searching for the right word, "— incorrect, isn't that so?"

"Maybe I forgot some details, I guess."

"Getting back to the incident, Mr. Connally, you were the theater manager, correct?"

"Yes, I was."

"You had keys to the building?"

"Yes."

"You had the authority to hire and fire people?"

"Yes, I did."

"If a worker was doing something not to your liking, you had the authority to tell him or her to do the job differently, yes?"

"Yes."

"You had the authority to order items to be sold at the snack counter, soda and candy and such?"

"Yes, I did."

"But it's your sworn testimony, here before this jury, that you didn't have the authority to give a little old lady, crying and weeping over her lost money, a refund because she couldn't find her ticket stub, is that right?"

"Objection. Fact not in evidence," said Armstead.

"Well, sir, was there a little old lady in line in front of Mr. Rooney crying and weeping over the fact that you wouldn't refund her money because she couldn't find her refund?"

"I don't remember. The only guy from the line that I remember was the guy who assaulted me."

"Very well, then. Is it your testimony that you didn't have the authority to give Mr. Rooney back his refund?"

"That's right."

"You thought he'd been skulking around the theater, hoping a projector would break so he could scam you for the price of two tickets. Is that what you're telling us?"

"Look, no stub, no refund."

"Where did you announce that there was going to be a refund?"

"Inside the theater."

"That particular one, the one where *Black Swan* was playing?"

"Yes."

"So only those people sitting there waiting for that particular movie to begin would've heard the announcement, correct?"

"So?"

"So you didn't post a notice on the outside door or announce it in the lobby, am I right?"

"No, we didn't do those things. So?"

"How on earth would anyone have known about the refund if they hadn't been in the theater?"

"That's not my problem."

"And if they were in the theater, wouldn't that mean they were entitled to a refund?"

"Not without a stub."

"How much does a ticket to the movies at the Rialto Theater cost?"

"Ten bucks."

"So you thought my client—a middle-aged, tenured professor at RPI with a wife and three kids—somehow managed—without buying a ticket—to find out that the projector at the Rialto Theater that was about to show *Black Swan* was broken and a refund was being offered, and decided to sneak into line to scam Maiko out of twenty dollars. Is that your testimony?"

"Objection! Form." Mr. Armstead was on his feet.

"Withdrawn," said the Cowboy. "Mr. Connelly, have you been taking it easy since this incident, generally speaking?"

"Yeah."

"Because of the pain?

"Yeah."

"Do you wear those earrings all the time?"

"What's it to you?"

"May I have an answer, please?"

"When I'm awake, yeah."

"Mr. Connally, I'm going to show you something, with the court's permission, if we can just have the clerk take this to the reporter to have it marked to identification."

Sheridan produced a photograph from under some papers on his desk and handed it to the clerk.

"Now, please take a look at this photo and tell me if the man in the photo is you."

Connally peered at the picture for a long while, eyebrows furrowed.

"Take your time, Mr. Connally, but I want you to know I've got the man who took that picture waiting in the hallway to testify if need be."

"Objection!" yelled ADA Armstead. "Move to strike!"

"Yes," said His Honor. "Sustained. Mr. Sheridan's last comments are stricken from the record. We'll have none of that, counsel. Just tell us if you recognize what's depicted in that photo, Mr. Connally."

"I guess that's me."

"That's you on a boat on Lake George, isn't it?

"Yeah."

"And you were in that boat, on that lake just two weeks ago, were you not?"

"Yeah, so? I'm just along for the ride."

"Yes, you're in a boat that's pulling a water skier, isn't that correct?"

"Yeah, but I'm not driving and I'm not skiing."

"You're doing what is commonly called riding shotgun, isn't that right?

"Right."

"And for those who don't know, that means, you look back to see if the skier falls, so you can tell the driver to stop and turn around and go pick him up, correct?"

"Yeah."

"Now the driver has to look forward, for obvious reasons, right?

"Right."

"But you're turned, or twisted in your seat so as to be able to see behind, where the skier is, isn't that right?"

"Right."

"One last thing. What's that thing in your hand?"

"A can."

"A can of what?"

"I don't know."

"It's not Budweiser beer?"

"I said I don't know."

"No further questions."

Every pair of eyes in the courtroom was on Sheridan as he took his seat, with the exception of Armstead's.

"Mr. Connally," the ADA said, not waiting for the judge's cue, "when was the last time you were treated by a health care provider for the injuries you suffered in that car crash?"

"About three years ago."

"And in that three-year span, have you had any treatment at all for your neck?"

"No. None."

"Have you had any cause to miss work or take medication during that intervening three-year period because of pain in your neck?"

"No, not at all."

"The moment before the defendant grabbed you, how did you feel?"

"I felt fine."

"Any problems with your neck then?"

"No."

"But now?"

"It hurts bad."

"Now, do you have a boss at the theater?"

"Yes, Charlie Remlinger."

"And while you order the food for the snack counter, if Mr. Remlinger tells you to order it from a different vendor, do you have to do it?"

"Oh, yeah."

"If he tells you to hire or fire someone, do you have to do it?"

"Yes."

"And if he tells you the policy is no refund without a ticket stub, do you have to enforce that policy?"

"You bet."

"Mr. Connally, how much effort is involved in riding in a boat?"

"None. None at all."

"Thank you."

Sheridan stood up again.

"One more thing, Mr. Connally. Did anyone, as far as you know, check the receipts to compare the amount of money refunded to the amount taken in?"

"I'm not sure about that."

"That would not have been your job, is that what you're telling us?"

"That's right. Mr. Remlinger has somebody else do that."

"Do you know how to do it?"

"Yeah, they showed me how. I've done it a couple of times, but he usually has an accountant come in."

"Tell us Mr. Connally, how long does it take to perform that function?"

"It's all computerized. Five minutes, tops."

"To this day, have the receipts for that night ever been checked?"

"I don't know."

"Thank you. No further questions." Sheridan sat down.

"Mr. Armstead, call your next witness," said His Honor.

"The People call Dr. Sharma Patel to the stand."

Dr. Patel was the radiologist who read the MRI taken of Connally's neck. Under direct questioning by Armstead, he told the jury that Mr.

Connally had a slightly herniated disc between the fifth and sixth vertebra of the cervical spine and that was the reason for the pain and weakness in his left shoulder, elbow, and arm.

"The term herniation is something of a variable thing, would you agree, doctor?" asked Sheridan for his first question.

"Somewhat. There are discs between the vertebrae in your spinal column, and they can move, they can rupture, they can move and rupture. Two doctors will look at the same film, and one will say the disc is herniated and the other might say it's only bulging. The key is whether the disc is impinging or touching the thecal sac through which the spinal cord runs. If it is, there's pain. If it isn't, the bulge or herniation, whatever you want to call it, is insignificant."

"Is it clear to you that the cord is impinging in Mr. Connally's case?"

"No. But it could be. It's close."

"So you're compelled to tell us the disc injury is the cause of his arm pain because he tells you he hurts, is that so?"

"Yes, plus the fact that the films do show an abnormality."

"And if what he tells you about his pain isn't true, your diagnosis would be wrong, correct?"

"Of course."

"You've seen presentations like this where the patient has no pain, have you not?"

"Yes, I have."

"Can you tell us for certain when this disc problem, if it is a problem, first appeared?"

"Not really. It could be an old injury. It could be an aggravation of an old injury. It could be a new injury."

"Will this injury become permanent?"

"Can't say for certain. In most cases, with a patient as young as this, no. But it's possible."

"Well, Mr. Connally was in court just before you were, and he was not wearing his neck brace. Is that a good sign?"

"I really can't say. Either he's feeling better, or he just doesn't like the brace, or maybe he doesn't want to wear it in public."

"Is it possible that his disc is back to where it belongs right now?"

"Yes, it is. I wouldn't know without another set of films."

"Can you injure a disc in this fashion in a car crash?"

"It's possible."

"Is it possible the disc, as shown on these films, is just where it's been since Mr. Connally had an automobile accident three years ago?"

"I didn't know he had an automobile accident, but it could be. I wouldn't know without checking the films from that time."

"If Mr. Connally alleged three years ago that he had weakness in his shoulder and elbow resulting from an injury to his neck at C5 to C6, would that be consistent with his having herniated the same disc then that he's claiming is herniated now?"

"Yes, we're talking about the disc at that same location, and if it's herniated or bulging enough, it will cause those symptoms. As I understand it, he has some of those same symptoms now."

"Has anyone from the DA's office asked you to look at the films taken of Mr. Connally's neck from three years ago?"

"No, they have not."

"Would you have been better able to tell this jury exactly what the extent of Mr. Connally's injury is from the incident at the movie theater if you had seen those old films and been able to compare them to the new ones?"

"I would."

"And without having looked at the films from three years ago are you able to tell this jury how much of the injury to Mr. Connally's neck was caused by the car crash and how much was caused by the incident at the movie theater?"

Dr. Patel, whose answers had been coming as quickly as Sheridan's questions, hesitated.

"Take your time, doctor." The Cowboy oozed graciousness. Five seconds ticked by. Ten. Fifteen.

"Not really. But I do believe he suffered some injury to his neck from the incident at the theater."

"Okay, but given the fact that he's no longer wearing his neck brace and the fact that you've no follow-up film to look at, it's possible Mr. Connally's injury is nothing more than a simple sprain from which he's already on the mend, isn't that correct?"

"That's correct, yes."

"And even if someone were to conclude he has a herniated disc in his neck, that disc could have been herniated because of the car crash three years ago, isn't that also correct?"

"Yes, it is."

"No further questions."

"Ladies and gentlemen," said His Honor. "It's time for lunch."

"If the DA rests his case, you're going on this afternoon," said Sheridan as he nodded at his client. They were in a conference room inside the courthouse eating a pizza Ms. Whit had brought in. Alexander and Cindy Hammermill were there too. "You first, though," said the Cowboy, pointing to the bearded sculptor. "You know what I'm gonna ask and I think you've got a pretty good idea of what Armstead is gonna ask. Do either of you have any questions?"

"Yeah," said Alexander. "How're we doing?"

"I don't sit on that chair till the paint is dry," said Sheridan.

"Of course not," said Hammermill, rolling his eyes as his wife pinched his thigh under the table. "Whatever possessed me to ask?"

Armstead rested his case as soon as court reconvened. Sheridan then called Alexander Hammermill to the stand. Wearing blue overalls over a white long-sleeve shirt, with work boots on his feet, the big man nearly trotted to the witness stand.

Out in the audience, Mario Lambruzzo leaned over to Scott Gezunterman and whispered, "He's the guy whose sculpture started it all. It was in my store. A laughing woman came in one day and understood the whole thing. Then this skinny Rodriguez kid follows right behind her and . . ."

"Wait," said Scott. "Was the laughing woman a blond? Great shape? Blue jeans?"

"Yeah. How did . . ."

"Sha!" said Mrs. Gezunterman.

"Mr. Hammermill, please tell the jurors what happened the last time you went to the movies at the Rialto Theater on Campbell Avenue in Albany."

"Well, we went to see a movie called *Black Swan*, but the movie wasn't shown. We just sat there until a kid who worked for the theater announced the projector was broken and that everyone would be given a refund along with a free pass to come back and see another movie. So we all went out to the lobby and lined up at the ticket booth."

"You were in line with your wife?"

"Yes. And the line was moving along and then there was an argument."

"Tell us about that."

"Objection. Hearsay."

"Mr. Sheridan?" said Judge Rheingold.

"These words are not being offered for the truth of their content but, rather, to establish my client's motivation at the time of the incident in question."

"Then my objection is relevance," said the ADA. "His motivation is irrelevant. I don't have to prove it, and it doesn't matter what it was."

"In chambers, gentlemen. Ladies and gentlemen of the jury, ten minutes."

Sheridan and Ms. Whit followed the judge through the door behind the bench, with ADA Armstead right behind.

"Take a seat," the judge offered. "Now, Mr. Sheridan, why isn't this testimony hearsay?"

"First off, there's already been testimony about having to show your ticket stub to get your refund and free pass, so there's no dispute about that. As to the rest, the issue is not whether the old lady in front of my client had lost her ticket stub or cried about not getting her refund or was there with her grandchildren. The issue is what my client heard. It goes to intent. He had no intention to hurt Mr. Connally. He was pushed to the brink in defense of the little old lady."

"Mr. Armstead?"

"Nonsense. Uh, with all due respect, of course. There's no evidence, nor will there be evidence, that the old lady was in physical danger. Nobody was attacking her, which means there was no need to attack anyone else to protect her. So there's no justification argument. In addition, Connally was on the stand. Mr. Sheridan asked him about the old lady, and Connally said he didn't remember her. There was no further testimony on that topic. Now counsel wants to backdoor the thing by having Mr. Hammermill, who was not a party to the conversation, testify about what was said."

"Mr. Rooney was charged with intentionally assaulting Mr. Connally. Rooney's state of mind is relevant," said Sheridan.

"There's also a count alleging reckless assault, isn't there, Mr. Armstead?"

"Yes, Your Honor."

"Are you willing to drop the count alleging intent? It would take away defendant's relevance argument."

"That depends on how you rule on my objection." With that, Sheridan shot a look at Ms. Whit, his eyebrows raised in approval of the young ADA.

"Well, is that it, Mr. Sheridan?"

"No, Your Honor. There's a bigger picture here. These jurors are free to find my client not guilty no matter what the proof. They're free to apply their own sense of justice, to do what John Adams and Thomas Jefferson said they should be able to do."

"Aha, we're back to jury nullification, aren't we?"

"Yes, we are. Look, it's bad enough I can't tell these jurors they have the right to do what you and I know they can do. But don't make it even more unfair by preventing me from presenting all the facts of the case. If they're going to view the case as a whole and render a verdict based on fairness and justice and truth, don't they need to know what happened that night? Why present a case to them piecemeal, constricted by some hyper-technical view of the law? We're not accountants from the IRS going over someone's tax return. We're in a court of law deciding the fate of a man who's never been in trouble before in his life. I'm seeking justice here, Judge Rheingold. Please don't tell me I've come to the wrong place."

Judge Rheingold sat back in his chair, contemplating how many votes he could get by handling this moment just right. Going back into the courtroom and saying simply, "Objection overruled," would be an unforgivable waste of an opportunity. On the other hand, quoting from the Book of Deuteronomy might be laying it on a bit thick, and no judge running for election wants to appear overly concerned with justice for the defendant.

"Don't drop any of your assault counts, kid," the judge said to the ADA. "I'm letting it in either way."

They shuffled back to the courtroom.

"I'm going to overrule the objection and allow this line of questioning to continue," he announced to the courtroom. "I'm sure this jury is more than qualified to make sense of what they hear."

Brilliant, he thought, *the populist route. Putting it all on the jury's shoulders makes it look like I'm a man of the people. Never mind that it's my job to decide what the jurors are supposed to hear in the first place.*

The jury then heard from Alexander about the old lady's tears at having lost her ticket stubs and how Frank Rooney was next in line, seemingly picking up the banner of her cause.

"Is there anything that made you take particular note of the events of that evening?" asked Sheridan.

"Yes—my membership in an organization called T.U.L.P., which stands for Treat Us Like People. We're a group dedicated to fighting corporate abuse of individuals, and what was going on in the theater that night seemed exactly the kind of thing we should get involved in. There you had this theater manager refusing to offer a refund unless the customer had a ticket stub when everyone in the world, including him, knew perfectly well that the old lady and Mr. Rooney were entitled to one. I mean, who other than people inside the theater would've known to get in line for the refund? Yet because of some arbitrary policy the manager was holding fast. It was ridiculous. It was also magical."

"Why magical?

"Because there, right in front of me, was the whole issue, an issue I'd thought for years was so important. And here this little old lady and this ordinary-looking guy were reacting just like I thought everyone should."

"Thank you. No further questions."

Jesse Armstead had been wildly scribbling notes until the witness began talking about magic. Then, as if suddenly realizing exactly where he wanted to go, he put down his pen.

"Magic? Did you tell us you believe in magic, Mr. Hammermill?"

Valerie Whit looked sideways at her boss.

"Yes, I did."

"Can you give us another example of magic, Mr. Hammermill?"

Whit looked at her boss again, this time imploringly. Still, no objection.

"This whole affair had a magical beginning," said Hammermill.

"Tell us about it," said Armstead.

Whit put her head down and stared at her lap.

"The way this entire protest has coalesced around this issue has been magical. No organization can create this kind of response out of whole cloth. The energy for it has to come from somewhere. It's as if it's been lying dormant, just beneath the surface, for years and then suddenly it springs to life in a way that's entirely positive. I think that's magical."

"Mr. Hammermill, how much of what you do is determined by magic?"

"You know what, Mr. Armstead? Life can be frustrating and tough. I try for as much magic as I can get. That and some good barbeque once or twice a week and I'm good to go."

The courtroom responded with a warm round of laughter. Judge Rheingold tapped his gavel a couple of times and it stopped.

"No further questions."

"And you, Mr. Sheridan?" said His Honor.

"Thank you, Your Honor. Mr. Hammermill, how many people do you estimate have joined T.U.L.P. in the six weeks since Frank Rooney's arrest?"

"That's a moving target, really. They've been signing up so fast. But when last I checked, which was a couple of days ago, it was about a quarter of a million."

"That's about two hundred fifty thousand new members?"

"Yes, it is."

"With more joining every day?"

"Yes, we're having a hard time keeping up."

"And the big rally in support of my client that took place just right here in Albany following Frank's arrest—did you help organize that?"

"Yes, I did."

"What was your main contribution to that effort?"

"I hosted the campers. The people who set up tents and so on. The newspapers called it Little Woodstock. That was on my property."

"How many people would you estimate stayed on your property that weekend?"

"I'd say at least twenty-five hundred, maybe more."

"And all this was arranged within a matter of days and hours, isn't that so?"

"Yes, it was."

"That's all pretty magical, wouldn't you say?"

"There isn't a doubt in my mind."

The Cowboy sat down.

"Next witness, Mr. Sheridan."

"The defense calls Frank Rooney to the stand."

Cheers erupted from the crowd. Mrs. Gezunterman rose to her feet, as if to signal that clapping from a seated position was not good enough. She had to be steadied by her son because when she arose, her blood pressure did not come with her. All the while she continued to clap, which only inspired those who hadn't yet stood to do so, and the entire crowd began to make noise. His Honor tried to get them to quiet with a downward wave of his hands, then finally resorted to the gavel.

The testimony began slowly, methodically, with Frank describing a life that was successful, if not gloriously so, and had, until the date of this incident, been led with nothing resembling fanfare. Working-class Irish family in the Bronx; Columbia University on full academic scholarship; graduated magna cum laude, and then on to Cornell for his master's and Ph.D. in chemistry. He was a tenured full professor and had been teaching for over twenty years at RPI, during which time he'd been the source of a number of lucrative research grants for the university. He never had a single complaint filed against him by faculty or students. He had three loving daughters who were all seated in the front row with his wife, to whom he'd been happily married for a quarter of a century.

He had a distant recollection of marching in protest of the war in Vietnam when he was in high school or maybe junior high school. He couldn't recall ever protesting anything else.

Frank enjoyed classical music and fiction. For exercise he swam, a sport he'd picked up while at Columbia and become moderately good at. His girls followed suit and as a result Frank spent a lot of his free time coaching them and their swim teams, as well as driving them to practices and meets. For vacations, Frank took his family to one or two national parks every summer where they hiked, rafted, and looked at wildlife.

He'd never been arrested, always paid his taxes on time, and drank an occasional beer in the summer. He'd had nothing to drink the night of the incident.

And the last time he'd ever raised his hand to another human being in anger?

"Never, Mr. Sheridan. I've never tried to hurt another human being in all my life."

"Just so it's crystal clear, Frank. Does that include the night of this incident?"

"Yes. Absolutely. Never."

"So what happened at the movie theater?"

"The part with the old lady and their refusal to return her money was pretty much as Alexander Hammermill described it. But suddenly, a light went on. It was as though I'd been storing up frustration for years and the nonsense over the lost ticket stub was the last straw."

"Tell us about that frustration."

At this, Rooney sat back in his chair, as if preparing for the emotional drain of a long, revealing answer.

"I'd been working on a grant proposal for my department at the university and it seemed there was another professor who felt his interests would be better served if I didn't get it. It was childish, really. We should've been working together, but it's as if no one thinks that way anymore. Whether it's at a university or a theater or anywhere, cooperation is viewed as weakness.

"And I'd been reading the newspaper before we left for the theater. There was a sex scandal involving a congressman—an alleged scandal, anyway. It's all so tiring. From politics to work to something so simple as going to a movie. It's as though life has become a giant game of Gotcha.

"The banks are the worst. They keep terrible records, then sell their so-called bad debt to debt collectors. But since the record keeping is so bad, the collectors' records don't conform to what the bank has, and neither conforms to what the customer has. And who gets taken advantage of? The debtor, the poorest guy in the chain. The credit card contracts are unbelievably one sided. Most don't even require that the bank provide proper documentation, so the customer has to do it. Most of the card holders have no lawyers and don't know their rights. They just get steamrolled.

"Now, while this is happening, the original bank that you dealt with is out of the picture. It has repackaged and forgotten you. Good-bye and good riddance.

"And the only way any of this comes to light is if some bank gets nailed in a multi-million dollar lawsuit or a government agency fine. Left to their own devices, they'll eat our lunch every day.

"I mean, it's like our entire culture is devoted to people taking advantage of each other. And the guys who figure out how to do that best are hailed as heroes. The concept of pulling together for the common good is not only gone, it's laughable.

"But the Rialto Theater is not a bank, Frank. Why that moment and that place? What was it about that very situation that made you react the way you did?"

"I think it just struck me that we've allowed ourselves to get to this point by behaving as if we're all strangers. One guy in a bank may come up with an idea to fleece a million customers, but he can't do it alone. He needs thousands of employees to help him pull it off. Customer representatives, accountants, lawyers, secretaries, the list is endless. The guy at the head of any big company can't abuse anyone alone. He always needs help.

"And banks are only the tip of the iceberg. Insurance companies are right behind them. Investment brokers, airlines, department stores, hotels—any large corporation, really. Once the entity has lost the personal connection to its customers and can get others—its employees — to do these things for it, all sense of decency is gone. That's the key, Mr. Sheridan. Personal identification.

"But we're still human beings. We still feel and think and cry and hope, and no corporate policy can take those things from us unless we voluntarily give them up.

"If any one person in that line at the theater knew that woman, he'd have come to her aid. But since no one did, they were content to let her be abused. That's what the corporations do to us. In the long run, they take away our sense of community and with it, our humanity.

"I decided I wasn't going to let that happen. I decided that for that one moment, that person was someone I knew."

"What did you want to accomplish when you grabbed that manager?"

"I wanted him to stop. That's all. I just wanted him to stop behaving like he was behaving. I wanted something human from him. I wanted him to stop doing the corporation's dirty work."

"Did you wish to hurt him?"

"No. Not at all."

"Frank, did you hear Detective Zito describe how he separated you from Mr. Connally and had you sit in the lobby to wait for a patrol car?"

"Yes, I did."

"And Mr. Connally wanted to get back at you and fight some more and you said, 'Let him go, I'm ready for him,' or words to that effect."

"Yes."

"Did it happen that way?"

"Yes, it did."

"What was that all about?"

"You know, I think I was as surprised by that as anyone. I think I just felt I had no choice. I'd decided to step in and help that old lady and this guy, this corporate guy, was daring me to maintain that position, and I wasn't going to back down. It was a matter of principle."

"Did you feel confident you'd prevail if there were fisticuffs at that point?"

"Strangely, I did. I knew I'd never been in a fight before, but I knew I'd win. I had right on my side and he had—what? Company policy?"

"Thank you, Frank. No further questions."

ADA Armstead was on his feet before His Honor could say, "Your witness."

"Professor Rooney, did Mr. Connally threaten that elderly lady?"

"Well, that's kind of a moot point, isn't it? He was making her cry."

"But did he threaten her with physical harm?"

"No."

"Did he threaten you?

"No."

"Did he threaten anyone else?"

"No."

"True or false, professor: if you hadn't grabbed Mr. Connally, there wouldn't have been any violence whatsoever that evening."

"I'm not trying to be cute, Mr. Armstead, but I think making an old lady cry for no good reason is a kind of violence."

"I mean no physical violence. There would have been no physical violence if not for you, isn't that correct?"

"I guess so."

"Well, nobody grabbed you, isn't that so?"

"That's so."

"And certainly Mr. Connally didn't grab anyone, isn't that right?"

"That's right."

"Other members of the Rialto staff came to Mr. Connally's aid while you had a hold of his throat, isn't that right?"

"I'm not clear on that. I know other people were there."

"But you wouldn't let go until Detective Zito waved his badge under your nose and ordered you to let go, isn't that right?"

"That is when I let go, that's correct."

"And as you just told us, you were ready for more just a few minutes later, weren't you?"

"If Mr. Connally had forced the issue, yes, I was."

"Professor, don't the kids who sit in your classroom have rules they have to follow?"

"Rules, yes. Rip-offs, no. What the Rialto was doing was ripping off this woman."

"I see. And you get to decide which is which?"

"We're all given some responsibility for that decision."

"Well, what about you, sir? Don't you have rules set down by your university? Codes of conduct? Conflict of interest rules? Workload requirements?"

"Yes, of course, but all those rules are designed to help the university achieve the higher goal of teaching students. You're an educated man yourself. I don't know you personally, but if you're an Assistant District Attorney that means you've completed college and law school, and I'm sure the schools you attended had similar rules to the ones you've just described, and you benefited from them. However, the rules we're talking about in this case, the rules put in place by the Rialto, were not meant to help that woman. They were meant to hurt her and at the same time help the Rialto and its parent corporation, Maiko. That's my point. They're preying on the helpless in order to help the strong."

"So everyone decides for themselves what rules they will and won't abide by and if the verdict is a thumbs down they reach for the nearest throat and grab for all they're worth. Is that the world you propose to have us live in, professor?"

"Not at all. I say everyone treats each other with kindness, kindness, and more kindness, and if someone tries to stop you, grab *that* fellow by the throat, but don't hurt him too badly."

With that, Frank Rooney couldn't help but flash a smile at the jury. A few jurors smiled back, Cowboy Bob grinned from ear to ear and about one hundred reasonably shod spectators clad in environmentally friendly clothing chuckled out loud.

"Listen," said Alexander Hammermill, leaning over to his wife. "Is that a pulse I hear?"

"No further questions," said the ADA.

"Ten minutes," said His Honor. "Counsel in chambers, please."

"Okay, gentlemen," said Judge Rheingold. "Will there be anything else?"

"I'll need a moment to consult with my assistant, Judge, as to whether we're going to call our own doctor on the issue of physical injury. I'm thinking right now we're not. We'll just take our chances with what the DA's doc said. Either way, I do have a written brief on the case law on that issue that I'd like to submit, along with my motion."

"That's fine. I'll take your motion and your brief and give you a few minutes to talk it over. Mr. Armstead, how about you?"

"Well, Your Honor, I may have a rebuttal witness."

"Rebuttal? We don't see that down here in local court very often. This is in response to what issue?"

"The little old lady crying over not getting her refund. She was news to me."

"And who do you plan to call to rebut that testimony?"

"I have Charlie Remlinger on standby."

"He's the owner of the Rialto, is he not?"

"Yes, he is, and the president of Maiko Corporation."

"Was he there?"

"No, he wasn't."

"Well, then, how is he going to rebut the testimony?"

"He can't rebut it directly. That is, he can't say the old lady did not have her ticket, or that there was no old lady, but he can explain the policy, which Connally couldn't do. Defendant's position is Mr. Connally was making up these rules on the fly, that he was withholding the poor woman's refund out of pure meanness, and I should be allowed to prove it's not so."

"Sounds reasonable to me. Mr. Sheridan."

"Let's have at him, Judge."

"I've got him on phone alert, Judge. May I have a half hour's recess?"

Scott Gezunterman grabbed hold of Mario Lambruzzo's arm the moment he heard the word recess. "I have to know about the blond," he said.

"I can see that."

"*Is mishuga*," said Mrs. Gezunterman. "Your mother finds you a nice girl and that's not good enough, but you hear about some strange woman who looks at statues and that's the one you want?"

"Did she tell you her name?" said Scott to the captured vintage clothier.

"Jane, maybe. Or June. Could've been Gillian."

"Congratulations, Sherlock. Now you're really narrowing it down," said Mrs. Gezunterman.

"What kind of car did she drive?"

"An SUV of some kind."

"A Pathfinder?"

"Could be. I really don't know."

Mrs. Gezunterman looked at her son and made a face that was one part disgust, two parts frustration, and a touch of what-do-I-have-to-do-to-get-through-to-this-knucklehead. It was a face that required no explanation, but she nonetheless added, "From this you're going to find romance?"

Bill Coleman had known that any time spent trying to educate his client to be a less abrasive and therefore more effective witness was time wasted. But he also knew that the meeting to prep Remlinger, should he be called to testify about the Rialto's ticket policy, was what lawyers got paid for, so at least Coleman had been able to bill for it.

"I suggest a sport coat and tie. Something that suggests you've got respect for the court, but you're not the corporate millionaire fat cat that Sheridan is making you out to be."

"I'll wear what I want."

"If you're called, be respectful and courteous at all times. That doesn't mean you don't fight back and it doesn't mean you don't stand up for yourself. It only means you must do so politely. No arrogance and no wise guy stuff. The judge is Your Honor. The ADA is Mr. Armstead. The defense lawyer is Mr. Sheridan, and the defendant is Mr. Rooney."

"That lawyer is a pinko fag. Rooney is a tree-hugging chicken-shit. I can't believe they're letting a rookie DA—and a black one at that—handle this case, and if that skinny little spokesperson sonofabitch punk shows up, I'll break his fuckin' neck."

"Well, this is moving along swimmingly. Now, as for your policy of having to show a ticket stub to get a refund . . ."

"What about it?"

"Yes, that's my question. Why do you have to show a ticket stub?"

"Oh, come on, Bill. Am I the only guy left with a brain that works? It's a multiplex! We got seven screens going. So you see one movie, it ends, you walk over and sit your ass down to watch another. The projector dies in the second theater, they announce a refund and bingo you get a free movie."

"You can't be serious."

"Man, are you naïve. How about this: the people who really were in the theater with the broken projector come out and they're talking. They pass through the line of people waiting for popcorn and those people decide to take a quick detour to the ticket booth to score a freebie. Or maybe some people coming out of another theater on their way home see what's going on, and they decide it's time to rip off old Chaz."

"I suggest in the strongest possible terms that you not give those reasons as the basis for your policy."

Remlinger mimicked his attorney. "Suggest in the strongest possible terms. What does that phrase mean, Bill? Because when you say 'strongest possible terms,' you don't even raise your voice. Those are the reasons, kiddo, and that's what I'm telling them, and assuming they're not candy-ass Ivy Leaguers like you, they'll understand."

"You know what I'm doing, Chaz? I'm charging you double for this consultation, because every minute with you is like two minutes with anyone else. You're a true paranoid.

"My final piece of advice is that you tell that jury you really never gave the matter much thought one way or another and that the simplest thing seemed to be to ask that the customers show their ticket stubs. Tell them that whenever you went to the movies you always put the stub in your pocket, and whenever you ran the ticket booth when you were younger, the customers always seemed to do the same and it never occurred to you that someone would lose a ticket or discard it and that a projector would break and this problem would arise. My advice is that you play it down the middle. Tell them you would not have been upset if Mr. Connally had given the old lady back her money, as well as the Rooneys, but on the other hand Mr. Connally is a valued and trusted employee who was only doing as he was told. Tell them what's truly outrageous about this case is that the focus seems to be on the loss of the price of a ticket to the movies instead of the fact that an innocent human being was assaulted. Tell them that if Mr. Rooney was that upset about your policy he could have come to see you personally and you'd have been glad to speak with him about it in a calm, civilized manner in your office, without violence and without anyone getting hurt and that if, after listening to Mr. Rooney, you felt the policy was unfair, you'd have changed it. But now that Mr. Rooney has taken the tact of assaulting your employee, you're standing behind Mr. Connally one hundred percent and you're asking the jury to do so as well.

"That's my advice to you, Chaz. Tell them that and they'll convict him."

"You know what, Bill, don't charge me double. Charge me triple. That's my good-bye present to you. You're fired."

Max Rodriguez, standing outside the courthouse, watched in wonder as a black BMW 740i with a license plate that read CHAZ, this time with no blond in the passenger seat, charged past him on Pearl Street and pulled into a parking garage. The event caused him to become suddenly taken with the circular nature of things, so taken that he failed to observe that the Nissan Pathfinder he'd noticed the day after first seeing the same big BMW had itself pulled in to a metered parking spot just yards from where he was standing. And since Max decided to remain there and watch the entrance to the parking garage to see if he recognized the man who might walk out as the man from Dr. Java's, he never saw Jane exit the Pathfinder and head toward the courthouse, nor did he notice two storefront neon signs—one that had been shouting Pizza and another Fresh Bagels—that started blinking erratically as Jane passed by.

Chaz exited the parking garage a block north of Pearl, depriving Max of the closure Max thought he desired.

Jane sat outside in the lobby, having brought her daughter into the courtroom to provide moral support for her dad.

"Thank you for coming down on short notice, Mr. Remlinger," began the questioning from ADA Armstead.

"No problem, kid."

"How did you come to own Maiko Theaters?"

"I've always liked the movies and I thought it would be fun. I bought the theater back about twelve years ago. It only had two screens then, just foreign movies. I expanded the building, remodeled, turned it into a movie destination. We started running low-brow and high-brow movies, not just the foreign stuff. If a movie was really packing 'em in, we'd run it on two screens, maybe even three, yet we always had at least two foreign flicks going. That way we kept our profitability and the loyalty of the foreign moviegoers at the same time."

"It was a good formula?"

"Oh, yeah. We've expanded to seven cities so far, with more on the drawing board."

Chaz seemed immediately comfortable on the witness stand, giving Armstead a gnawing feeling of discomfort.

"Now, to the main reason I asked you to testify in this case. Tell us about Maiko's policy regarding refunds when shows have to be canceled for one reason or another."

With that, and as if to add an extra dose of reproof to his ex-attorney, Chaz gave the explanation for his policy that he'd given his lawyer the night before, only with more variations on his themes and greater gusto. Not a single paranoid possibility was left untouched. He ended with, "And there's a tea house/coffee shop/God-knows-what place right next door to my theater. It would be nothing for people coming out of there, walking by my lobby, to look inside the window, see what's going on, duck inside my place and glom some freebies at my expense."

When he finished, he reached for a glass of water, appearing to the stunned ADA like he was expecting the courthouse to break into applause.

Silence, punctuated by suppressed giggles, filled the room. Several jurors looked at each other for visual confirmation of what they'd just heard. The audience was a sea of rotating heads topped with un-dyed gray hair.

Searching, Armstead alit upon a question to which he already knew the answer. "Was Mr. Connally just doing what he'd been told to do?"

"Damn straight he was."

"No further questions."

"Mr. Remlinger, you started your business empire with a landscaping business, isn't that right?" asked the Cowboy.

"Yup."

"And the way you started out was at the very bottom, by mowing grass, right?"

"Bottom of the barrel and worked my way up to the top. You got it, mister."

"Well, work was only part of the story. The truth is you muscled the competition away by slashing the tires and smashing the windshields of the trucks of your competitors, isn't that true?"

"Nothing of the sort. Look, a lot of people don't like my success, and I'm sure that's where you're getting this stuff. The fact is business is not for sissies."

"But you like muscling people even when it's not business, don't you, Mr. Remlinger?"

"What do you have, my dossier?"

"Well, you like to boast about the things that you've done, so compiling a dossier on you is not too difficult, would you agree?"

"I'm proud of what I've accomplished."

"One of the things you did was to beat up your new brother-in-law so badly he needed to go to the hospital after the first time you met him at a family Thanksgiving dinner, isn't that right, Mr. Remlinger?"

"He was a jerk. A real jerk."

"Although now that you're a more successful man you don't beat people up anymore. Now, you pay other people to beat people up for you, isn't that right?"

"Watch yourself, fella. I can still take care of myself."

"You sent teams of goons out to harass and beat up T.U.L.P. marchers who were peacefully marching along Utah Street a few weeks ago, isn't that right, Mr. Remlinger?"

"It was my guys who got beat up!"

"Oh, so you admit you sent teams of men into the crowd. Why did you do that?"

"What's the difference? Some big blond guy beat them up."

"Really? One big blond guy? How many of your men did he beat up, Mr. Remlinger?"

"Two, three. What's the difference?"

"But why were your guys out there in the first place? You still haven't told us that."

With that, Charlie Remlinger's head and upper body began shifting around as his eyes scanned the audience in what looked like an effort to find the big blond guy. But the Cowboy had anticipated something like this. As soon as he heard Remlinger was coming to testify, he had ordered Johann Mathison back to the Brindisis.

"I'm right here, Mr. Remlinger," said Sheridan, standing in front of the witness box. "You want to stop squirming and tell us why you had teams of men roaming through the crowd that day?"

"Objection!" called out ADA Armstead.

"Yeah," said His Honor. "We've gotten a bit far afield here. Now let's get back to . . ."

"Son-of-a-gun. You miserable little punk!" Screaming, Chaz rose to his feet and pointed into the audience. Sheridan turned and followed the pointed finger, along with everyone else in the courthouse, to Max Rodriguez, who was seated in the third row of the audience.

"I'm gonna get my hands on you, you little punk. Nobody messes with Chaz Remlinger like you did!"

For a split second, there was silence. Then Gus DeMauro got up and moved from a seat two rows away to take a spot next to Max. As he did, the courtroom exploded.

"Mr. Remlinger!" His Honor boomed. "Mr. Remlinger!" Chaz was still shouting something. No one could hear it over the din. "Sit down and keep quiet. This is a court of law, and you are one very small step from being removed from it in handcuffs. Do you understand me?"

Chaz sat down, and the courtroom quieted.

"I asked you a question," continued the judge.

"Yes, I understand."

"Answer questions that are put to you. Do not do or say anything else. Is that clear? If you do or say anything else from the witness stand, I'll hold you in contempt. Now, you've just stood up and said something nasty to someone in the audience. I don't care who that person is or what you have against him, but if you threaten him or harm him while he is in my courtroom, I'll have you arrested. Is that clear?"

"Yeah."

"Mr. Sheridan, have you any further questions of this witness?"

"I do, Your Honor." Sheridan walked back to counsel table, picked something up, and returned to where he'd been standing. "Mr. Remlinger, the man in the audience you just yelled at is Max Rodriguez, Spokesman for T.U.L.P., is he not?"

"Yeah." Remlinger sounded like a pit bull growling.

"And about a month ago, you sent two thugs to his home in Niskayuna to threaten and intimidate him into quitting his activities with T.U.L.P., correct?"

"Objection!" yelled Armstead.

"Overruled," said His Honor.

"I've no control over what my men do on their off-hours."

"Really? Even when they're driving your company trucks? This is one of your trucks, isn't it, Mr. Remlinger?" And with that, the Cowboy placed a photograph of a pickup truck in front of Chaz. Chaz stared at it, saying nothing.

"Let me help you out. Here's the registration. It says, Maiko Industries, Inc. Now, isn't that one of your trucks, Mr. Remlinger?"

"So what? It's one of my trucks."

"So it's in front of Max Rodriguez's home at seven in the evening last Tuesday, that's what. What business would Maiko Industries have with the Rodriguez family, Mr. Remlinger?"

"None. That's why this truck being over there had nothing to do with me."

"You didn't send a couple of your boys over there to intimidate Max, to send him a message?"

"No."

"So you're telling this jury that even though you jumped up out of your chair just two minutes ago when you spotted Max in the audience, that you were practically shaking with rage and pointing at him and threatening him, it's just a coincidence that a couple of guys driving one of your trucks went over to his home a few nights ago to strong-arm him to stop working with T.U.L.P."

"I don't know what you're talking about."

"Of course not. No further questions."

"Redirect?" said His Honor.

"No," said the ADA.

"Tomorrow morning at 9:30, ladies and gentlemen. We'll sum up and charge and conclude this case tomorrow. We're adjourned until then."

Chaz Remlinger walked slowly from the courtroom, past Scott Gezunterman.

"Now there's a man who's not afraid to take a punch. The press is going to carve him up," Scott said to Mario Lambruzzo.

"I think you're reading him all wrong," said Mario. "He may be headed for trouble, but I think he's looking forward to talking to the press. I think he thinks he did a great job."

"A *geferlicher mischugena*," said Mrs. Gezunterman.

"What does that mean?" said Mario.

"It means even among crazy people, he's crazy."

Remlinger strode right past the three onlookers, chest out, chin forward. His daughter ran to his side and threw her arms around him. Trailing her was Jane Blake, whose unintentionally protective presence prevented any of the three local TV crews from getting recorded interviews with her ex-husband.

"I knew Mommy's talent would come in handy someday," said her daughter as the combined personnel of the three local TV crews worked keyboards, pulled plugs, screamed into cell phones, reinserted plugs, screamed louder into cell phones, and typed more furiously on keyboards in efforts to get their machinery to work.

"What are you talking about? Wouldn't you like to see your old man on TV?" said Chaz. "I'll just tell your mom to go on home. The cameras will start back up as soon as she leaves, and then I'll take you home."

"I don't think so, Dad. I'm not feeling well. Actually, I've got a problem in school and I think it's something I need to talk to you about," said the teenager, pulling and pushing her father away from the reporters and toward the street. "And besides, I'm really hungry."

Remlinger hesitated for a moment, but the combined impact of his daughter's triple offensive proved too much to resist. He let himself be led away while the reporters, faced with unprecedented technical problems, barely noticed him go.

Jane, standing still amidst the commotion of exiting courtroom observers, reporters and their fumbling technical crews, was watching Sarah depart with the ELF when Ava and Bartholomew came along.

"I wonder if he appreciates how lucky he is to have her?" said Bartholomew.

"Hard to imagine," laughed Jane. "The question I have is whether to be more proud of my kid for showing compassion to someone who doesn't deserve it or for being able to think quickly enough to get the buffoon out of harm's way."

"See you back at the lake," said Ava, and they took off.

Jane stood still for a bit watching her friends walk away, then felt a hand on her shoulder and was spun around and brought face to face with the man who'd sung "Jacob's Ladder" so very badly just a few days before.

"I've found you," he said.

She looked up at the man she'd been waiting for since she was her daughter's age, and placed her hands slowly around the outside of his hips.

"You sure took your time about it," she said.

"I'm sorry. If only I knew. But I got distracted."

"Yes. Life is that way, isn't it? My name's Jane, by the way. Jane Blake."

"Scott Gezunterman."

"No. Not . . . You're not . . ."

"Wait a minute. Are you the artsy woman my mother has been . . . "

With that, Florence Gezunterman, escorted by Mario Lambruzzo made her way to the couple. Mrs. Gezunterman, whose eyes, in eighty-one years of loyal service, had yet to convey a single image her brain had not overruled, concluded that as a matter of metaphysical principle, nothing could have happened between the two people because she was only just arriving.

She said, "What a lucky coincidence. You're both here. Jane, this is my son Scott, the substance abuse counselor."

"Yes, Mrs. Gezunterman. We've met. We were just talking about how you . . ."

"Scott, this is that nice girl Jane I was telling you about. She sews or paints or something. Right, Jane?"

"I paint, Mrs. Gezunterman, but mostly walls," Jane said, laughing.

"Again with the laughing. So," Mrs. Gezunterman said, turning her attention to her son, "you can shake her hand, it wouldn't kill you. And since when do you grab a girl by the shoulders when you're introduced? This, yet, I have to teach you?"

Turning back to Jane, "You'll pardon him, darling, he doesn't get out much, but he's a good boy, and smart. Always at the top of his class. That's why his teachers wanted him to be a doctor. So, okay, he's only a counselor, it's not the end of the world. Yet he makes a good living, although you wouldn't know it from the way he dresses, but a woman like you could straighten him out one, two, four if you know what I mean."

"Hey, you're the woman who wanted to know about the statue," said Mario. "Remember? At Your Father's Child, the store up in Latham. That's my store. I'm Mario. Remember me?"

Jane removed her hands from Scott's hips in order to shake hands with the shopkeeper. "Yes, Mario. I remember you."

"What are you doing here?"

"My ex-husband was testifying. My daughter wanted to come to give her father some moral support."

"He wasn't that Remlinger guy, I hope," said Mario.

"I'm afraid so."

"*Oy vey iz mir*," said Mrs. Gezunterman.

Chapter 39

"If he's smart, he'll disavow Remlinger completely," Valerie Whit said. "In fact, he'll do more than that. He'll throw him under the bus. He'll argue that the judge was absolutely right in slapping old Chaz down like he did, that we have rules of conduct that we live by, and that just as we have rules in the courtroom, so too do we have rules outside the courtroom, like at that movie theater, and if Charlie Remlinger's behavior was unacceptable in this courtroom, Frank Rooney's behavior was unacceptable in that movie theater."

They were gathered around the Hammermills' kitchen table—Sheridan, Whit, Max, Christina, Lucy, Gus, Boris, Irena Poppadapoulos, the Rooneys, and their hosts.

"He is that smart," said Bob Sheridan. "I'm very impressed with this kid. Quick on his feet. Good instincts too. But let's not forget that I go first. So I'll just beat him to the punch. I'll tell the jury that you can't have it both ways. You can't call someone to the witness stand hoping he'll be credible only to turn on him when he's not. Remlinger is callous and uncaring. His corporation is callous and uncaring. The theater manager took on those traits and he became callous and uncaring. The only person in this whole misadventure with the dignity and the courage to behave like a human being is Frank Rooney, and in return for the one brief moment of kindness that he exhibited that night, he asks for a dollop of justice, a statement of understanding, and a verdict of not guilty. Frank Rooney didn't attack justice that night. He defended it. It's not the Frank Rooneys of the world you need to fear. It's the Charlie Remlingers. Frank deserves to hear you the jury say that. Charlie Remlinger and his manager need to hear you say that. But most importantly, you need to experience how wonderfully American it feels for a jury of citizens to face down callousness and greed and announce to the world: Justice have we sought and Justice have we found."

"Oh, my," said Christina Clark. "Oh, my."

Jane Blake and Scott Gezunterman were sitting on Jane's living room couch, watching the local TV news, and Scott started humming "If I Loved You," which made Jane laugh.

"Is my voice that bad?"

"No. Well, yes, but that's not it. It's just that . . . never mind."

"Anyway, you're telling me this TV works because it's a newer model, is that right?"

"No," she laughed. "It works because it's a cable hook-up. But if we want to change the channel we'll have to do it manually. The remote won't work unless I go outside, and you stay in here and use it."

"But how is it you're able to work on cars?"

"I've not sure but I think it has something to do with the size of the battery. If it's big enough, the signal can get through."

"Trains?"

"So far, so good."

"How about airplanes?"

"I've never been on one."

"We'll have to remember that."

On the tube, Meagan Swoboda was detailing Chaz Remlinger's "crazed courtroom outburst" and extolling the nimbleness of the Cowboy's response. "It was a trap that had been set days in advance. Instead of being thrown off his game by the shocking turn of events, the veteran defense lawyer saw an opening, and in the short space of two or three questions had Charles Remlinger all but admitting to having sent a team of thugs to the Rodriguez home several days before to intimidate the T.U.L.P. Spokesman into leaving the movement. Our viewers may recall that that story was a WTXY First and Fair exclusive."

"I think she and that Max kid have a little thing going on," Jane said.

"Is clairvoyance one of your powers?"

"I dabble."

They kissed just after Meagan Swoboda turned it back over to the anchorman, who was reporting on the continuing debate over the Financial Crisis Inquiry Commission's report on the causes of the 2008 financial meltdown. The report strongly criticized government agencies such as the Federal Reserve Bank for not exercising their regulatory powers enough, harshly condemned banks and Wall Street for corporate mismanagement and heedless risk-taking, and concluded that the disastrous recession they caused was both foreseeable and preventable. In the face of those conclusions, Republicans in Washington were nonetheless seeking to reduce government budgets for regulatory agencies, insisting that deregulation of banks was the way to go.

As Scott began unbuttoning his shirt, a congressman was being quoted as saying, "Limited government also means effective government."

Then another congressman, with no evidence to support the statement, was quoted to say, "Of one hundred thirty-two regulations put in place in the last two years, many of which will cost our economy one hundred million dollars or more . . ."

"You know," said Jane as she reached underneath her blouse and removed her bra from one of the sleeve openings, "I read somewhere that this recession has cost the country almost three trillion dollars. Do these congressmen live on the moon?"

"Corporate hypocrisy turns me on," said a now breathless Scott. "But government hypocrisy just drives me wild."

"Reach over and turn off the light, will you?" Jane said.

"Can't you just wiggle your nose or something and make the place go dark?"

There was no gospel music coming from the protesters outside the courthouse the next morning, although most of the choir members were there, along with the Reverend and Mother Ethel.

"Ccwe not want push too much," Boris had said at the previous night's meeting. "By silence, ccwe emphasize solemn occasion, that now is in juror's cchand's and we respect that."

"That's fine," said Christina Clark, "but we don't want to disappear completely. I think we should make up in numbers what we're losing in sound. And we should continue to emphasize the local slant. We want those jurors to think that the Assistant DA is the one guy from the Capital District who's out of touch with the community. So I suggest we get on Twitter and Facebook and get all the locals out again, all the high school team jackets, hats, jerseys, et cetera, and put all those people right in front of the courthouse door where the choir has been so that the jurors will be sure to see them when they enter the courthouse. Then we use the same database to bring in a far bigger crowd than we've been bringing in. With the locals so visible at the front door and the out-of-towners down the street, it'll look like the whole place is filled with locals. The size of the protest, combined with the silence, as Boris suggests, will make the jurors feel like they're being called upon to do something far bigger than decide a simple assault case. It'll make them feel like they're entering a chapel."

"Oh, my," said Alexander Hammermill, who'd been standing behind his wife, sipping a cup of hot chocolate. "My, oh my."

"Sit down, dear," said Cindy, rising to give her husband her seat. "I'll go get the smelling salts. If Christina says anything else, just put your head between your legs and breathe deeply."

His Honor reserved on the defense motion to dismiss, and the summations began.

The Cowboy made sure to hit the mundane aspects of the case before moving into the flashier parts of his closing, so he argued that the theater manager never suffered a serious injury, the injured disc had been there from a previous car crash, and that Frank Rooney had no intent to hurt the man. Then he turned his attention to God, Country, and the Founding Fathers.

"It is for you as citizens and as human beings to determine who the real criminals are here. Is it the fire-breathing bully who stood up in open court, right before you and threatened a fellow citizen, who sent his minions out to intimidate and harass innocent people—your neighbors—in their homes? Is it the obedient soldiers of those bullies who felt, and continue to feel, unburdened by the constraints of decency and honesty, like that theater manager, who came before you and lied about his medical history and insisted, for reasons we still have not had explained to us, that the little old lady couldn't get her money back? Or is it Frank Rooney, a decent family man, who spends his free time coaching his daughters' swim teams and taking his family to our National Parks—a chemistry professor, a man who cares about civility and compassion for strangers so much that he was the one person willing to stand up for that old woman on that fateful night?

"You've got corporate might on the one hand and American justice on the other. Which side are you on? You've got the arbitrary rules of the Maiko conglomerate on the one hand and the legacies of John Adams and Thomas Jefferson on the other. Do I really need to tell you how those two great men would vote on this one? But most importantly, you've got lifetimes, your own lifetimes, to look back from this moment on and ask yourselves, Did I seek justice? And I'm not talking about the narrowest kind of justice that you can shoehorn into the smallest box you can find. No! I'm talking about the kind of justice your parents and teachers and clergy and holy books have taught you, taught all of us for generations. That justice. Because that justice cries out for a not guilty verdict here. It cries out for it."

ADA Armstead rose to his feet.

"That was quite stirring. I was moved myself. But it was a speech about everything but the facts of this case. Who really is the person who started a fight over the price of a theater ticket? It's the defendant, Frank Rooney. You can say whatever you want about Maiko Theaters, Biblical justice, the Founding Fathers, and an alleged little old lady and her two granddaughters, but the only reason we're here today is that this defendant got violent over the cost of a ticket to the movies. All Mr. Rooney had to do was get in his car and go home and get up the next morning and call Charlie Remlinger on the phone and make his complaint. If Remlinger gave him his money back, case closed. If not, Mr. Rooney could have gone to small claims court. That's what the courts are for. That's how we resolve disputes in a civilized manner, which is what he claims he wants. But no, he just grabbed Mr. Connally by the neck and smashed his face against the glass, and that's why we had to have this trial.

"As to Harrison Connally and Charlie Remlinger, I'm not going to apologize for them one bit. The reason I'm not going to apologize for them is that I didn't choose them. Prosecutors never get to choose their witnesses. We take them as they come. Frank Rooney chose to assault Harrison Connally, so Harrison Connally became my witness. The assault took place in a theater owned by Charlie Remlinger, so Charlie Remlinger became my witness. You can like them or dislike them as you please because it doesn't matter. Why? Well, ask yourselves this question: Does anything you saw or heard about those two men change the fact that Frank Rooney committed an unprovoked, illegal act against Harrison Connally? No. Not a thing. He did it, and three days of smoke and mirrors cannot change the simple truth of his guilt."

There followed the usual exodus of courtroom spectators unwilling to bear the pain of the judge's instructions to the jury. Included in the stampede were Ed Armstead, who'd taken the morning off from work to see his son in action, along with his nephew Barry.

"Well," said the older Armstead, as he slapped his nephew on the back. "What was that you used to say about my son's tennis outfits?"

After the instructions, the Rooneys and their attorneys left a cell phone number with the court clerk in case the jury reached a verdict and headed out to a pizzeria on Pearl Street. But before they did, Cowboy Bob pulled Jesse Armstead aside for a quick private chat.

"Kid," he said, "they're gonna acquit him. For all our fireworks, the fact is your victim lied about his injury. There's nothing wrong with that guy's neck and if there is, it's from a car crash he had years ago. But I gotta tell ya, you did a helluva job."

"Thank you."

"They let you try any felony cases yet?"

"Not yet."

"They should. You're more than ready. How many misdemeanors have you tried?"

"This is my fifth."

"No kidding. I am very impressed, kid. Listen, here's my card. Once you get a few felonies under your belt—if you're interested, that is—I want you to give me a call. Maybe I'll have something for you. And if I don't, I'll know someone else who will. You put this thing somewhere safe, you hear?"

"I will, Mr. Sheridan."

"It's Bob. You take care now."

Laura Rooney stared at her husband in disbelief as he woofed down three pieces of pizza and a large Coke. She could eat nothing. Val Whit and the Cowboy were right behind Frank Rooney on the consumption trail, but Max Rodriguez, who'd shown up by chance at the same restaurant with the Hammermills and Boris Petrovich, had all he could do to get through half a piece and a glass of water. He sat with his head down, rubbing his thumb over his mother's old Binghamton meal card.

"At that rate will rub out mother's picture ccompletely," said Boris. "Perhaps want to rub back of card instead."

"I don't know how you lawyers do it," said Cindy Hammermill. "I'm so nervous I can barely speak. And Mr. Rooney! You've the appetite of a stevedore!"

"It's remarkable. I could eat a horse. I think it's the relief of being done with the trial, regardless of the outcome."

"So, Max, you've not said a word. Where will you go from here?" said Alexander.

Max looked up from his mother's picture, as though someone had just woke him up. "I hadn't really thought about it," he said.

"I have," said Alexander.

The Cowboy's cell phone rang.

"They've got a verdict," he said.

Chapter 40

"I don't know what's worse," said Scott Gezunterman, "watching or participating."

They'd gone through all the "Have you a verdict" and "Would the defendant please rise" drama Judge Rheingold and his clerk could muster and now there was nothing left to do but have the jury foreman read it.

"And what if the defendant won't rise? What would they do then?" Scott sneered.

"Sha! I'll have to hire a lawyer for you, yet," said his mother.

"As to the first count, intentional Assault in the Third Degree, what is your verdict?" said the court clerk.

"Not guilty," said the foreman, and the place erupted. Judge Rheingold started banging away with his gavel immediately, but it wasn't until some of the larger people in the crowd, including Johann Mathison and Reverend Walker, stood up and motioned for silence, that order was restored.

"As to the second count, Reckless Assault in the Third Degree, what is your verdict?"

"Not guilty," said the foreman.

This time there was a tense silence as the uncertain crowd waited for a signal. The judge banged his gavel one time on his desk and said, "Case dismissed!" and the place erupted.

Within minutes, the scene outside was pandemonium. People hugged, car horns honked. Members of the Sweet Honey Gospel Singers had shown up and begun to sing, though it was hard to tell what the song was.

Judge Rheingold stood next to the court stenographer as they looked out the window from the courthouse.

"My father grew up in Brooklyn," he said. "He used to tell me stories of how crazy it was the day the Dodgers won the Series in 1955. In my mind's eye, it always looked like this."

Max Rodriguez tried making his way out of the courthouse to find Meagan Swoboda, but Alexander Hammermill wouldn't let him. The man practically dragged Max into a quiet corner of the courthouse.

"We need to talk," Hammermill said.

"Okay."

"Max, I'm thinking permanent constituency here. Does that mean anything to you?"

"Not yet."

"The problem with grassroots movements like this is they have no permanent constituency. They have people who are outraged, impacted, troubled by a corporation's actions at a particular place and time, so they come together and, if motivated enough and properly organized, can accomplish something like we did here. But then they disperse. They've no staying power. The corporation, however, is permanent and will reorganize itself to fight again. In the long run, it will win. We need a permanent organization. We need a building, an address, a membership, and a budget. We need to be able to bring pressure on the perpetrators of the next outrage. And we don't want to have to reinvent ourselves every time we do it."

"Which means what, Alexander?"

"Which means you, Max."

"Now you've lost me."

"You're our most recognizable member. When you show up, it means T.U.L.P. is on the job. You stand for thousands of members, or at least the perception of thousands of members. I want to build a staff around you, a permanent staff with you as our Spokesman. I'll supply the money, at least to start with, including your salary. Maybe we can have our members pay a nominal annual fee as dues, say five bucks, to help out."

"Wait. You're saying I can do this for a living?"

"For a while, anyway. Why, have you got a better offer?"

"I haven't got any offers. Hey, I've got to make a quick phone call. Will you excuse me for a minute?" And with that the new paid Spokesman for T.U.L.P. walked down the hallway, pulled out his cell phone, and called his father. Strangely, as his phone indicated he'd connected with his father's, Max heard a ringing sound coming from right behind him. When he turned around his father was right there, with a full-blown smile on his face.

"I wanted to get here before the verdict," Chuck said. "But I see I'm a little late. I guess it went well for you."

The Spokesman, now silent, was trying to remember when he'd last seen his father with a smile that broad, trying to figure out why the man had wanted to get to the courthouse before the verdict, and was coming up empty on both counts.

"I wanted to tell you, regardless of how this all turned out, that I'm proud of you."

"You . . . really?"

"Yes. Okay. I've got to get back to work now. You'll be home for dinner?"

"Yeah, sure."

"Good. See you later then." The boxy engineer turned round and headed back down the hallway. Max remained there for the next two minutes unable to move.

As Chuck approached the doors nearest to where he'd parked his car, he stood aside to let a couple of sheriff's deputies and their three handcuffed prisoners enter the courthouse. One of the prisoners was an old woman. The others, also females, were very young, maybe even teenagers, and Chuck had the feeling, because of the way their heads were bowed all in the same exact manner, that they were related.

Acknowledgements

I'd like to thank two wonderful friends, Barbara Strauss and Gene Fackler, who began helping me with this book when Mrs. Gezunterman was but a youngster. I also want to thank Ellen Larson, my excellent editor, who offered up unerring insights and rock solid advice, and did it all with the patience of Job.

Made in the USA
Charleston, SC
18 May 2013